THE FALL WE FELL

OCEAN PINES SERIES, BOOK 1

VICTORIA DENAULT

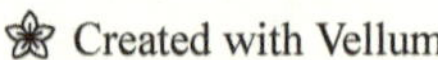 Created with Vellum

For Sarah Jillain, my Fryman soul sister

PROLOGUE

TERRA

ASPEN GRABS MY HAND AND PULLS ME INTO THE CENTER OF THE dank basement where all the other girls are dancing. The boys are all huddled up in clusters around the wood paneled walls. Some stare at the girls, some stare at the disco ball Aspen bought from the dollar store and hung from a water pipe in the center of the room. Some stare at their feet. None of them are staring at me, though. Except my brother Logan.

I glare back and he laughs as he does this stupid little twitch thing, like he's having convulsions and I know it's his impression of my dancing. He's mocking me, which isn't surprising. He's been such a dick lately. I don't know why. Mom says it's a phase because he's a teenager. But I'm fourteen and I'm not a dick. And his twin brother Finn isn't either. My oldest brother Declan is seventeen and he's not a dick… I don't think. He barely leaves his room lately, so I don't really know. I'm actually really surprised he's here. After all, he's older than the party's host, Aspen's older brother Abbott Barlowe. But they are both on the varsity track team at school so I guess they're friends.

"Isn't this the best co-ed party ever?" Aspen says into my ear over the blaring music. She's dancing her cheerleader ass off, swinging and swaying, and I'm barely moving now because of Logan and to be honest, because my legs are achy and stiff. I have a low-grade temperature I'm ignoring too, so the basement feels extra hot and sweaty to me. I yank at the collar on the green sweater I'm wearing, the one I borrowed from Aspen, because she swears I look 'killer' in it. I didn't tell her I'm feeling too warm to wear a sweater because she would tell my parents, or hers. Everyone is on high-alert since I was diagnosed with lupus last month. No one really understands it so everyone who knows is treating me like I'm some kind of alien or atomic bomb or something. Well, almost everyone.

I don't even really get what lupus is, but I know it basically means I'm going to feel shitty for the rest of my life, like I have for the last year. And I feel like a freak show.

"It's the *only* co-ed party I've ever been to," I remind Aspen, who grins. It's her only one too.

Our parents are friends from church, which is how we know each other. Aspen's mom Cynthia, who is even more hardcore religious than my mom, decided her kids weren't allowed co-ed parties until they were sixteen and convinced my Mom to implement the same rule. Aspen's brother Abbott just turned sixteen so this is his inaugural co-ed party.

Aspen and I were supposed to be upstairs decorating gingerbread men for the church Christmas social tomorrow but we snuck down here when her parents went outside to shovel the elderly neighbor's driveway for her. So far no one has ratted us out.

I'm usually cool with the boundaries my parents set, but since I found out all my symptoms—the sluggishness and fevers and aches and general relentless pains—aren't ever going to really go away, I have been itching to do stuff. Stay up late, watch R-rated movies, skip school, whatever. I just want to do everything, because I'm angry that I'll never feel normal again. I feel like my life has been short-changed.

"Your brothers… oh man." Aspen starts fanning herself as her eyes land on Finn and then Logan before sliding over to Declan. "I wish one of them would ask me to dance when a slow song comes on."

The music stops suddenly as I'm making a gagging sound and pretending to stick my finger down my throat. Everyone gets quiet and a few people are drawn to the noises I'm making, including Finn and Logan's mutual best friend Jake. He's staring at me with an amused smirk and now I want to die. Abbott claps his hands, pulling everyone's focus. "Who's in for a little game?"

He grabs a Santa hat that was lying next to a bowl of pretzels on the food table and holds it up. His birthday party is Christmas themed since his birthday is just four days before Christmas. "In this hat are a bunch of pieces of paper. Half of them say truth. Half say dare."

You can literally feel the tension in the room rocket, like a power surge that makes everything snap and crackle. The boys stand straighter, all the girls' eyes get wider, and some start fussing with their hair nervously. Abbott's grin widens. He's really handsome. Tall with a thick, athletic build, blue eyes and thick blond hair. But for me it's the kind of good-looking I can acknowledge but am not drawn to… I like dark hair with even darker eyes and an angular jaw and full lips and… Jake. Finn and Logan's best friend. He's the person I can never stop staring at. He's the guy that makes me feel like I'm caught in a riptide whenever he walks into a room.

Declan rolls his eyes and makes that sound in his throat he makes when he's unimpressed like when Dad tells him to shovel the driveway even though it's Finn's turn. "This is a lame idea. And it's not even the proper way to play the game."

"Rules are meant to be broken, Hawkins," Abbott shoots back

at Declan and then turns to everyone else. "You pick a piece of paper with truth or dare. You say the truthful answer to the question I give you or do the dare I give you, and then and only then, you get your secret Santa gift."

My eyes flitter over to the plastic tree in the corner with the wrapped gifts under it. Everyone was told to bring something that costs seven bucks or less. Aspen and I didn't bring anything, so we should probably slink away now and head back upstairs. I glance at her and she's standing as still as a deeply rooted tree. We're not going anywhere.

"I'll go first!" Finn volunteers easily because he's a daredevil. Always has been.

"Good man, Finn. You are my new favorite Hawkins," Abbott announces and holds out the hat. Finn shoves his big mitt in there and pulls out a folded piece of paper.

"Dare," he says with a happy grin. Of course he's happy. He's the kid who tobogganed solo down Demerit Hill when he was five, hit a rock, and his little body launched from the sled, careened over the road at the bottom of the hill, and almost landed in the barely frozen lake, then immediately asked to do it again.

"I dare you to spend two minutes in the closet with…" Abbott's icy eyes scan the room, and I am horrified to notice all the girls look excited. About being locked in a closet with my brother? Gross. "Casey."

Casey Andrews, a bubbly brunette with the highest voice I've ever heard, turns this ridiculous shade of pink that somehow makes her look more attractive. When I blush I just look like a tomato. Casey's in Logan and Finn's class and I think she's in love with both of them. Or maybe it's just one of them but she can't tell them apart. She spent half the summer at our family restaurant, sitting at the counter ordering sweet tea after sweet tea just to moon over them. Now Finn walks over to her. "You game?"

Her answer is to giggle and I want to make the gagging sound again. Finn and Casey walk over to the little closet next to the bathroom. He gallantly opens the door for her. Inside, there's a vacuum cleaner and a water tank and probably forty spiders. I try not to shiver. I hate spiders.

As soon as Finn closes the door, Abbott walks up to it and leans on it, pulling his cell phone from his back pocket. He stares at the screen. "Time starts now, kids. Make it interesting."

I try not to think of what Abbott considers interesting. He may only be sixteen but I've seen him making out with girls, like big time, after hockey games tucked into the alcove where the pay phones used to be in the corner of the arena by the public restrooms. He knows what he's doing.

"Casey must be over the moon," Aspen whispers. "What I wouldn't do to be locked in a closet with one of your brothers."

"Are you trying to make me puke?" I whisper back with a frown. I grab the front of my sweater and subtly move it back and forth, trying to cool off. I don't know if my fever is getting worse or it's my anxiety that's warming me. I am low-grade freaking out about the idea of playing this game.

She nudges me and laughs. "Come on. There's got to be someone here you want to be locked in a closet with. Boy or girl. No judging."

My eyes flicker over to Jake who has his head tilted to the left, talking to Logan. His voice is only a low rumble of undecipherable sounds from where I am but it still makes my stomach flutter. He is so… perfect. Aspen gasps and grabs my arm. "Do you wanna get locked in a closet with Jake Grady!"

"Shut up!" I whisper back angrily and feel my face get hot. "You are insane. You don't know what you're talking about. Also he's changing his last name when he turns eighteen. He told Finn that the other day. He's going to be Jake Maverick."

I don't know why I've told Aspen about all my crushes so far in life but not him. I feel like I can't tell anyone. It's like if I admit it, it will grow even deeper and I don't know how to handle that level of infatuation. Also, I'm feeling more than a little vulnerable these days since being diagnosed with this albatross known as Lupus, and I'm worried she'll disapprove. She hates my crush on Chuck on *Gossip Girl*. She's always trying to get me to be Team Dan. Aspen continues to stare at me and I know this conversation is far from over.

"Maverick? Why?"

"He doesn't want to be attached to Grady because of his family issues. Turns out his mom gave him the middle name Maverick, after some character on a popular eighties movie about pilots or something. I don't know, anyway, he likes it better and thinks it'll make people forget his family and his past," I explain and I know it's insane that I know all that personal Jake information, and that it rolls off my tongue like a memorized soliloquy. After all, Jake said all this to Finn while he was working as a dishwasher at my family's restaurant and I just happened to be prepping food for the lunch rush, but I remember it better than the book I read for English class last week. What I don't tell her is that I immediately found the movie online—it's called *Top Gun*— and stayed up until midnight watching it on my computer that very night. The name is perfect, he's a total Maverick. And I'm longing to be his Charlie.

"He's been arrested twice," Aspen says, not with judgement, but more like with awe. She's always wished she was a wild child, but she's almost as tame and boring as I am. "And he's the only emancipated kid this town has ever had, I think."

"The two theft charges were both dropped when the store owners realized his mom had made him try and steal those smokes and those groceries," I remind Aspen, my voice a harsh whisper. "And the word is emancipated. You know Jake works hard at our restaurant and he's even talking about finishing high school by taking night classes. He really doesn't deserve the bad rep this town gives him."

Aspen's eyes get bigger, as does the shape her mouth has dropped into, and I know I'm screwed. I won't be able to deny these feelings any longer because she has this uncanny way of seeing the truth even when you don't tell it. I sigh and shrug like it's no big deal. "He's hot. And he's nice to me—really nice. But I can't tell if it's because he feels he has to be because he's always at my house hanging out with my family or if he's nice because… he thinks I'm cool too."

And Jake is the only one who didn't look at me like I was some pathetic weirdo when he found out about the lupus. My brothers, God bless them, keep squinting their eyes and examining every move I make, trying to figure out what it is. Hoping to see something that they can understand. So far the only real outward sign I've had from lupus was a faint rash on my cheeks and the fevers. My dad is just a grumbling mess who won't talk about it but is hugging me too tightly now. Mom cries and prays. Jake found out, I guess one of my brothers told him, and all he said was, "I heard about your illness thing. That sucks, Terra. I know you'll handle it because you're a badass, but if you need help with anything, let me know." And that was it. No weird looks, no grumbling or avoidance or tears or stares. My crush grew even deeper that day.

"He likes you," Aspen declares in a firm whisper. "Your brothers aren't even that nice to you half the time so he's not doing it for their benefit. He probably gets teased by them for being nice to you. That's how brothers work."

I want to believe her so badly.

Abbott suddenly grins and swings open the closet door. It hasn't been a full two minutes. He's short by probably 30 seconds and so Casey and Finn are in full-on make-out mode. Her arms are around his neck and his arms are circling her waist, his hands both palm-down on her ass. And I swear his tongue is in her mouth. "Oh my God I really am going to barf," I hiss and grab Aspen's arm. "Let's go."

"Hell no," Aspen replies. "I want a turn."

"You'll get truth and it'll be boring because we have nothing to confess. We have no life yet, remember?" I tug at her wrist. "Please. Let's go before your mom figures out we're down here."

Finn and Casey have jumped apart and emerged from the closet, both flushed. I avoid looking at Finn and focus on Casey. I'm fascinated by her expression. Her eyes are glassy. Her lips are puffy and pink like she applied lip gloss to them but she didn't. She looks… *euphoric*. I don't think I ever understood the true definition of that word until this minute. Abbott slaps Finn on the back. "You just earned yourself a Secret Santa gift, Hawkins. Pick what you want. Casey you have to pull from the hat to get yours."

Casey tries to calm herself, taking a deep breath before she pulls a piece of paper from the hat. "Truth."

Abbott's grin gets deeper. "Easy. Are you a virgin?"

"Abbott, come on!" Declan barks. "That's not cool."

Casey doesn't seemed bothered though. "Technically."

A round of oohs starts to echo from around the room. Casey flushes again and bounces over to the gifts piled under the fake tree covered in horrible pink tinsel. She grabs a gift I know my brother brought—a tin of homemade caramel popcorn and a gift certificate to our restaurant. That'll come in handy next time she wants to drink sweet tea all day and stalk my brothers.

"Casey you also have to pick the next person to go," Abbott announces.

Casey doesn't even bother to look around the room she just says my name so quick and easy I don't even register it at first until Aspen gasps. "O-M-G."

She always says the text version of oh my god so her mom doesn't get angry about taking the lord's name in vain.

"Terra," Casey repeats. 'Let's go, girl."

"The children aren't playing," Abbott announces and waves his hand in our direction.

"Yeah, no. They aren't," Declan adds and Finn is nodding in agreement so hard I'm surprised he doesn't snap a vertebrae in his neck.

"No one wants to be *their* first kiss," Logan calls out and people snicker.

"It won't be my first kiss," Aspen retorts and snickers erupt. "And you're just scared you'll learn a thing or two, Hawkins?"

"From you?" Logan rolls his eyes. "I dare you to teach me."

Aspen turns beat red at that and I panic. I do not want my brother making out with my best friend.

"You guys are lame," Jake announces suddenly turning the attention to himself. "Let them play. It's not a big deal. They might pull truth and not every dare has to involve making out."

Aspen leans right into my ear. "See? He wants you to play. He likes you."

Spurred on by my anger at my brothers for humiliating me in front of everyone and the growing confidence I have at Jake's defense of me, I march over and stick my hand in the hat and snag a piece of paper between my fingers before Abbott can yank it away.

I unfold it and panic pierces my heart as I read it. I swallow but there's no saliva in my mouth suddenly. "Dare?"

"Are you unsure?" Abbott looks over my shoulder to read the paper himself. "Yep. Dare. Okay… I dare you to—"

"I should get to pick since I just went," Casey interrupts forcefully and turns to me. "I dare you to… pick a guy and go into the closet for one minute."

"What? Pick someone? Me? No," I stammer out. I can't pick. If I pick then it's my choice. I'm showing everyone who I like. I won't pick. I'll die before I pick.

"It can be a girl if you want," Casey shrugs. "So… pick. Unless you are really a toddler like Logan said, then you can go upstairs where the adults can babysit you."

More people laugh at that than I would like. I feel humiliated and panicked and angry. I hate this girl so much suddenly. I hope she chokes on that tin of caramel popcorn she's holding. Everyone is watching me. Aspen gives me a nudge. "Make a pick, Terra. You know you want to."

"Leave her alone. Terra, go upstairs," Logan says and he looks deadly serious. Like Dad when he's barking orders at Tom Brady from his recliner during a Pats game.

"Bite me, Logan," I bark and start walking towards Jake. I stop right in front of him and poke him in the chest. Hard. "You. Let's go."

The room erupts with so many whistles and oohs and ahs that Abbott actually shushes them. I walk toward the closet and pray with every fiber of my being that he is following. I'm shaking on the inside even though I'm not on the outside. It makes no sense but it's like my blood and guts are in an earthquake right now that no one else can feel or see. I would probably puke if I'd eaten any of the cookies, candy, and chips on the long table next to the Christmas tree. Luckily I didn't. I fling open the door and only then do I turn around and see… Jake is following me.

Oh my God this is happening.

I step into the darkness of the closet before anyone can see my face explode in heat or my arms and legs shake with nerves as that earthquake inside me starts to breach its confines. Jake hesitates for the briefest second on the threshold but then, he steps inside. Casey walks up and shuts the door saying firmly. "Sixty seconds starts now. Have fun kids."

And now darkness. And Jake. And me.

"Terra," Jake whispers, which is the only reason I know he's close. I can hear him crystal clear. "I'm too old to be in here with you."

"No you're not."

"You're a freshman and I'm… well I should be a junior."

Jake was held back in seventh grade. He's also dyslexic so school has always sucked for him and it's why he dropped out this year. I wish he could see my face right now. I know my expression is one of adoration. Admiration. I think Jake failing a grade is not a big deal. I know he's thoughtful and kind and funny, and all of that matters more than how you do on stupid standardized tests.

"So what?"

"It matters. I mean, juniors shouldn't take advantage of freshman."

"I'm the one who hauled you in here so you aren't taking advantage," I remind him. "Are you mad at me?"

I blink out of confusion. My eyes adjust the slightest bit to the inky, tiny room and I can make out a vague outline of his tall, lanky frame. He's actually less than a foot from me. "No. Of course not. Why would you ask that?"

"Because picking me is going to make your bothers want to kill me," Jake announces. "Or at the very least, stop hanging out with me. If you aren't mad at me then why would you do this?"

Because I want you to be my first kiss. My mouth is open but the words don't come out. "Because I… you're… because I don't hate you."

He doesn't respond. I can almost hear the time ticking away and nothing is happening. *Nothing.* Except all those spiders I know must be in here are probably inching closer to us. I take a step forward and my nose bumps into his chest. "Ouch!"

"Are you okay?" Jake asks and I feel his hands hit me in the stomach. "Sorry. Damn. Is there a light in here?'

"No light!" I say in a whisper yell and gently reach forward, palms out, and I hit his chest and slide my hands slowly towards his shoulders. "Just… don't make this worse."

"Terra," his voice has changed. It's deeper. It's rougher. He sounds older than sixteen somehow. My belly becomes a butterfly sanctuary. "I can't… do what Finn did with Casey. Not to you."

"Oh…" I feel the belly butterflies disintegrate under the burn of humiliation as clearly as if battery acid has been poured over them. My hands that have reached his shoulders suddenly feel cold. I start to pull them away from him. But then his hands are on my hips. Firm and warm, holding me right up against him.

Those butterflies rebuild themselves like a Terminator. "Terra, your brothers are the closest thing to family I have. Your mom treats me like a son. No one else does that. You know that. I've never said it, but I know you know. You're the smartest person I know."

His grip tightens on my hips. No boy has ever held me like this or at all. I tilt my head up to where his must be hovering above me. "I won't tell them. If you just kiss me once no one has to know."

"I'll know," he whispers back. "You'll know."

"I won't tell," I promise. "You want to… don't you?"

I suddenly feel like Aspen is right. I feel it right down to my soul. Jake likes me. In *that* way. He does. A countdown starts outside at ten. Everyone must be doing it because it's loud.

I feel his breath on my cheek and then… he breaks me. "No. I'll never want to touch you. Like that. Can't happen."

I step away, stumbling over the vacuum and slamming into the water tank so hard it makes a gong-like noise.

"Shit, you okay?"

"I hate you," I hiss as the door swings open.

Casey scans our faces as I squint against the intruding light. "You guys didn't do anything?"

"Smart choice, Jake," Logan calls out, happily. Asshole.

"He's gross," I say righting myself and pushing past Jake. "It would be like kissing my brother or our family dog."

I ignore the relief on Logan, Finn and Declan's faces and the confusion on Aspen's and head right up the stairs. I'm going to finish the gingerbread men for the Christmas social. Then I'll make one just for me, one that looks like Jake, and I'll take it outside and stomp on it with my boots until it's dust. Then I am going to go home and cry. Forever.

1

TERRA

ELEVEN YEARS LATER

"I HAVE TO PEE." I TURN AWAY FROM THE CROWDED RESTAURANT and the front door where he's standing, and make a beeline through the opening between the counter and the bar and push my way through the swinging door into the kitchen. Everyone is so busy that no one pays attention to me. I pass the cooks and the line prep team and march into the break room.

I give a curt wave to the two employees in there before heading straight into the bathroom and locking myself in one of the two stalls. Then I let go of the breath I didn't know I was holding and cover my face with my hands as it heats up like a log thrown on a bonfire.

I have to pee?

I haven't seen Jake Maverick in almost three entire years and that's the first thing that comes out of my mouth? Yeah, that was pure and utter genius. Ugh. I'm a semester away from being a certified trauma and addiction therapist and that's how I act under pressure? Someone should call my school and have them kick me out.

I knew Jake was coming home today. The whole damn town knew. If they didn't hear it from his excited best friends, my brothers Finn and Logan, then they saw it on the Ocean Pines News & Notes Blog. Last week they did a lengthy post on how the new Lieutenant for the OP Fire Department was a returning local boy. Jake Maverick was leaving his post as Lieutenant on King's Rock, Maine's Fire and Rescue team to return to his hometown, as a hero no less, since he won the Medal of Valor last year. My Mom has spent all week planning a little party for him tonight so I *knew*. And yet, when he walked through that door and our eyes connected for the first time in seventy-one months, it wasn't just the bell above the door that jostled. It was my emotional equilibrium.

The fact is though I *do* have to pee, I realize as I stand in the bathroom stall, drowning in humiliation. But what else is new? I pull my hands from my face and undo my jeans, turn around and yank one of the seat covers out of the dispenser. As I go about my business I wonder what the hell he's doing here already. Finn and Logan said he wasn't getting into town until the evening and it's only a little after one in the afternoon.

My entire plan has been obliterated. I was going to finish my shift at four, go for a walk on the beach and meditate, then shower, spend stupid amounts of time doing my hair and make-up and put on that cute new sundress I picked up last week for this specific reason. And of course pair it with a shrug I found in the same sage green color that's in the sundress' flowers so he doesn't notice my arm. It's still kind of misshapen and discolored from my dialysis treatment this morning. Nothing to worry about but ugly as hell to look at.

But he's here. Now. And he already saw me, makeup-less, in my grubby work jeans and my Hawkins Lobster Shack shirt that I'm certain has some stains on it from the vanilla bean milkshake that sloshed everywhere when the machine started to act up again.

When I'm done actually peeing I flush and head out to the two sinks, washing my hands and staring at my reflection in the mirror. I look tired. I have a gray tinge to the skin under my eyes and I'm pale and not just because I haven't been to the beach once this summer. I use my damp hands to try and fix my hair. It barely hits my shoulders, but because I work in food service I have to pull it back. So it's in a short stubby ponytail at the back of my neck and there's a billion clips holding the sides back. I stupidly bought children's clips covered in glitter and unicorns. Because clearly I don't mind looking like a quirky goofball when my lifelong crush lives a seven hour drive away. But now he's seven seconds away and I look like an idiot.

I resign myself to two facts: I can't do a damn thing about any of it, and we're in the middle of a lunch rush so I can't hide in here any longer. I turn, face the door, take a big breath, and head back to face this disaster head-on.

I step out into the bustling restaurant from the kitchen. Jake is sitting at the counter now. Finn is on the other side of it grinning at him like it's Christmas and Jake is Santa. I suppose it is exactly like that. Finn, my other brother Logan, and Jake were inseparable until three years ago when Jake took a job at a fire station clear across the state of Maine on the Canadian border.

Finn pulls his phone from his back pocket. "I'm going to tell Logan you're here."

"No personal phones while on shift," Declan announces. He's in a suit as always. Deck is in charge of our advertising and marketing at Hawkins Lobster Shack, mostly because he refuses to serve customers. But also a little bit because he's got a degree in it from Harvard. He smiles at Jake. "This time I'll make an exception. Welcome back, Maverick."

Declan and Jake grab hands in one of those stupid bro hand-shake-hugs that are all clapping and slapping. I grab my tray off the counter where I left it as a table waves their hand in my direction, probably for the bill. I step through the opening between the bar and counter and that's when he touches me. Jake wraps a big, warm hand around my wrist.

I freeze. Well, my forward motion freezes, my insides are actually melting and swirling like chocolate in a double boiler. I'm suddenly thrilled my long-sleeved work shirt shrunk a little in the wash so his fingers are touching my skin and not the fabric. I turn and look at him. Big freaking mistake. He's better looking than I remembered and I remembered well.

"Not even a hi, Tink?"

My nickname. The one he invented. The one only he uses. My insides are officially nothing but goo. And I hate him for it. "Hi Jake. Welcome back. Bye Jake."

I tug my wrist free, take my tray, and head over to the table that flagged me. Wow. That was not at all a great beginning. I throw myself into the rest of my shift like I'm up for Waitress of the Year and am currently being evaluated by a panel of judges.

But by two-thirty the lunch rush has evaporated. The gaggle of tourists that have remained a week after labor day are back to the beach or one of the amusement parks, water parks, or other attractions peppering Route One just up the road. The locals are back to work. So now it's just staff, which is ninety percent family, and Jake. He's been sitting on that same stool at the counter this entire time and people have shown up to shower him with greetings. First Logan came. Then Dad sauntered in from the docks where he was cleaning the fishing boat after a morning out switching the lobster traps. Some of the locals walked over too before leaving to say welcome back or congratulate him on the new position.

I've been cleaning the countertops of all the tables and booths but now that I've finished that, I decide I should head back into my office where I can finish up next week's schedule and sneak out the back door in the break room to avoid Jake a little longer. If he sees me disappear he doesn't try to stop me this time. I make it into my office, which is the closet-sized room next to the walk-in freezer, and close the door.

I move my textbooks out of the way and then stare at the schedule on my computer screen for fourteen minutes while I think of Jake and nothing else. He looks… incredible. And he called me Tink, which is short for Tinkerbell. He's started that trend after the first time Logan and Finn had him over to our family house. Jake was fourteen. He'd been working two shifts a week as a dishwasher at the restaurant for almost a month. Logan and Finn loved having him around since most of the staff was way older. We were all shocked when Mom and Dad hired him because he was so young and well… everyone knew about Jake Grady, the skinny kid with the troubled mom and no dad, who bounced in and out of foster care.

Because Logan and Finn liked him so much, they started hanging out with him outside the restaurant and inviting him over to dinner. Mom and Dad never minded an extra mouth at the table. Anyway, the first time he came to the house he saw the picture my mom had on our mantle. It was of Halloween when I was six. She had somehow coaxed me and my brothers into theme costumes. I was Tinkerbell, Logan was the crocodile Tock, Finn Peter Pan, and Declan was Captain Hook. He's called me Tink on and off since he first laid eyes on that picture. But I never expected him to remember that now. After a solid three-year gap, I wasn't even sure he'd recognize me.

There's a single rap at my door. I yell that it's open, and Nova pops her head in. "Don't yell at me but Mom said we had to check on you anytime you disappeared for a longish period of time."

I roll my eyes. "You faint once at work and suddenly everyone is on high alert."

Nova opens the door farther and steps inside. "Five stitches and blood on the floor in the middle of a dinner rush earns concern, Sis."

"That hasn't happened since," I remind her. Nova isn't my actual sister. She's my sister-in-law, married to Declan. But she feels more like a sibling than he does most days. "I was getting used to the dialysis. I'm a pro now."

Nova frowns. "Nothing yet?"

"You mean donor-wise? Nada," I reply. "Hey, has anyone said anything about this to Jake?"

Nova shakes her head, her thick wavy chocolate brown ponytail swaying like a horse tail behind her, but then she blinks and her face lights up. "But I bet he would get tested if he knew!"

"No!" I bark and it causes the excitement on her face to disappear. "I don't want him to know. Not yet. And I am definitely not asking him to get tested."

"Terra, you should be asking *everyone* in town to get tested," Nova lectures and I try not to get pissed off. She, like the rest of my family, just wants me to get a new kidney from anyone I can. I want that too, frankly, but Jake? No. I mean I won't ask him. He has a habit of turning me down for things I really want. "Yeah, eventually maybe someone should tell him but not now. Not today. He just got back. And besides what are the chances he's a match? Slim."

Your luck at getting a kidney match is best with direct family. I have three brothers and two parents and sadly only two of them were matches—my dad and Declan. But Dad was disqualified because of age and his type one diabetes. Declan was not deemed an acceptable match because he has had mental health issues in the past. The kidney donor regulations are strict and vary from state-to-state, and Maine is stringent with emotional issues. It's not just that he has ADD and takes meds for that or that he suffers from depression. He tried to kill himself a week before his eighteenth birthday, and there's also concern the carbon monoxide from that almost-successful attempt that involved a car and a locked and sealed garage might have damaged his kidneys without anyone knowing. He's appealing the decision, meeting with psychiatrists, and getting doctors to run more tests on his kidney function, but I'm not holding my breath.

"You never know, Terra." Nova is the Queen of optimism. "If Selena Gomez can get a kidney from her best friend, you can certainly match with your brother's best friend. And I bet it's an extra strong, extra tough, extra handsome kidney. Like Jake himself."

I laugh at that and Nova joins me. "He looks good though, huh?"

I can't believe I just said that out loud. I shouldn't have.

"To be clear, I'm just stating the obvious. I'm happily married but…" Nova's chuckle dies out and she grins. "He looks hotter than the fires he puts out."

I laugh again. "Not a lie. And to be clear, I'm also just stating the obvious."

"Like hell you are," Nova challenges, and I no longer want to laugh.

"Seriously. I'm with Tom, remember? And I like Tom," I say pointing to the framed picture on my desk of my boyfriend Tom and I.

"We all like Tom. Tom is swell," Nova says, her voice as cheery and bright as it always is but somehow it feels false right now. "Is he coming to town this weekend?"

"Yeah. He'll be here for the party actually," I say and shut-down my computer, giving up on doing the schedule today. I scribble a note on a post-it and stick it to the corner of the screen with the other To-Do reminders I have stuck there.

"Has he been tested yet?" Nova asks, her tone judgy. I'm running out of excuses to call her on it.

"He was supposed to go this week now that he's got the clear from his insurance company and his college faculty," I reply and keep my eyes focused on my desk, absently tidying up the papers strewn there instead of meeting her eye. She is less than impressed that Tom's first thought about becoming a living kidney donor was how that worked for insurance purposes rather than how it would be giving me my life back. "I'll find out how it went tonight when he gets in."

"Cool," Nova says lightly. She opens the door as I grab my purse and make my way around my desk. "See you and Tom tonight."

I nod and blow her an air kiss. "*Hasta luego, hermana.*"

"Ugh. Your Spanish is horrible," Nova moans. "*Es doloroso para mis oídos.*"

"That's because I took French in high school," I remind her.

"I've been your sister-in-law for four years and worked here for four before that, you'd think you'd pick something up by now," Nova complains as we walk through the kitchen. I cut right while she cuts left to head into the restaurant again. "Leaving through the back door? Chicken!"

"*Pollo!*" I yell back and grin. "See you are rubbing off on me."

I'm making my way through our small parking lot, the building and the ocean and dock beyond at my back when I hear him call my name. "Terra!"

I pretend I don't hear but then he yells. "Tink!"

I stop and turn around because I am helpless against that nickname. It takes my eyes a minute to find him, but when they land on him my heart skips. On the right side of Hawkins Lobster Shack is a flight of stairs that lead to the two bedroom apartment above the restaurant where Finn lives. Jake is on the tiny landing in bare feet, a wetsuit covering him up to the waist, but rest of it hangs off his body leaving his upper body completely exposed. And what an upper body it is. Muscle ripples his stomach. His broad chest is well-developed and bronzed because clearly he hasn't spent this glorious Maine summer at the dialysis center in Casco Bay Memorial Hospital.

"Wanna come surfing with us?"

"No. I've got plans."

He smirks at that. Oh lord how I've missed that smirk. It's easy, lazy, and somehow just a little bit sweet. "You used to love to surf with us, Tink."

"Been three years, Jake. Things change," I say, and it's true but I actually am too tired and rundown lately to get my butt out on my board. "But I've gotta get ready for tonight. I don't know if you've heard but there's an award-winning firefighter who just moved back to town."

"You mean that scrawny foster kid who failed outta high school, got his GED and stumbled his way through the fire academy?" Still same old Jake. He'll never forget where he's from, so he's not going to let you do it.

"Like I said, things change." I smile. He smiles back. Everything inside me warms like it's been laying out on the sandy beach in a cloudless July sky.

"Tonight then, Tink," he points to me with a perfectly sculpted arm. "I wanna hang out and catch up."

I wave and get in my truck. Boy, that's going to be a fun conversation. *Hey Jake. Yeah I'm good. Managing the restaurant now and met this guy who's nice and cute. I got my degree in social work and I almost finished my second degree in addiction therapy but had to take my last semester off when my kidneys dropped dead. I'm shopping for a new one. Turns out they aren't one-size-fits-all so it's taking a while, but yeah, I'm good. How about you?*

Yeah, can't wait for that.

2

JAKE

It's not good to be home. It's great. The second the posting came up for a Lieutenant position at Ocean Pines Fire Station, I wanted it. Because I wanted a second chance to prove to everyone in this town I'd turned out better than they'd expected. Because I missed my friends. Because even though there were a lot of bad memories, there were some good ones too and like it or not, this tiny coastal town was home. And because… she was here.

I had the qualifications and experience, but I applied without telling anyone. I was still in contact with Finn and Logan. We text each other all the time and video chat, and they both came up to King's Rock a couple times a year to visit. In summer for the fishing and in winter for the skiing. But I hadn't gone back to Ocean Pines once. Finn and Logan kept telling me how much I was missed, how the regulars at the restaurant asked about me. How their parents, Charlie and Lucy Hawkins, kept telling them to invite me back for Thanksgiving or Christmas or Easter or anything. But I just couldn't bring myself to go back to visit. I hadn't accomplished enough yet. I wanted to go back knowing that I was a better, different person. The town couldn't see me as more than a foster fuck-up that depended on the Hawkins family for survival if I didn't feel like I was more than that. It took three years, a promotion and a medal of valor, but I was finally ready.

Ocean Pines was a seven hour drive from King's Rock and a lot of the road was through some pretty hairy mountain passes. I wouldn't recommend traveling them at night to my worst enemy. That meant I'd have to spend the night. Instead of staying with Finn, or anyone else, I booked a motel room outside of Ocean Pines. There was a chance I wouldn't get the position and I didn't want anyone to know about this if I failed to get it. Especially Terra. The next time I saw her I wanted to be confident and sure. The interview was in downtown Portland, at the Southern Maine Emergency Management office. Since there were applicants from all over the State, the decision was made by a board of battalion chiefs, so I didn't have to set foot in Ocean Pines. But I did. And I shouldn't have.

It was after four when I got out of the interview and after checking into the hotel and changing out of my dress uniform, and into some jeans and a Henley, I threw on my leather jacket and drove to Hawkins Lobster Shack. The interview had gone well. *Really* well. The battalion chief for Ocean Pines stopped me afterward in the hallway and told me that the captain of Ocean Pines, D'Amato, remembered me from when I was a proby there and was adamant he wanted me back. So I felt like I had it in the bag and suddenly, all I wanted to do was see my unofficial adopted family, the Hawkins. Especially Terra.

I had this overwhelming sudden need for her to know how accomplished I'd become. How worthy I was now of the attention and affection. I wanted to know if the cold indifference she'd shot my way since she was fourteen had thawed a little. And if it hadn't, well for the first time in my life, I wanted to try and change that.

I had no idea if Terra would be working but I would find her if she wasn't. Lucy and Charlie would gladly tell me where she was. I didn't exactly know where I would begin with her, but I wanted to begin… I mean, at least a friendship, which we'd lost. And hopefully a lot more.

I pulled into that parking lot full of nervous energy and naive hope. But before I could even get out of the car, it was all gone. As I sat there, parked at the back of the lot, Terra walked out of the restaurant holding hands with a blond guy. He was well dressed, well built, and smiling at her with an ease and intimacy I could *feel*. And that hurt. He opened the door for her on a Range Rover and carefully helped her in even though she didn't need it. Terra was tiny but she had always been able, even with her illness. Still I saw her pretty little mouth form the words 'thank you'. If I'd tried to help her into a car like that, she'd swat at me in ire.

And then they kissed. Just a lingering peck on the lips, but it was enough for my bubble of excitement to pop. I sunk lower in my seat and averted my eyes until they drove away. And then I drove back to my rundown motel and marched my ass over to the dingy little bar in the strip mall across the street and berated myself over four Moscow mules. What the hell did I expect? That she'd be single for the rest of her life? That every guy she liked would be as stupid and as easily intimated by her over-protective brothers as I had been as a teen?

Nah, this was what I deserved. I'd lost the girl because I was not good enough or smart enough. This guy wore expensive clothes and drove a Range Rover. Probably a doctor or a lawyer or some fancy shit. Terra didn't give a rat's ass about that kind of classism—and deep down I knew it—but I did. I never felt good enough, not even for the working-class Hawkins family.

"Hello..?" Finn waves a hand in front of my face. I glance up and see him staring down at me, the beer bottle in his other hand half empty. "You need to do less day dreaming and more drinking. Logan will be home any minute and I don't drink in the house when he's home."

"He's still on the wagon?" I ask, concerned that something has happened no one told me about. It wouldn't be the first time. Just before I transferred to King's Rock Logan was shipped off to a rehab in Florida before anyone even told me he had a drinking problem. He was my best friend as much as Finn was and I considered them my family, but they hadn't included me in this huge family moment so I became acutely aware the feeling wasn't mutual.

"Oh yeah, straight and narrow," Finn nods brings his beer bottle to his lips and tips it back to finish it and then continues. "He's so straight and narrow you would swear there was a stick up his ass. The perma-scowl completes the look."

I swallow down a big gulp of my own beer, almost finishing it off. "So same as your last visit to King's Rock. Since your face doesn't know any other expression except goofy grin, it actually makes it easier to tell you two apart."

Finn lets out an incredibly fake laugh and flips me his middle finger. I grin back and finish my beer. He swipes the bottle from my hand and carries them into the small kitchen, shoving them deep into the recycling bin. This apartment above the restaurant is all too familiar because I called it home from age sixteen until twenty-three.

"All joking aside, he's been a model son, part-time fisherman, full-time paramedic, brother and father. But yet, that last role he still doesn't get to do on a full-time basis."

"Bethany still not into shared custody?" I ask about Logan's ex and the mother of his four year old son, River.

"Nope. Ma finally convinced Logan to get the courts involved. There's been a hearing and a social worker got assigned to assess the situation. He's worked out a non-nego-tiable schedule where Logan picks up River after pre-school two days a week and gets him one day a weekend. It all fluctuates based on his work schedule. Still no overnights, but after the social worker gets a better look at everything I'm sure that'll change."

I think of River. He was fifteen months old when I moved to King's Rock. He wouldn't remember me. Finn scrubs at the short beard on his face. And then motions for me to stand. "Get up. If we don't get downstairs soon, Ma is going to come up here and drag us down. You are, after all, the belle of the ball."

I roll my eyes. "Please don't say this is a big thing. I'm not ready for a big thing. I just want to hang with Hawkins and Hawkins-adjacent crew."

"That's who we invited," Finn says as we leave the apartment. He doesn't bother to lock the door, just swings it shut and starts down the stairs. I follow. "But you know Ocean Pines. Word gets out. People want to see the new and improved Jake Maverick."

"I'm not improved," I reply and grin. "Because you simply can't improve on perfection."

"Someone got cocky living in the middle of nowhere, huh?" Finn chirps, his blue eyes twinkling. "FYI hot shot, there's some real competition for attention—and women—in Ocean Pines. Not like King's Rock where your only competition for the six available women were mountain men who don't shower and geriatric fisherman."

"There were only four single women near my age and I never hooked up with any of them," I clarify and Finn stops so abruptly I bang into him.

"Wait… so you never had sex in King's Rock? For three whole years?" He looks like he might faint. I laugh.

"I did, just not there," I pause. Should I tell him? I know I can trust him. "I came back down south for my interview for this position and… I got some then."

"Why didn't you tell me when you were in town?"

"I hadn't even told you guys I was applying for the job yet," I explain with a shrug. "I didn't want to jinx it I guess."

"So instead you snuck into town and had sex with a stranger," Finn grins. "I would have picked that over hanging out with me too, I guess."

"Not a stranger. Aspen."

His jaw slowly descends, leaving his mouth wide open in shock. "What. The. Fuck."

"I know. I just happened to run into her and we were both just… desperate, I guess," I think about that night with my ex. It was truly just two people who needed a fix. "It was fun, but not anything more than that. We're on the same page."

"If you say so," Finn says clearly not believing me. "Ex sex has a way of biting you in the ass, my friend."

"Not this. I mean it was over two months ago and knowing Aspen, she doesn't even remember," I say.

"So you're that good in bed, huh?" Finn jokes, and I flip him off this time.

We round the corner of the restaurant to the front door. "I take it you're still single."

"Happily," Finn replies. Unless there's something I don't know about that occurred in the last three years, Finn Hawkins has never had a long-term girlfriend. He has semi-long-term arrangements, with willing bed buddies, but that's about it.

"Logan?" I question.

"No one since Bethany," Finn replies. "For a while there I thought Declan would be the only Hawkins to give wedded bliss a shot, but Terra—"

"She's married?" I blurt out because the idea is so upsetting I lose it for a second.

Finn stops, his hand on the door to the restaurant and looks back at me like I'm insane. "Oh fuck no. But she's finally dating someone. Seriously. Although it's long distance. He works and lives in Portsmouth New Hampshire so they don't see each other more than a couple times a month."

"Oh. Cool." *So not cool.* "How long has that been going on?"

"Six or seven months," Finn shrugs. "Dude is nice. She seems happy. I mean, she's Terra so you know, it's hard to tell. Girl likes to keep her emotions locked up in a vault somewhere in that head of hers."

I've never agreed with that assessment of Terra. Her whole family sees her that way but I know if you look close enough, every feeling that girl has is visible. I guess the guy I saw her kiss is this Portsmouth guy Finn is talking about. I was really hoping that he'd have gone away by now.

"How's she been feeling? You know, health-wise?" I ask as we walk into the restaurant. I can't help but notice the hand written note on the glass door that says 'closed for private party'. "They closed for me?"

"Hell yeah they did," Finn replies. He doesn't answer my other question about Terra and I'm about to repeat it, but his dad cuts me off.

"Finally!" Charlie Hawkins's voice booms through the restaurant as we cross the threshold. "I thought maybe you'd come to your senses, turned back around and got the hell outta this water-logged crackerjack box of a town."

"You're not fooling anyone, Charlie," I say with a smile as I walk into the restaurant that has only Hawkins and Hawkins-adjacent bodies in it, like Javi, Nova's brother, and staff members I remember from working here. "I know you love it here in OP and would never live anywhere else."

"But I'm batshit crazy," Charlie counters.

"We don't use that word, Dad," Terra reprimands, and my gaze floats across the room until I find her. And when I do, I wish I didn't. She's sitting at table near the center of the room next to the dude I saw months ago, her boyfriend. His hand is casually slung across the back of her chair. "Making jokes with the word crazy perpetuates stigma, and that can make it more difficult for people to seek treatment."

"Right," Charlie clears his throat. "Sorry, what I meant was I'm looney tunes."

"Not better Dad!" Terra's tone is no longer light.

Charlie grins. He's purposely pushing Terra's buttons, like the ornery old New England fisherman he is.

"Jesus Terra, can you put the PC police work on hold for a night? I'm the one who spent time in a psych ward, and I'm cool with it," Declan calls out.

Boof. Lucy Hawkins has managed to rock up high enough on her tip toes to gently whack her eldest son's head. Quite the feat considering she's five-one and Declan is six-one. "Do not take the Lord's name in vain in my house, Declan Eammon Hawkins."

Declan rubs the back of his head, scowling, and I chuckle. "Some things never change."

My eyes find Terra and she's smiling right back at me and mouths the words, "I told you so."

My heart beats faster. Then the door opens behind me and Logan walks in with River on his hip. Oh my God, he's so big. His hair is darkening a little to a golden color from the bleached wheat color it was when he was one, and of course there's much more of it. He's looking more and more like Logan—and Finn if you want to get technical. "Do you remember your Uncle Jake? He gave you your Ewok stuffie."

River stares at me, little pudgy face scrunched up as he really gives it his all trying to remember me. I smile and wave and although I don't think he remembers, he announces. "Tank woo unkie Jake."

"My pleasure," I say as Logan puts him down and he toddles straight over to his granny Lucy. More people start walking into the restaurant behind them.

"The guys from the station found out there was a little welcome back thing here for ya and wanted to tag along," Logan explains.

"Thought we could have some fun before you start ordering us around like a big shot," Murphy Ross announces. I remember her well. She was in the academy with me and we both started at Ocean Pines together. A few other faces are familiar like Dan Keribo, who was my favorite co-worker back when I started. So good to see him again. And Ronan Green. He's a few years older than me and was already a firefighter when I started but unlike Dan, he was far from my favorite. You always haze a probie a little bit, but Ronan was relentless and a total dick. He gives me a nod and a smile, but it's insincere. I ignore him and make a point of introducing myself to the co-workers I don't know yet.

A few hours later, the party is going strong and I'm enjoying every minute of it, as long as I don't look at Terra and the boyfriend, who's name I have inadvertently found out is Tom Kowalewicz. I overheard him introduce himself to Murphy and Ronan. Later, as the party is winding down and I'm grabbing a lobster bomb—Lucy Hawkins's famous homemade appetizer—off the food table, Tom walks right over and introduces himself. I pop the bomb in my mouth, wipe my hand on a napkin and give his hand a shake, firmer than I need to.

"I thought I should say hey since, you know, this get-together is for you and we've never met and Terra talks about you all the time," he says with a friendly smile. "I'm an associate professor of social sciences over at Darby College in Portsmouth. That's in New Hampshire."

"Yeah. I know where Portsmouth is. Grew up in Ocean Pines," I explain. I toss a smile at him hoping it takes the edge off my words. "You're dating Terra?"

He nods and shrugs. *Shrugs?*

"Yeah. For a while now. Long distance," he explains. "We're

both super busy. I have work and she's got this place to run and school and between that and my cycling club commitments and her doctor's appointments it's been hard. Which is too bad because she's a great girl."

Why does it sound like he's breaking up with her as he talks about her? Is that my wishful thinking? He makes eye contact. He has to look up to do it, but that's normal. I'm six-four, tallest guy in the room tonight, and most nights. Tom is probably about five-nine. "Someone like Terra is worth it, though."

He nods. Slowly. "Sure. Yeah. Of course. But the lupus thing… it's tough."

I officially do not like him.

"Tough on *her*, you mean?"

Before he can respond the devil herself is in front of us. "Why are you two talking?"

"Umm.. because we haven't met yet because you haven't bothered to introduce us," I tell her and she snaps her head up to glare at me.

"Tom Kowalewicz, my boyfriend, meet Jake Maverick, best friend of Logan and Finn," Terra says cordially. "I'm tired. I'm heading home now. You coming Tom?"

But Tom isn't looking at her or paying attention. The front door has opened and two people have walked in. "Is that… Abbott Barlowe?"

Terra swings her head around. "It is."

"Like *the* Abbott Barlowe? Who plays for the Boston Eagles?" Tom is fangirling so hard I'm almost embarrassed for him.

"Yeah." Terra's tone is hard and cold like stone but Tom doesn't notice.

"You know him? How did this never come up? Can you introduce me?"

"Nope," Terra answers, and finally Tom looks at her. He's

visibly startled by the hardness in her chocolate eyes. "Because that blonde he walked in with is his sister and my ex-best friend and I've exiled the whole family. But Jake here might be able to help you out. Since it's his party, and she's his ex-girlfriend."

Terra storms off toward the doors to the deck that overlooks the dock. Tom doesn't follow. Jerkoff. I'm about to turn around and follow her to explain I definitely didn't invite Aspen or Abbott when Abbott calls my name. "Hey bud. I'm leaving tomorrow for training camp but I had to swing by and say welcome home."

"Yeah, thanks."

Abbott shakes my hand and actually pulls me into a hug. Abbott and I were never close. He's a good guy and everything, we just don't gel. He was closest to Declan growing up, but they don't really talk anymore. Of course they didn't have the colossal blow-out fight that Terra and Aspen had. Speaking of … my eyes land on her. "Hey Aspen. How are you?"

I lean down to give her a hug because it's expected. She hugs me back. "Oh you know…"

Tom clears his throat. I pull away from Aspen. "Have you guys met Tom? He's with Terra."

Tom immediately starts talking to Abbott about hockey. I back away and turn to make my way out to the deck. Aspen's voice calls my name. "Jake! Can we catch up for a sec?"

"Yeah. In a minute. I have to do something," I call back and make my way to the deck doors. I'm worried Terra won't wait for her man to stop gushing all over Abbott and just leave by herself, and I don't want to miss her.

Out on the deck Terra is leaning against the railing. It's still unbelievably warm outside and humid. My clothes start to feel clingy as soon as I step outside, and there's zero breeze. I notice for the first time she's wearing a long-sleeved sweater over her cute dress. "Aren't you melting in that?"

She nods, keeping her eyes on the inky black ocean churning in front of us. The moonlight is slicing a perfect silvery line down the middle of the water. It's really pretty and I realize how much I missed this, the tranquility of the ocean.

"So take off the sweater."

"Nope. I'm good," she replies firmly. It makes no sense but I don't push her.

"So Tom…" Now she looks at me, her expression anxious. "How'd you meet?"

"He gave a guest lecture at my school. I attended and asked him a couple questions afterward and he asked for my number," Terra replies. There's no awe in her voice. No excitement or sweet nostalgia as she recounts the tale.

"How old is he?"

"Thirty-one."

"Wow. Older than Deck," I say without thinking.

"Let me guess, you think he's too old for me," Terra says but doesn't stop talking so I can answer the question. "I mean if you thought a junior was too old for a freshman, this must be totally unacceptable to you. Tom was already in college when I was a freshman. Gasp!"

"You're feisty tonight," I remark and wink at her before growing serious. "And I don't think he's too old."

"Age was one of your excuses not to touch me when we were in high school," Terra replies, turning her eyes back to the ocean.

I laugh. "Okay well, if we're following the stupid things we said when we were teenagers, then why aren't you and Tommy boy married with twins named Chuck and Blair?"

She swings her head back to stare at me. The freckles on her nose are gleaming in the moonlight and it's fucking adorable. I want to cup her face and run the pad of my thumb across them. "You told your family you wanted to marry by twenty and have twins and name them after those *Gossip Girl* characters, remember?"

"I was thirteen and an idiot," Terra replies. "I don't actually want kids now. And marriage is a big maybe … and I'm not talking with Tom, I'm talking with anyone."

I love the Tom part of that revelation but not the anyone part.

"Oh, so you've changed, but I haven't?" I cock an eyebrow.

"Maybe you did but how would I know?" she asks softly after a long pause where we just stare at each other. "You didn't keep in touch."

Ouch.

"And that's exactly why I'm out here," I lean on the railing too, making sure my forearm rests against hers. I can't feel her skin through that damn sweater, unfortunately. "I'm trying to catch up with you. I've missed you."

"What?" I can't decide if her tone is shocked or offended.

"I missed you," I double down. "I thought about you a lot when I was in King's Rock."

"Okay…" Now she sounds cautious. Like she's expecting a punchline or a backhanded compliment.

I laugh. "This isn't a set up for a joke or something, Tink. I mean it. You were on my mind a lot."

"Over three entire years?"

"Yeah."

"And you didn't call? Email? Visit?"

"No. I didn't." She's got me there. "I'm sorry about that. It wasn't because I didn't want to but I just… needed some space."

"From?"

"This town. My past. My own demons," I reply and those dark eyes of hers are locked onto mine. So piercing, so fabulously intense. Terra doesn't look at you, she looks through you. I love it and am terrified of it at the very same time. Always have been.

"You can't leave your demons behind," she reminds me in a calm, confident voice. "They follow you."

"Sometimes you need to go somewhere else to realize that," I explain and she just nods, like she gets it. "I'm sorry I didn't keep in touch."

"So am I."

That tiny confession sends a ripple of warmth through my chest. I need to remind myself she's taken. So I say, "Tom mentioned your lupus. How is it? Are you doing okay?"

The soft smile that had been flirting with her mouth, disappears. "Tom mentioned it? Why?"

"I… I don't know he just did," I say, wondering what the hell is up with her. "Said you had a lot of doctor's appointments."

"He's talking to you? About my doctor's appointments?"

"Look I'm not trying to start a fight between you two," I say and want to feel worse than I do, but the fact is I don't like him. I didn't like the way he talked about her like she wasn't fucking amazing and perfect and better than he could ever deserve. Her eyes glint in the moonlight. Her hair looks thicker than it has in the past and it's loose and skimming her shoulders except for the couple strands kind of stuck to her cheek because of the dewy humidity. I want desperately to brush them away. "You look great, Terra."

"I do?"

"Yeah. Beautiful actually."

"Hey Jake!"

Aspen. Fuck.

"Oh. Hey Terra," Aspen says, and I hear her heels clicking on the wooden deck as she approaches. "How have you been?"

"I'll leave you two alone to get reacquainted," Terra says, and just like that she's gone, scooting by Aspen and back into the party.

"Tink, wait!" I call and her steps slow. I turn to Aspen. "Can I talk to you in a minute. I haven't finished with Terra."

"Honestly, Jake, it's fine," Terra argues, glancing at us from over her shoulder. "I told you earlier, I'm exhausted and heading home. I'm sure I'll see you again soon."

Terra continues on through the deck doors into the party. Aspen stands awkwardly a foot and a half away. I turn to face her, exhaling loudly as I lean back on the railing.

"Why do I get the feeling I was interrupting something?"

"Because you did," I reply, bluntly. "Did you know she's dating that douche canoe trying to kiss your brother's ass?"

Aspen smiles, but even in the dim moonlight I can tell it's not her usual smile. Aspen is hard as nails and passionate. Everything from her smile to her laugh to the way she speaks is no holds barred. But not tonight. Tonight she's reserved, uptight. "I knew she had a boyfriend. I mean, she didn't tell me but I heard she had met someone who was from out of town. And Mrs. Green told me he's rich. Family money. They own camp grounds all over New England or something. It's Ocean Pines, Jake. People can't fart without someone talking about it."

"Yeah … I didn't miss that," I reply.

"You know we're lucky no one's talking about what happened with us…" Aspen says, her voice significantly lower than it was a moment ago. She walks closer, basically taking over Terra's position, against the railing next to me. Her blue eyes are so pale they look almost white in this light as she stares at me, willing me to know exactly what she's talking about. "You remember that … right?"

"Aspy I was drunk but not that drunk. Of course I remember," I reply. "And thankfully no one was hanging out in the Wagon Wheel Motel parking lot at four a.m. that night so they didn't see our unexpected walk down memory lane."

"Yeah… we were discreet. I'm still kind of amazed out of all the bars in Scarborough you walked into the one I was working an undercover case in," Aspen says in awe and something in my stomach tightens uncomfortably. If she starts talking about fate or something… But then her expression gets serious. "And just for the record I'm still on the same page I was then. It was a one-time thing."

"No strings attached," I agree. It's what I said then, before we got naked, because there was no way I was doing it if we weren't both emotionally on the same page. "So we should probably stop talking about it."

"Sure thing. After I tell you this one thing," She turns to face me. Her expression is serious. "I'm pregnant. Full disclosure, there's a fifty-fifty chance it isn't even yours. But I'm telling you because … well there's a fifty percent chance it is, and even though I won't ask a single solitary thing of you financially or emotionally, I thought you should know. Because like we said earlier, it's Ocean Pines, and people will start talking when I start showing, so that means you'll find out eventually anyway."

I … what? She did not just say … She can't be. Is she? Oh my God this isn't a joke. "Okay. Great. You know. Tick that one off my To-Do list," She starts to walk away. I reach out for her but miss. I'm moving like I'm up to my neck in quick-drying cement "Oh, and tell anyone and I'll kill you. This is my news to share, okay? Thanks! Later Jake."

"Aspen, wait!"

"No. Later, Jake."

She disappears back inside. My eyes follower her through the plate glass window as she weaves through the remaining guests to the front door and then out, where she disappears from view.

Holy shit. What the hell just happened?

3

TERRA

Tom is more handsy than I would like in the back of the Uber – AKA Jay's nineteen ninety-nine Toyota Corolla. He's tipsy and affectionate. This should be every girl's dream, I think for the hundredth time. But I have never been one for PDA.

To be fair Jay has probably seen worse. He is literally the only Uber driver in Ocean Pines. No joke, you pull up the app and you'll always only get his little icon, parked at the trailer park he lives in. Luckily he's a great, reliable driver with his eyes always on the road and not glancing in his rearview at his passengers. Still, when Tom kisses my neck I pull away. "Busy night tonight, Jay?"

He shrugs. "Not especially. I guess for Ocean Pines it's been a little busy. Mostly people coming and going from Jake's little welcome home bash."

I nod. "Yeah there were a lot of people there."

"He's a popular guy," Jay replies. "Even got Abbott Barlowe to make an appearance. That says something."

"You drove him to the restaurant?"

Jay shakes his head and he turns left onto my street. "No. But I drove Aspen home from the party. She was fighting with Abbott on her phone the whole ride because I guess she wasn't supposed to leave without him. Anyway, she was upset about more than that. No idea what though."

Huh. Aspen left before I did? It took me about twenty minutes to say goodbye to my family members and peel Tom from Abbott but I assumed Aspen would have still been outside with Jake.

"We have arrived at your destination," Jay declares in a robot voice like he's a human GPS as he pulls to the curb in front of my building, which is an old, massive Victorian house that was converted into apartments in the seventies.

My apartment is on the top floor, accessed by a very long staircase on the side of the building. The outside of the house, which was constructed in 1881 when Ocean Pines was founded, is weathered blue-gray shingles with white-framed windows. There's only five apartments in the whole three story building and I'm the only one on the top floor and the only one with a balcony, tiny as it may be. I have enough space for a suspended rope chair and a tiny table which is all I need. And if I stand up as tall as I can and look to the right, I can see the ocean on a clear day. The males in my family and Tom complain about the sloped ceilings because it's technically the attic, but at five-foot-three, that never bothered me much. Lately it's the stairs that bug me. So much climbing and I'm always exhausted. I dread them even now, just thinking about them.

"Jake have a good time?" Jay inquires as we unbuckle our seatbelts.

I nod. "Yeah. I guess."

Jay chuckles. "I heard he won some big fancy medal over in King's Hill or wherever the hell he was."

"King's Rock," I correct. "It's on the border with New Brunswick Canada and yeah, he saved a baby in a big fire when he was actually off-duty. He was given the medal of Valor. Youngest firefighter in the State to receive it in the last forty years."

"Wow. Who would have thought that fucked-up little orphan kid would turn into a hero?" Jay says and he means it as a compliment but it bugs me. Still, I know Jay is essentially a good guy so I bite my tongue and nod as Tom opens the door, climbs out, and reaches out his hand to help me. I wave at Jay, who calls out, "Five-star ratings are always appreciated!"

Jay drives off. He doesn't have to be so nice. The town doesn't have a taxi service, so it's Jay or walking. It's adorable how seriously he takes customer service and how his Corolla is always immaculate. By the time we make it all the way up the staircase to my apartment I am beyond exhausted and fighting the urge to pant from exertion. I've only been on dialysis for nine weeks now but I swear my body feels like it's been ten years. Oh God, I can't even imagine what I'll feel like if I'm actually still on it in ten years.

The last thing I would want right now is sex, even if I didn't have a serious topic to discuss, but it's clearly the only thing Tom wants. He is lifting my hair and kissing the back of my neck as I lock the apartment door behind us. I turn around and face him, placing a palm on each side of his handsome face. "Tom, I'm wiped out. And... I kind of think we need to talk about some stuff."

He looks disappointed but nods. "Whatever you need, T."

I am not a fan of the way he shortens everyone's names to initials. I'm T. His sister is B. My brothers are F and L and D. "Okay let's start with an easy one. Can you drive me to and from dialysis Monday, before you head back to New Hampshire? I know Logan has River and Finn and Nova are working at the restaurant. Declan has some marketing meeting in Boston or something. Dad has to go out on the boat and Mom... well she makes me nuts when she comes with me. She hovers and asks the nurses too many questions and tries to pray over me while the treatment is happening and it just stresses me out."

He walks into the living room, ducking to avoid a beam the runs through the middle of the room, and I follow. When he turns to face me he looks contrite. "I can drive you there, but I won't be able to drive you home. I know I usually leave late afternoon but I have to get back early this time because my bike club is doing a late afternoon ride, and I kind of organized it, so I can't bail. Your treatment takes so long. I wouldn't make it back in time for the ride."

Oh. Okay. So much for that being the easy ask. "Okay…. I guess I can find someone else."

"Ask the new guy," Tom suggests as he walks past my breakfast bar that divides the kitchen from the living room and dips his head a little so he can walk over to the fridge where the ceiling slopes. He grabs my filtered water jug from there and makes his way over to the glasses stacked on the open shelf. "He's probably got nothing to do."

"Jake isn't exactly the new guy." I have no idea why I feel the need to explain that, but I do. "I've known him since I was twelve. He was born and raised in Ocean Pines. When he was emancipated from his mom, he lived above the restaurant and he worked for us for like seven years before he became a firefighter."

"Wow. You know a lot about him. Are you President of his fan club or something?" Tom chuckles at his joke and takes two glasses off the shelf, flips them over and starts to fill them with water. "Anyway, whatever. Ask him."

"I'll figure something out," I mumble and shake my head when he offers me a glass of water. "I pee enough as it is, I don't need water before bed."

He cringes uncomfortably because I brought up peeing. Tom is supportive as long as I don't get into gory details of kidney issues and lupus in general . I have told myself repeatedly not to take it personally. His sister said she once cut her hand on a glass she was washing as a teenager and Tom bolted as soon as he saw the blood. Like, ran out of the house and left her bleeding all over the place. He did run to the neighbors, screaming, and got them to come over and help her and drive her to the hospital, but Tom himself was useless. And he was seventeen at the time.

"Okay. No water," he puts the glass he poured for me down on the counter. "What else do you want to talk about? How about how you've never told me you know one of my favorite hockey players, ever?"

"No, not that," I shake my head and dive head first into my next topic. "Did you get a chance to talk to your insurance company? About the testing and stuff?"

Everything about Tom suddenly changes. His shoulders tense, but his head sags. His eyes hit the floor and stay there. He doesn't seem casual, calm and collected anymore. He seems… awkward, tense and maybe even a little… guilty?

"I just ask because you said last week when you couldn't come for our regular weekend visit that it was because you were figuring out stuff with your insurance company and your work union about whether or not you'd be covered if you donated?" I say and I feel suddenly like a beggar on the street with my hat out. Which infuriates me.

"Yeah… Terra… listen," he pauses, finally lifting his head. He looks at me. His wholesome, handsome face is suddenly void of warmth or that friendly easy smile he has that I found so attractive when we first met. "My family thinks it's a lot to ask of anyone to donate a kidney."

"I didn't ask you," I reply flatly. "You said you wanted to see if you were a match."

"Yeah well what the hell else was I supposed to say?" Tom says, and now that guilty vibe has switch to annoyed. He puts his glass down on the counter behind him and runs a hand through his blond hair, which doesn't ruffle because it's too short to be displaced. "I mean I really like you. We're a great match but we weren't even dating all that long when you told me about the kidney problems. I just … I felt cornered."

"You were not cornered," I argue and I'm fighting a hot flush to my cheeks that is sheer and utter humiliation. "I was never going to ask you to donate. I made a pact with myself when I found out that I was only going to ask family, direct blood relatives, and I have stuck by that. You volunteered."

"I know. But I never expected to have to do it. I thought for sure someone in your family would match." he pauses. "My parents flipped out when I told them I was thinking about it. They said I was too young to live on one kidney."

"Not scientifically accurate." I can't keep my mouth shut when someone spews misinformation about anything. It's not who I am. But I should keep my mouth shut here because it makes it seem like I'm making an argument for him to donate. I'm not.

"Well, what if something happens in five or ten years to my only kidney? What if my parents need one in the future and I gave the extra one to you?" Tom asks, and in that very second I know that this relationship is over. Not because he won't get tested or donate but because he's made me feel so utterly unimportant and defective—like a burden.

"Those are all valid concerns."

I walk out of the kitchen and back into the living room. Tom follows, still talking. "I mean they haven't completely shut the door on Declan donating, right?"

"They have."

"But he's fighting it, right?"

"He is."

"Maybe he'll win," Tom says, hopefully.

"Tom, is that hope dripping from your tone over the idea that I'll be healthier if they allow Deck to donate or that you'll be able to stop feeling like such a cowardly asshole?" I walk to the front door. He follows behind me.

"That's not fair. I am not a coward because I have other family members to think about, Terra," he tells me. "We've been together five and a half months. I just…"

"You just never should have volunteered to be tested," I finish the sentence for him. "And I agree. That's why I *never* asked you to be tested. Not once. You said you wanted to be there for me."

"I am! I've driven you to doctor's appointments and dialysis," Tom defends himself and I try not to smile. He drove me to the doctor once and to dialysis once. "And I've given up all my weekends at home because you can't drive to Portsmouth anymore because of all the medical stuff you're dealing with here. I haven't complained about that even though it totally sucks that I have to do all the sacrificing now with the distance thing."

"Well, there's a problem I can fix," I say and unlock my locked front door. "You don't have to do that anymore. We're done. No need to spend weekends here or ever set foot in Ocean Pines again."

He looks stricken. "Terra. Come on. I don't want to break up."

"Yeah but I do." I say. "Can you go home now?"

"It's almost midnight."

"Well head up to Route One. There's about forty motels to choose from." I open the door and hold it wide for him to exit. The bag he brought with him for his weekend stay is still packed and lying on the floor of my front hall. I pick it up and hand it to him.

"I've been drinking Terra."

I pull my phone from the pocket of my cardigan and pull up the Uber app. I punch the screen and turn back to Tom. "Jay is on his way."

"Terra…" he pauses. Our eyes lock and then I see it… the relief. "I'm sorry."

"Yeah, me too."

He steps through the open front door and I watch him disappear down the stairs before I close my front door and lock it again. I take three deep breaths, the last one ending in a small hiccup of a sob and then I slide down the door and dissolve into a puddle of tears.

4

TERRA

My dad, Charlie Hawkins, isn't a talker. If you looked up 'Salt of the earth New Englander' in a dictionary, you'd find his picture. He's tough, rough around every edge and also a giant teddy bear. The one thing my brothers and I have never doubted is his love for us. And I'm thinking of him right now, on the beach as the sun crests and creates a shimmering golden glow on the waves. Because it's his rare but sage advice that I'm taking right now. He once told me, when I was crying over teenage drama of some sort, that the best medicine for any emotional ailment was the beach. So I should pick my sorry self up and go take a walk, get my toes buried deep in that sand, inhale that salty air and let the waves crush my worries as they break.

I'm doing that now, only to be honest I'm picturing Tom's face getting crushed under each breaking wave. Jerk. As I left the apartment for this walk, before sunrise, I noticed Tom's car was already gone from my parking lot. He didn't even try to talk to me again and fix things. It stung even though I realized halfway through my sleepless night that I was more humiliated than heartbroken. Tom triggered my worst fear—that someone I cared about felt this fucking illness that was an albatross around my neck was something I had tried to wrap around their neck too. I never outright asked him to try and be my donor. I promised myself when my doctor told me I was going to need a new kidney that I wouldn't ask anyone. But did it hurt that he didn't volunteer to help me like my family and even Nova's brother did? Hell yes.

"Tinkerbell?"

The voice booms over the surf crashing to my left. It's deep, friendly and oh so familiar. I turn to my right where a group of surfers who have just come in from the ocean are standing around talking, boards at their feet. My eyes lock with Jake's right away.

Shit. I should have known he would be at the beach. He'd spent the last three years in the mountains, nowhere near the sea that he grew up loving, so of course he's going to be here surfing for the second time in twenty-four hours. After a curt wave, I turn and walk the other way.

"Terra!"

Fuck. I pause at the very same time I consider pretending I didn't hear him, which makes that idea impossible. I slowly turn around. He's jogging toward me. Damnit all to hell. I try to transfer the seven sand dollars in my hands to one hand so I can use the other to pull the sunglasses holding my hair back down over my eyes. I get the sunglasses down but drop two sand dollars. Before I can bend to pick them up, Jake is on his knee in front of me doing just that. He holds them up to me, still on his knee in his wetsuit, and gives me the most dazzling smile. "Terra Lucille Hawkins, will you take these sand dollars as a symbol of my love and affection?"

My whole body heats up, and my ovaries do somersaults. Sweet baby Jesus, this man has no idea how much he affects me. And I've learned not to tell him.

"Very cute, " I reply and try not to smile too big as I take the sand dollars out of his hand. "Don't you have work in an hour? Your first shift."

He laughs. I've missed that sound. Jake's laugh is a deep chesty rumble. Hearing it for the first time at almost thirteen was the first time my girl parts tingled. "You took the sand dollar, that means you accept my affection. "

"Uh-huh." I start walking. "I'll let you get back to surfing."

"I can skip another wave. I'd rather chat with you. I told ya last night I missed you. That wasn't a lie," he replies and smiles. I know he means my family, not just me alone. But his smile isn't its normal light, casual, lazy smile. It's … intense. I must be hallucinating from exhaustion, right?

I stop walking and just stare up at him, a tall wall of muscle wrapped in neoprene. His hair is glimmering like wet coal in the sun turning the sky orange above us. He cocks that head and his full mouth quirks upward. "This sun is barely up, so the sunglass thing is overkill."

He reaches out and lifts them off my face, pushing them back onto my head. He squints. "You've been crying."

"Nope. Collecting sand dollars. Got sand in my eyes." The lie is ridiculous and he will see right through it.

His dark, delicious eyes fall to my little pocket of sand dollars. "Yeah, you've been hunting sand dollars since you were three. And like the perfect girl you are, you don't keep the live ones, and dead ones don't spit sand at you."

"Live ones don't either. They have no defense mechanism against predators except to hide in the sand," I explain and it makes him smile.

"I love that you know all these weird facts."

"I love that you called me perfect because I'm far from it." I had no intention of blurting that out but there it goes, flying out of my mouth before my brain can stop it.

One of the other surfer guys yells his name. I can't make out their faces from here, but I'm sure I know them. I know almost everyone in Ocean Pines. "You coming to breakfast, Mav?"

He shakes his head. "I'm gonna go straight to work from here. Later guys."

"You can go, Jake. I'm sure you're hungry," I say and start to walk away.

"I can eat at the fire house." He falls in step beside me and for ten paces we both say nothing, we just walk the velvety wet sand, as the edge of the surf dances over our toes. "Where's the boyfriend? Not into some early morning beach combing?"

"Did you know the larvae of the sand dollar are able to clone themselves?" I ask.

"Don't distract me with your hot nerdy girl facts, Terra Hawkins," Jake says sternly but he's grinning and oh my God, with the coral colored sky bouncing off the tanned skin covering his high cheekbones I'm just… enamored. And it's wrong and dangerous. It did teenage me exactly zero favors to fall head over heels for Jake. "Where's the boyfriend?"

"He had a name. Tom."

A charcoal eyebrow lifts. "Had? And yeah I know his name I just don't like him enough to use it."

Now both of my own eyebrows raise. "You can't dislike him. You don't know him."

"I can and I do," Jake replies defiantly. "I am an excellent judge of character. He isn't good enough for you."

"I have three brothers and a dad. I don't need another overprotective, testosterone-filled protector in my life. It's not eighteen-eighty-one, Jake," I reply and stop walking, turning my body away from Jake to stare out at the waves as they crash. "Anyway, it's over with Tom. Ended last night."

"You broke up? Last night?"

I nod. There's silence. I don't want to look up at him. And then I hear a chuckle. A fucking laugh! So I can't help but snap my head up to look at him.

"Of course you did. Of course you're single now. Not in June, but now."

"What are you talking about?" His smile has turned trite and he's looking up at the sky like he's arguing with the universe.

He sighs, runs his hands through his wet hair and then faces me again. "What happened? He made you cry."

"Don't all people cry when they break-up?" I reply.

He shrugs those broad, neoprene covered shoulders. "I don't. I've never dated a girl who has."

"Not in front of you," I correct him but I hate myself for it. I do not want to discuss his past relationships. Especially not now when I feel so vulnerable. "Anyway, I don't want to talk about Tom, okay? It's over and in all honesty, it's for the best. Even if it sucks."

I start walking again but all of a sudden his arm is around my shoulders and he's pulling me into him and I'm tingling all over at the feel of his body against mine. "Let's sit. Talk."

The beach in Ocean Pines is wide and long. When it's low tide, it creates a bit of a sandy hill to get back up to the board walk. Jake walks me halfway up the hill and stops us. Slowly, I let him turn me toward the water and pull me down to the sand. Now we're sitting side-by-side staring at the rolling surf, his arm still around me. "I hate that you cried over him." His statement is star-tling, mostly because he says it in such a deep, low voice, stuffed with emotion.

"I'll be fine."

"I know. You're the strongest Hawkins. Also the prettiest, but don't tell Finn I said that," Jake replies, and when I steal a glance up at him he winks. I smile and swallow down a laugh. His arm around my shoulder tightens. "A smile? Wow, it's almost like you're happy I'm home."

"I never understood why you left," I confess. Afraid to keep looking at him, I lay my seven sand dollars out in front of my crossed legs.

"There's not enough time to really get into that since, as you mentioned earlier, I have to be at work for my first shift in twenty-five minutes," Jake replies quietly. "I got a new place too and I'm supposed to swing by and grab the keys."

Now I can't help but look up at him again. "So fast! Man, Logan has been searching for his own place for like a year and you're back fifteen minutes and snag one."

"I lucked out. Friend of a friend knew a guy," Jake explains. "I actually got it lined up before I even got here. You should come by and see it sometime soon. It's right on the water."

He tells me the address. I know exactly where it is because it's only four short blocks from my place. I like the idea of him being so close. After he explains a little about how he found it, and how small it is but the views make it worth it, he pauses. "Tell me another silly sea fact like you used to do when we were kids."

I smile, eyes back on my sand dollars. "Ninety-four percent of the earth's living species exist within the oceans you call silly. And the world's oceans contain more artifacts, thanks to shipwrecks and such, than the world's museums."

"I've missed you in all your nerdy glory," he flops back on the sand after letting out that beyond-sexy grunt.

I smile and my heart swells more than it should. My brain yells '*Take that, Tom!*' I rearrange the sand dollars in order from smallest to biggest the way my mom used to line us up for family photos.

"Did you miss me?"

My breath catches. That's a loaded question because I don't know how to answer. Things definitely feel different between us. I know it's only been twenty-four hours—not even, technically—but he feels less… walled off. I'm no longer filled with teenage humiliation over that shun way back when or the fact that he dated my best friend instead of me… okay well maybe that one still irks me a little. But not enough to keep me from being happy he's back.

"The pregnant pause isn't doing anything for my ego, Tink," Jake warns me.

I turn and glance over my shoulder at him, lying in the sand, a careless smile on his pretty mouth, a glimmer of something mischievous in his coal colored eyes, sand granules peppered into his inky, still damp hair. "I missed you. I'm glad you're back but I also wish you never left."

The smile deepens, but not in a cocky way. "I needed to go, but I also needed to come back."

"Why?" I whisper. I don't mean to but I don't seem to be able to find my voice.

He sits back up. Sand is everywhere – the shoulders of his wetsuit, his hair, his cheek. "I needed to prove something to myself, and to others. I wanted to prove I wasn't just the town charity case."

"You were never that to my family or me and you know that," I can't help but gently chastise him. "We helped you out because you were a kid. All kids in your situation need help, but you especially deserved it. It wasn't charity, or pity."

"Yeah but… I was leaning too hard on your brothers and parents. I expected too much." He looks suddenly uncomfortable like there's a deeper issue he doesn't want to disclose. There must be.

"Children who grew up with the lack of stability you did, tend to have fight or flight reactions to situations," I explain, my schooling kicking into high gear. "So what exactly triggered your flight three years ago, Jake? There is something more concrete than just a vague idea of proving yourself. Which, by the way, you never needed to do."

His eyes shift from the ocean in front of us to me. We're

shoulder to shoulder. If I wasn't wearing a cardigan I would be able to feel the neoprene of his wetsuit. I can almost feel his breath on my cheek. Oh how I wish we were just a little inch closer. "I see you finished you're therapy degree, huh?"

"Close. One semester left, but I'm taking a break," I reply without elaboration. He's trying to change the subject and I want to force him to open up but I'm distracted by the sand on his cheekbone. It's the perfect excuse to touch him and that's what I want more than anything right now. So I reach up and softly brush my fingertips across it from just under his eyes to his hairline. The sand tumbles off. His skin is warm from the sun and slightly sticky from the salt water.

He reaches up and circles my wrist with his hand, freezing my movement, keeping the tips of my fingers against his cheek. His own fingers curl around the edge of my sleeve. "What's with another long sleeved shirt, Tink? It's already high seventies out here."

"Long story," I whisper back.

"Don't feel like talking?" He questions, his voice also a whisper, but a rough one that makes a tingle start to spread inside me. I shake my head. "Yeah, me either."

His head moves a fraction of an inch closer to mine. And just when he gets close enough that he blurs and my stomach clenches in anticipation … his cell phone alarm goes off a few feet away, by his surfboard. It might as well be a cannon going off. We both jump apart and he leaps to his feet. "Fuck. I have to leave like right now or I will be late for my first shift."

"Seven a.m. to seven a.m.," I mumbled. "Just like the paramedics."

"Yeah, I'm actually working with Logan this shift which will be great," Jake says and walks over to his stuff. I follow. I don't know why. I feel like I'm not ready to walk away. I'm clinging to whatever the hell that almost was and am not ready to let it go. He grabs his phone off his towel and I watch as he turns off the alarm.

"Man, timing is everything, and I don't seem to have it," His smile disappears. "I wish I could stay longer and talk more."

It doesn't feel like talking is what we were going to do, but I don't say that to him because I'm never sure of anything with Jake. And right now, that's a can of emotional worms I'm not ready to open. So instead I nod and smile back at him. "No worries. We have all the time in the world to catch up now that you're back for good."

"I hope so," Jake says and reaches for his board. "Okay. Well, I'm gonna go."

"Knock 'em dead on your shift!" I say cheerily but then realize how stupid that expression is for a firefighter. "I mean, don't actually knock anyone dead. Keep 'em all alive. And yourself too."

Everything is suddenly and completely awkward. My head clears instantly. I walk back over to my sand dollars and pick them up. "Have a good shift!" I call over my shoulder and without looking back, I walk down the beach away from Jake.

5

JAKE

OF COURSE LOGAN CATCHES ME UPCHUCKING IN THE BATHROOM at work on my very first damn shift. When I heard about the opening in Ocean Pines, one of the pros for applying on my pros and cons list was getting to work with Logan. He's on the paramedic team, which is also based out of the fire station, so I would be spending a lot of time with him. I figured it would give us a chance to get close again. We never had a genuine falling out but, well, we've had some issues most of which, like stereotypical manly men, we've never discussed. He was one of the main reasons I decided to leave Ocean Pines in the first place. The one I didn't want to discuss with Terra this morning. He doesn't know that though.

"Jesus, Mav, do you need to go home?" Logan asks as I walk out of the stall. He's standing there in a towel, soaking wet. I knew someone was in the shower when I rushed in here to heave up that lobster roll I ate before my shift started, but I didn't have an option to do this anywhere else.

"Nah. I'm good. Just… nerves," I say with a shrug and walk over to the bank of sinks and turn the cold water on full blast.

First I splash it on my face and then I drink from the faucet to wash out my mouth.

"Nerves? You still do that? Like, a lot?" Logan's stern expression says he's unconvinced I'm okay.

When I was a kid I had what the doctors called a nervous stomach. Growing up, my life was more than a little unpredictable and I used to puke if I was really stressed or scared. Logan and Finn knew about it because I'd upchucked in front of them before. A lot. "Nah. But, you know, I just changed my whole life, so I guess it was bound to happen."

Oh and this morning I almost kissed your sister on the beach but then spent the last several hours spiraling over the fact that I might have impregnated her sworn enemy and my ex-girlfriend, so there's that.

"You look pale," Logan says as he studies my face. "You sure it's not more than nerves? Flu maybe? You're never pale."

I glance at myself in the mirror again. He's right. I'm olive skinned so for something to make me pale, it's serious. Potentially knocking up an ex is pretty damn serious. Logan of all people would be the one I should tell about this since River was an unplanned pregnancy. But Aspen told me to keep my mouth shut.

I catch his eye in the long mirror above the sinks. I've always been jealous of how the Hawkins kids look like their parents. You can visibly link traits to both Lucy and Charlie in each kid. I don't look a lick like my mom. She's fair skinned with medium brown hair and pale hazel eyes, narrow lips and an upturned nose. The only thing darker than my skin is my eyes, and the only thing darker than my eyes is my hair, which is jet black. My nose is straight and narrow, my lips full. I must look like the accidental, unknown sperm donor. But if you took a quick glimpse at Lucy and Charlie Hawkins you could pick out their four kids in a group of hundreds. Logan and Finn have their dad's chestnut hair that turns golden with enough sun and their dad's light blue eyes, strong jaw, and rugged build. Declan has a Charlie face but with Lucy's lighter hair and dark eyes. Terra got Lucy's dark eyes and her fair hair, and height, but there's Charlie in her wide set eyes, dimpled chin and freckles, which he had when he was younger too.

Terra.

I physically shudder at the idea that I may have to tell her I got Aspen pregnant. It's crazy that I feel worse about that than telling anyone else. It felt like something was finally happening with her this morning, but that's impossible… right? She just broke up with someone. I just got back to town. That alone would be enough to say the chemistry, the pull between us at the beach, couldn't be real. But it *felt* real. And right. But if she knew Aspen might be carrying my kid, she'd be even colder and more emotionally blocked off than she was before I left three years ago. And she would likely stay that way forever if the kid is mine. Suddenly the idea that I may have to go all my life without ever telling her how I feel seems ludicrous. Why the hell did I leave it so long?

"Dude… let me get my kit and check you out," Logan says.

I shake my head, making sure to hold his eye when I do it but not daring to speak. I don't want to tell him about this until I talk to Aspen again. I didn't have her phone number, because she's changed it in the last three years, and I'm not even sure if she's at the same apartment she was when I left and I didn't have time to drive by and find out. So since I can't see her or text her, I've sent her emails. Fourteen of them since last night, all begging for more information. She hasn't answered one of them.

"You've been a firefighter since you were twenty-one. You've worked this exact station and you were a lieutenant back in King's Rock for a year so that role's not new either. This shouldn't make you stressed, buddy," Logan claps my shoulder. "And you know this town like the back of your hand."

It's sweet he's trying to give me a pep talk. I wish this was my real issue because it would make me feel better. To be fair, it is something I worry about, just not my biggest worry anymore. "Yeah, I know. I'm good. I swear."

He doesn't look like he's convinced but he nods and makes his way over to the lockers and changing room. I head for the door to leave but pause. "Hey, how's it been being a dad to River? I mean now that you're…"

"Not so drunk I don't remember I have a kid?' Logan finishes that sentence way more bluntly than I would have. He grins to let me know he's okay with his own bluntness. "It's great. He is the best thing I ever did. Even though it means I have to deal with the wrath of Bethany for the rest of my life, I wouldn't give him up for anything."

I smile. Logan looks so proud right now. So fulfilled just talking about River. I want to cling to that, make it a reason to hope that would be me if Aspen's baby is mine, but then I remember Logan had good roots. Charlie and Lucy are solid parents. He knows how to be a good parent because he was raised by them. I'm the kid who was essentially raised by no one and everyone and has no foundation for this. That's a big part of the reason I have never wanted kids.

"Jake? You're pale again." Logan pulls on his underwear and a T-shirt.

Logan will be able to talk me off this mental ledge I'm teetering on. I know Aspen doesn't want anyone to know but I need to tell someone. I need support. Logan is also not a gossip. He's in Alcoholics Anonymous so he understands and values privacy. If I told him, he wouldn't tell a soul.

"Something… might have happened and I just…" The alarm starts echoing through the entire building. Logan rushes to throw the rest of his clothes on as I sprint to the door and make my way down the hall to where the firetrucks and my gear are.

The dispatcher's voice booms through the intercom. "Structure fire. Apartment complex. 19 Union Avenue. One Truck and ambulance required."

Shit. I know that address.

I charge down the hall to the engine bay and scramble into my gear like everyone else. Logan and his partner are jumping into their rig as I climb up into the firetruck. Our firehouse serves two towns. Ocean Pines is the smallest. The town next door, Old Orchard Beach, is the biggest and it's where the fire is.

We get there quickly and see fire spitting out the broken windows of one apartment unit. The one above my ex-girlfriend Aspen Barlowe's apartment. At least it was her apartment three years ago before I left town. Does she still live here? I fucking hope not.

We all jump off the rig and Captain yells orders. He has me on lead to go into the building with Ronan and Murphy. Dan and the others are working the truck and hose. I flip the switch in my brain that I have to, that I'm trained to, the one that has me walking into a burning building following all the rules, procedures, practices that I've been taught and not worry about personal problems. It locks up the part of my brain that wants to be freaking out that my ex, who may or may not be pregnant with my kid, might be burning to a crisp.

There's a crowd of tenants already on the grass but no Aspen. Maybe she moved? Three years is a long time. We start a floor by floor sweep of the building. Because the fire seems fairly contained to one unit and the main sprinkler system is raining down on us, we split up to cover more ground. I go up to the second floor, Ronan the third, and Murphy covers the first. As I'm helping out an elderly lady cradling her cat in her arms out of her apartment and down the stairs to the first floor, I hear screaming. Not screaming in agony or screaming in fear but screaming in frustration. I know that scream. And then, as I enter the lobby of the building with this gray-haired lady and her hissing orange cat, I hear Murphy. "Ma'am. Please! Calm down!"

Across the tiled lobby soaked with sprinkler water, she's got Aspen over her shoulder. Aspen's got her head reared up as she yells. Her blond hair is hanging in long wet curls around her face which is red with anger. In her hands she's got two bags, the reusable grocery store kind. I follow Murphy and my tantruming ex out the front doors, my arm wrapped around this little old lady who I guide straight over to Logan and Lester for a health assessment.

Murphy has plopped Aspen onto her feet and now she's standing on the grass in front of her building digging through her bags. "Ma'am you should probably go see the paramedics and make sure you don't have any—"

"I'm fine but you won't be if you call me Ma'am again," Aspen warns. "Got it, lady?"

"Sorry but I don't do cat fights," Murphy quips, unphased by Aspen's tantrum.

Ronan exits the building. "Third floor clear."

Technically Ronan Green is a lieutenant, like me, and we should always be on alternating shifts, but he is supposed to be training me, or reacquainting me as Captain D'Amato put it, with the station so we're on this call together.

I call out to Captain. "Building is clear."

"That's my job, Maverick," Ronan says and frowns and then he turns to the captain and shouts. "New guy is correct. All clear, Cap."

Captain nods in our direction and opens his mouth to give more orders but suddenly Aspen jumps to her feet and runs back toward the building. Captain's eyes look like they're going to fly out of his head and he points.

"On it!" I say loudly and put a hand on Murphy's shoulder to stop her from following Aspen before I take off after her. Ronan scowls at me as I jog by him but I pretend not to notice.

I reach her as she's about to run into the lobby again. Wrapping my arms around her waist, I lift her off her feet easily. Aspen is tall, almost five-ten, but I'm taller and picking her up is something I've done literally and figuratively before. She screeches in protest.

"Aspen I know this is a nightmare, but you don't need to up the ante by repeatedly running into a burning building," I say sternly and she stiffens for a second but then starts thrashing in my arms again. But at least she stops with the screaming.

I finally put her back on her feet, which I notice are bare, on the sidewalk and stand in front of her blocking her path back to the burning apartment building. "Jake, my stuff. It's all still in there!" Aspen explains to me, her very pretty face all twisted with stress and panic. "Thousands of dollars of work equipment. Notes. My work laptop. Evidence!"

She tries to rush past me again but I grab her by her narrow shoulders, which I suddenly realize are covered in only a thin, long-sleeved T-shirt, which is a pale gray and soaking wet. Soaking, like her hair. It's a chilly night. "Aspen, it's just stuff. If your rental insurance doesn't cover it, the building's insurance should. Now let's get you into a warm blanket."

Still holding her shoulders I guide her over to the ambulance. Well, it's more like shove and pull her because she really doesn't want to go. "I grabbed as much as I could," she points to the bags as we pass them. "But I didn't get everything."

"I have to say a part of me is impressed you're trying to save your work stuff and not your designer clothing," Logan says with a snarky grin as he starts unfolding a silver emergency blanket for her beside his ambulance. "You're not the Aspen I knew in high school who would save her Coach purse from an oncoming car before she'd save a kitten."

"Ugh. Logan, you still suck," Aspen says tersely and rolls her eyes. But she shivers and I frown. Her eyes find mine and she whispers. "Not now."

"Is it your apartment on fire, Aspen?" Ronan asks as he strides over to us.

"No. The one above me," Aspen explains, her tone terse and cold. "But the smoke is pouring into my place and it tripped the main sprinkler system and I'm sure my place is completely flooded by now."

I feel bad for her. Her big blue eyes are swimming in tears. Ronan stares at her and she stares back, defiant. He opens his mouth, closes it and storms off. "Jake, don't spend all night coddling your ex. We have work to do."

Logan wraps the blanket over Aspen's shoulders as I head back toward the building. Green falls in step with me and I hear Aspen's voice, high and panicky again. "He's going in there again? But I can still see flames!"

I turn to look at her, walking backwards toward the building. "It's my job, Aspen. Don't go anywhere until I'm done. Or else."

"You two a thing again?" Ronan asks with a cocked eyebrow I can see through his shield.

"Nope. Just friends."

"Exes are never friends," Ronan says and shoots me a patronizing look like I'm clueless. "And dating the same person twice is something only idiots do."

"You and Courtney broke up and got back together like five times in the three years you were dating before I left town, didn't you?" I counter, not because I want to make a case for dating Aspen but because I want him to see he's a hypocritical asshat. "Are you still with her?"

"Shut up and follow my lead, okay?"

I manage a terse nod, then I flip that switch in my brain again, blocking out Aspen and how much Ronan Green still annoys me and get back to work.

Twenty-five minutes later, the fire is out. The apartment it started in is a burned out shell and the ones above and below like Aspen's have serious smoke and water damage. No one is going to be allowed back in until the morning. Sadly for Aspen and a couple of others, it will be more than just one night as their apartments will need a shit ton of renovations.

I start to pull off my gear as I leave the building and as soon as my helmet and face shield are off she visibly sighs in relief. I walk over to where she's sitting on the curb behind the ambulance and stop directly in front of her. "Two questions. Say yes or no and nothing else," I command. "Are you okay?"

"Yes."

I turn to Logan. "Did you check her out?"

"Yeah. Vitals are fine and she has no wounds or injuries," Logan tells me.

I turn back to Aspen who is scowling because I reconfirmed with Logan and didn't just take her word for it. "*Everything*. Feels fine," she hisses.

"Okay. Good. Now Please tell me Major is somewhere safe," I say.

Aspen nods. Her blonde ringlets are drying and frizzing a little, giving her a golden halo under the street lamp. "He's in my car across the street. He was, of course, the first thing I saved."

"And then you went back into a burning building?" I say like it's a question but it's not. I lower my voice and glance around to make sure no one is paying attention to us. "After what you told me last night? You still went charging back into a burning building over work files?"

She looks instantly stricken. "I forgot."

"You forgot that you're..." I see Logan watching us so I don't finish that sentence.

"It's still new to me and I just panicked and didn't think."

"Major is here?" Logan interrupts. He's smiling, which is a rarity nowadays.

Aspen points to her car again.

"Door unlocked?"

When Aspen nods, Logan takes off in a jog across the street. Aspen glares at me. "My work is all I have. You know that."

"You apparently have more than just work now," I remind her, my eyes dipping down to stare at her midriff. Her stomach is as flat as ever—at least it appears that way through her loose, damp shirt.

Her arms drop to cover her middle. Our eyes meet. "Sorry for the trying to ghost you. I still like to avoid emotional conflict."

"So… what are the chances, really, that this is … mine?" I whisper after I've squatted down in front of her. The look that passes over her pretty features immediately makes me feel like an asshole. She looks the way she used to look when her parents would critique her appearance or chastise her for not being Godly enough. It's humiliation. She gets to her feet. I rise to join her.

"I can't talk about this right now. I can't have someone over-hear us," Aspen hisses and then whispers quickly. "The chances are truly fifty. I mean maybe even less because you were one time and the other guy was … more than one time. And I also want you to know he and I and you and I were five days apart. Not much in the baby making game or for the god-fearing good girl my mother expects me to be, but it isn't like it was two guys in one night."

"Aspen I don't care about that stuff," I reply. "I'm not here to slut shame you on any level. I'm just … I'm fucking confused. Worried. Stressed."

"Join the club."

I really look at her. The fear on her face makes her look young, like she did when we actually dated, which was ten whole years ago now. I hadn't slept with her in eight years, and never would have thought to do it again if she wasn't working under-cover in the one bar I happen to wander into while I was in an emotional tailspin. So many little particles had to come together to make that meteor, and somehow they did. And now it's going to impact my entire life.

Aspen runs a private detective firm and had been hired by the bar owner to pretend to be an employee. He was trying to clean the place up and find out which employee was dealing Molly to customers on the side. She was working the bar and I played along and didn't blow her cover, and stayed until close because I had nothing else to do. When I was the only one left in the place, we talked candidly. She was just getting out of a relationship that had soured fast and I … well all I said to her was I'd been recently shot down. It felt true enough after seeing Terra with Tom. By three in the morning we were in my motel room. Neither of us were fucking each other, we were trying to fuck these other people out of our systems.

"If it's mine I *will* be involved," I find myself promising and I know, even before she frowns, that I sound despondent and resigned. Like I'm walking a plank.

"I'm begging you not to talk about this right now. Not with so many people around, Jake," Aspen replies and glances over her shoulder toward her car. Logan has let Major out and is holding him by the collar while they cross the street.

I nod and change the subject back to her apartment. "You can't go back in there for at least twenty-four hours. Maybe forty-eight. And after that you may be able to salvage some stuff, but you still won't live there. You'll definitely need massive reno-vations."

Aspen lets out a tortured growl that gets the attention of her oversized German Shepherd that is now on this side of the street. Major, cocks his head to the side and then sprints to Aspen's side.

He looks up at me and for a millisecond I think he might growl, but then he sniffs and his tail starts wagging wild as he jumps up on me. I bend down and let him shower me with kisses as Logan joins us and scratches him behind the ears.

"Wow. He is a smart dog if he remembers you after three years away," Logan remarks in awe.

I used to volunteer to dog sit him when she went on vacation or couldn't bring him on one of her assignments so me and this gentle giant had been tight.

As I stand, Major spins around and gives his full attention to Logan, who grins like he used to years ago before the wheels came off his life.

"You should really get a dog, Logan," Aspen says. "River would love it and you're a different person when you're around them. You look positively human again."

Leave it to my ex to speak her mind so fully she pisses everyone off. Logan looks up and his dark eyebrows pinch as a frown pulls his mouth down. "What do I normally look like?"

"Like a hipster who spilt all his oat milk on the floor," Aspen says, flatly. "Like a millennial who can't find avocado toast. A grandfather who starts every conversation with 'back in my day'. Or your dad when there's a storm and he can't collect the lobster traps."

Logan raises a hand in between him and Aspen. "Thanks for all that elaboration, Aspy. And for making me wish Jake had let you run back into that building."

"Shut up," she says with a confident smile.

"You gonna stay at Abbott's now? You still have a set of keys, I assume?" I ask Aspen and she shakes her head.

"He was actually staying at the Five Seasons most of the summer. Went back to Boston this morning for training camp. His house is being renovated. Again," She rolls her eyes. "He doesn't have electricity or running water right now. I'll figure it out."

I know exactly what she's going to do and it's stupid. "You are not camping out alone in your van, Aspen."

"I won't be alone. I'll have Major," she replies stubbornly. "And it's just until the insurance gets sorted or they let us back in."

I sigh. I can't believe I'm doing this, but she's pregnant and even if she wasn't I wouldn't let her sleep in that van she uses for surveillance work. Aspen isn't a monster. I look her in the eye. "Clover Road. The big building right on the water."

"You have a place already?" Aspen blinks.

"Yes. Rented it before I even left King's Rock. Ocean Pines isn't exactly a hot market, so it was easy to do," I tell her. "But it's kind of empty because my stuff is still en route with the moving company. I've got an air mattress and you're welcome to it since I'll be at the station anyway."

She doesn't say anything for a second. "Really?"

"Yeah. Spare key is under the door mat." I shrug. "Unit fourteen. Top floor, left corner."

Logan raises a curious eyebrow. I pretend not to notice.

"Thank you," Aspen says, her defiant armor finally lowering long enough to give me a grateful smile.

She whistles and Major trots off with her toward her car. Logan keeps glancing over to me as he packs up his rig and I work on packing the fire truck back up. "It's just a friendly gesture," I say before he can make the comments he wants to make. "Nothing more. We aren't a thing anymore."

"Uh-huh."

"Do not uh-huh me, Logan. I'm serious," I reply, my tone unwavering. I never loved Aspen the way I should have.

"Do you think Riv really would want a dog?" Logan asks me suddenly. "Is he too young?"

"Honestly?" I say as I finish rolling the hose back into the truck. "You're never too young for a dog. And you could use the company. It's been a while since your family had a pet and your Ma is so great with animals. Terra loves dogs too. Finn will probably be okay with it."

"I don't need his permission, Jake. I'm not his freaking tenant and I'm not going to live above the restaurant with him forever," Logan says defensively, his jaw tight. He gets so bent out of shape about his living situation. Probably because he doesn't have his own place yet but I do. He has been bouncing around from his parents' place to Finn's since he got out of rehab three years ago.

"I know you don't need permission, Logan." I pause. "I just admire how well you adapted to being a dad unexpectedly."

"I assume you mean after the rehab," Logan replies and gives me a dry, humorless smile. "Because for the first year of River's life I was going out for diapers and coming back swimming in whiskey fourteen hours later. Not exactly perfect parent behavior."

"Yeah but that wasn't because of River. You had a disease. You got it under control," I remind him.

"I did and knowing I had River to raise helped me do that, but it doesn't always work for other people," Logan explains as he walks toward the driver's door of his ambulance. "Alcoholism is a life-long battle that a lot of people lose. I have to think of it every day. I have to make the choice not to drink every day, and some days are harder than others. Really hard. Some people don't get sober or can't be good parents no matter what. It's not a reflection on the kid, though. I know you know this."

His blue eyes lock with mine and I think of Kelsey Grady, Ocean Pines' drug-addicted stripper, also known to me as Mom. "You should get a dog."

"Yeah. I am definitely going to look into it."

"See you back at the station," I say and climb into the truck as Logan nods gruffly and gets into his ambulance.

Luckily, back at the firehouse I'm able to get out of my gear and into the shower and then lock myself up in one of the private bunks. Perks of being a lieutenant, I don't have to use the cavernous bunk room. I get a private room. The bed is the same single bed, and the room is a shoebox, but it's got none of the bunk room rules like no cellphones and no talking. I drop the towel and crawl under the sheets, plug my phone in, and put it on the nightstand. I command myself to sleep, but of course that doesn't work, so I start Googling information about paternity tests.

6

JAKE

I HEAD HOME FROM WORK AT A LITTLE AFTER SEVEN IN THE morning. Our shifts are twenty-four hours on, forty-eight hours off, which is pretty standard in the industry. It means I have the next two days off, which is good because the moving company is arriving late this afternoon with my stuff and now I have Aspen and Major to deal with too.

The fire station is located on Smithwheel Road which is the road that divides Old Orchard Beach from Ocean Pines. There's a pine grove behind us, with the turnpike right behind that and the football field at the back of the high school in front of us. To the left of the station is a small strip mall with a laundromat, a fresh vegetable market, and a Chinese restaurant. To the right, a Dunkin', beyond which is the police station. I swear between the high schoolers and the fire department and the police, whoever owns that Dunkin' franchise is a millionaire. I swing through the drive-thru now and order two coffees. Aspen used to love their caramel iced coffee and I used to love their coconut macchiatos. Used to because I haven't had one in three years. King's Rock was rural and so small it made Ocean Pines look like a metropolis. There was no chain store in King's Rock. If you drove across the border into New Brunswick you'd get those creature comforts, but there it was Tim Horton's not Dunkin'.

I place my order. The girl at the pick-up window looks vaguely familiar. "That'll be five-forty." She looks up and blinks. "Jake Maverick?"

"Yeah." Shit. I hate when I can't remember a name. "How are you?"

"Good!" she chirps and her smile grows. "Terra mentioned you were coming back to town when I grabbed some lobster rolls last week. And of course it was on the town blog and everything, thanks to me. I gave the scoop to my mom, who still runs it. We get a thousand hits a month. Heavy traffic for a tiny town."

Right. Cassidy Green. Her mother is Nellie Green, renowned town gossip who used the guise of 'journalist' to excuse her noisiness. But Nellie didn't have any formal training. Her son Eddie, who is Declan's age, had set her up a web site when we were in junior high. Cassidy is Terra's age. And then there's Ronan, who I work with, the oldest Green and my least favorite. "I told her it was time to hand over the reins. I mean, I actually got a degree in journalism from South Portland Community College and I freelance. I even had an article on the new water plant published in the Mainer. A *real* publication."

She whispers those last three words like her mom is somehow eavesdropping and she doesn't want to get caught. I bite back a chuckle. "Anyway, one day she'll retire or die or something and I'll clean that site up and make it a much better news source for the town. Did you work with Ronan last night? He swung by about ten minutes ago for a coffee for him and his fiancé, Courtney. Have you met Courtney? She's… not my favorite person, but my mom loves her."

"Yeah he was dating Courtney before I left. Didn't know they were engaged though." I hand her the cash for my order but she suddenly waves my hand away.

"Yep. Never ending engagement," Cassidy rolls her eyes. "Been two years and no wedding. Just planning. So much damn planning. She's changed the bridesmaids dresses twice. And both times they were ugly so I'm hoping for a third."

I just nod because I never know what else to do when someone rambles on about shit I give zero fucks about. I hand her a ten dollar bill.

"This one is on me. I'm the shift manager here. Until my free-lancing takes off," she explains and adjusts the Dunkin's visor pressing her long dark hair to her head. "Consider it a welcome home present. And an apology gift on Ronan's behalf. I know he can be a dick, and he was a little irked when you got the job as the other lieutenant. He's worried you'll screw up his chances at getting the Captain's position when D'Amato moves on."

I blink. "D'Amato is leaving?"

Cassidy's eyes grew wide and she covers her mouth with her hand and then spits out a muffled answer. "I'm mean... maybe? According to Ronan. I don't know for sure."

"Huh. I didn't hear that," I mutter, wondering why the captain hadn't mentioned it. Or Logan. Anyone, really.

She uncovers her mouth and hands over the order. Her brown eyes glancing from one drink to the other. "Extra thirsty today or do you have someone hiding in your trunk?"

"Ha," I say and try to force a chuckle. "Bringing coffee to a friend."

Her eyes spark with curiosity. "Don't tell me you've been back in town fifteen minutes and are already off the market. That would break the hearts of so many single Ocean Pines girls."

Is she hitting on me or just mining me for info she can pass to her gossipy mom? I'm not sure either way so I lie. "Meeting Finn for surfing."

"Oh. Right. You musta missed that over in the mountains," she says. "I thought maybe it was Terra since she swings through here for a caramel iced coffee three or four times a week. Come to think of it, it's usually later in my shift though. Afternoon. And she's never driving, someone is always with her. Usually her mom but sometimes Nova or Finn or Logan."

"You're observant."

"Journalist's brain," Cassidy shrugs. "Hey, do you know what happened to her arm?"

"There's something wrong with Terra's arm?" What the hell is she talking about?

"Well most times when she swings through it's got bandages on it," Cassidy informs me. "Thought maybe she was donating blood or plasma or something but then I remembered she's got that disease… what's it called? Leppis?"

"Lupus."

"Yeah, so then I thought can they donate blood and plasma? Maybe it's something to do with that." Cassidy blinks and glances out the window. There's two other cars behind me now. "Okay well I should keep the line moving. Welcome back Jake. Come by anytime."

I hand her the money I was going to pay for my coffee with. "Thanks for the coffees. Pay it forward by letting me buy the next order, okay?"

"You are such a sweetheart," Cassidy smiles and I drive off.

As usual, running into a Green means receiving a dump truck load full of town gossip. Except Ronan. He spews cocky bullshit not gossip. Hell, he hasn't even mentioned a fiancé. The stuff about our fire captain potentially leaving is big news, but I focus on the more important information Cassidy dropped as I drive home. Terra has something wrong with her arm?

She *was* wearing long sleeves the two times I've seen her even though we're in an early fall heatwave. When I rolled into town the restaurant was packed, the AC barely cutting it, and she was in a long-sleeved tee while everyone else working was wearing short sleeves. *Everyone*. Huh.

I pull into the parking spot of my new apartment ten minutes later. Aspen's car is in one of the guest spots so she hasn't left yet. I was slightly worried she'd bail before I got home in an attempt to ghost me again. I walk toward the building, which in the sixties was a beach front motel. It was turned into apartments in the late nineties but still has a beach motel vibe big glass lobby and plunge pool and hot tub on the small patio that faces the dunes and ocean beyond. I got it so easily and quickly because the owner was the brother of Captain D'Amato and he put in a good word. Also, the units aren't huge so if you aren't single without much stuff, you probably don't want it even with the killer ocean views. My goal is to buy something by spring. I have a nice little savings account already. There wasn't much in King's Rock to spend your pay checks on. I'll be the first person in my family to ever own a home and that matters a lot to me.

I climb the stairs to the fourth floor, walk straight to the end, balancing the coffees one on top of the other while I unlock the front door. I do a horrible job and the top one leaks onto the front of my shirt because the lid isn't on right. Fuck.

Inside, a deep, heavy bark echoes menacingly, but when I swing open the door I'm greeted by a swiftly wagging tail and Major promptly throws himself down on my feet and rolls over to show me his belly. "I'll rub that in a minute, buddy."

I step over him and follow the scent of bacon into my kitchen. Aspen is leaning against the counter in there, sipping orange juice out of a plastic container. On the counter next to her is a full eggs-and-bacon breakfast with a side of baked beans. I'm stunned. "I found your camping dishes, ran to the convenience store at the end of the block, got the basics."

My stomach rumbles. "Aren't you little miss ingenuity?

Here's your favorite coffee as a thank you, but I spilled a little. Sorry."

I hand her the ice coffee, put mine down on the counter and tug off my coffee stained shirt. She looks at it, reads the label and gives me a smile that isn't really a smile. "Thanks but pregnant women can't drink coffee. And this is Terra's favorite drink. Not mine."

"What?" I ball up my shirt and put it on the counter.

"I love the iced coconut mocha. Terra gets the iced caramel coffee. Every time. Without fail since she was sixteen," Aspen sips her orange juice, puts the coffee down on the counter and motions to the plates of food. "Eat. Before it gets cold."

Did I really mix up their drinks? We started dating because Aspen asked me to be her prom date. By the time we went to prom, Aspen and Terra, who had been lifelong best friends up until that point, were no longer speaking. They had actually gotten into a food fight in the cafeteria one lunch hour. I wasn't there, having dropped out the year before, but I heard all about it like everyone else. Terra dumped a plate of the special—spaghetti and meat sauce—on Aspen's head.

They told people it was a fight over a prom dress. Aspen bought the one Terra had been saving up for. But damn, it was quite the fight over a dress. After prom night, when we started dating, Aspen wouldn't even let me say Terra's name without getting pissed off. It strained our relationships because when I wasn't with Aspen I was with the Hawkins family. Lucy and Charlie had really helped me out a few years earlier, when I was sixteen and applied for emancipation from my mom, by letting me rent the apartment above the restaurant. And although they weren't thrilled when I dropped out of high school, they gave me full-time dishwasher hours at the Shack so I was around Terra all the time. I always wondered if the real problem was that Aspen sensed how much I liked that.

But now she's clearly matured because she doesn't make a snide comment about the mix-up. She just drinks her orange juice and leans against the counter. She points to the shirt she's wearing, which is one of my T-shirts. "I didn't grab much clothes and needed something to sleep in," she says as I reach for the one of the plates of food. "Hope you don't mind."

"It's fine," I say and grab the fork from my camping kit that's beside the tin camping plate. I jump up to sit on the counter, since I don't have furniture yet, and Aspen walks over to the fridge. The shirt hits her mid-thigh but when she bends a bit to put the unwanted coffee inside the fridge, I get a clear view of the bottom of her ass, covered in lacey hot pink boy shorts.

I feel nothing sexual at the sight. That's new.

"You sleep okay?"

"I was out like a light. Pregnancy makes you sleep like you're in a coma. Probably because once the baby is born your body knows you'll never sleep again." She says it so casually, like the fact that she's pregnant and her entire life is about to change, is no big deal.

"How are you so calm about this?"

She shrugs. "I had a bit of a meltdown when I realized my period was M.I.A., and I was shaking so hard taking the home test I almost didn't even get enough pee on the stick. But I knew the minute I saw the little plus sign that this was just happening and there wasn't a thing I could do about it but accept it. I won't get an abortion, Jake. I'm not against them at all and fully support anyone who wants one, but I don't want one. So I'm at peace with this new, unplanned path and I'm rolling with it. And that's why I'm not keeping you on the hook. This is my decision. I'm not giving you a say."

"First of all I would never ever ask you to consider abortion," I reply. "This is one hundred percent your body and your decision. But if it's mine, I'm a parent and that's my decision. Don't try and take it from me okay? The way Bethany tries to take it away from Logan."

"Logan gave her good reason in the beginning," Aspen reminds me but then she smiles. "You'll be great at it, Jake. I know you don't think you will, but you will. I hope it is yours because the other guy … he wants kids less than you. And he's not the person you are."

"Who is he?"

She shakes her head. "Nope. Not telling. I mean, if he isn't the dad, you don't need to know I hooked up with him. If he is, well, he should know first."

I want to fight her on that, but she's right. "Fair enough. But it was more than a hook-up wasn't it?"

She nods. "It was for me. A lot more. Went on for months. But I don't think he ever saw it as more."

"Have you told Abbott about the baby?" I ask and she shakes her head. "But you will."

"Eventually."

"The parents?"

She laughs out loud at the idea she'd tell her parents. I'm not surprised. Mr. and Mrs. Barlowe are cold, rigid, mean people if you really looked past the money and power they hide behind.

"I have no intention of telling them," Aspen replies, her tone indicating there is no room for discussion on this. Not that I would talk her into telling those sanctimonious assholes.

"So… I Googled information about paternity tests," I say as she motions for me to continue eating, and I spear some scrambled eggs covered in melted pepper jack with my fork. "We can find out really easily as soon as we want. It just takes a couple blood tests and about five days wait time."

She glances up at me with puppy dog eyes. "Can I at least figure out the whole ruined apartment thing first? I can only handle so much at a time."

She has probably lost almost everything. She'll be allowed back in there today to assess the damage and see what can be saved, then there'll be a lot of debating back-and-forth with insurance companies because they're never easy to work with. "You need to tell Abbott so he can help you find a place to crash. It'll take a few weeks to sort stuff with the insurance companies."

She sighs. "He just got to training camp and he'll want to turn around and come back. That can't happen."

"Unfortunately, you can't stay here, so he's your best bet, Aspen," I say. "I'm not trying to be mean."

She frowns but reaches for her phone which is on the floor by air mattress. "You can feed Major my breakfast. I'm not going to want it after this call."

I nod and head back into the kitchen while she calls her brother. Major happily follows me. When I put the metal camping plate with the eggs, bacon and home fries down on the floor, he devours everything on it as I try not to eavesdrop too hard on Aspen's conversation with Abbott.

I sip my coffee and hear her explain. "I'm at Jake's. Yes *that* Jake…. No we are not back together… No. I am not lying. I just… well my apartment building kind of almost burned down."

I can hear him perfectly clearly. "WHAT THE HELL, ASPEN!"

"I didn't burn it down," she replies defensively and I try and stifle a chuckle because of course he thinks she did it. Aspen is the queen of getting herself into pickles. And pregnancies now, I guess. Oh man, if this kid is mine, Abbott is going to hunt me down and beat me with his hockey stick. He blames me for the heartbreak Aspen felt when we broke up. I felt it too, but he doesn't get that and he wouldn't care if he did. Because that's what family does—they rally behind each other and protect each other at all costs. That's why Terra Hawkins was off-limits way back when I was a lonely, struggling teenager. Because if things blew up with her, I would have lost all of them.

Aspen drops her voice to an angry and loud whisper. "Well, he offered and I had nowhere else to go. Did you want me to call *them*?"

Them would be their parents. Both of them have been estranged from their parents since Aspen was eighteen. She has never, ever told me the exact reason why. But there are a lot of reasons I could guess at. They're hardcore religious, cold, vicious people.

"What? No. Really? Okay, well I would be eternally grateful," Aspen says and I know he's just offered to pay for a new place for her to live while her dilemma gets sorted. "Thanks Abbott. Truly. Yeah I will call you when I get there. Bye."

I walk back into the living room as she drops her phone on the air mattress. "He's putting you up in a hotel?"

"Five Seasons," Aspen replies.

"Fancy!"

"They take dogs," Aspen says and pats the top of Major's head because he's moved to sit by her feet.

Then my doorbell rings not once, not twice, but three times in a row. Major goes berserk. His bark is beyond loud and super scary if you don't know him. Aspen glances at me in confusion, which I'm sure is the look I'm also giving her. I walk through the apartment to the front door and fling it open, thinking my movers might have gotten here way early. Instead, I find Terra standing in front of my door.

She's wearing a big cardigan, even though it's warm out, and leggings with tall Uggs. "Did you get a dog?" she asks but then swings into a new subject without giving me a second to answer. "I need someone's help tomorrow, and you're the only one I could think of."

"Umm…I'm flattered?" I scratch the back of my head and she

lets those big, endless dark chocolate colored eyes sweep over me. Major comes bolting down the hall.

"Are you dog sitting Major? Aspy off on one of her stake-outs?" Terra scratches him behind the ears and then barges right by me into the front hall.

Oh fuck.

Before I can stop her she's marched into the living room. Aspen is there next to the air mattress with the rumpled sleeping bag, still dressed in barely anything. She stares at Terra and Terra stares back. This is not going to go over well. Damnit.

"Aspen is just—"

Terra spins back around so fast she blurs and then she's storming past me back to the door. I chase after her. "Wait! Stop!"

Major barks like he's helping. I swear he's saying, 'Don't leave! It's not what you think!'

"This was a mistake," she mutters and waves a hand in front of me. I reach out and grab it.

"Stop! The only mistake is the assumption you're currently making. Aspen is here because her apartment burned down," I blurt out. "Yesterday. Call Logan. He'll confirm."

"Sort of burned down. Mostly just got drowned by sprin-klers." Aspen adds, now standing at the end of the hall. I don't think it's all that helpful and my expression shows it. Terra glances between her and me but when her eyes stay on Aspen and take in her outfit, or lack thereof, I know she isn't going to believe a word I say.

"Are you okay?" Aspen asks Terra and takes a couple steps closer. "You look like hell, Ter."

Way to make a bad moment worse, Aspen.

"Thanks!" Terra exclaims so full of passive aggressive perki-ness I can't help but smile. "I wonder why we don't hang out any more?"

She turns to me, placing Aspen at her back. Aspen slinks off into the kitchen with Major, hanging her head.

"Look, I just want to walk out that door and wipe this whole scene from my hard drive," Terra announces and I bite back another smile because she's dead serious but I love when she talks nerdy. It's adorable. "But I need help."

"You know I will help you with anything," I sweep my eyes over her outfit again. I'm shirtless and not even close to chilled. She must be sweating under that cardigan. "Can I take your sweater? It's warm in here."

"No." She glances over her shoulder again. "Can we talk outside?"

"Is there something wrong with your arms?" I ask bluntly. "I'm no detective or anything but you're constantly wearing long sleeves and it's hot and humid as f—"

She rocks up on her tip toes and slaps a hand over my half open mouth. Hard. Now her whole tiny body is pressed up against me. The open cardigan is positioned in a way that the buttons are rubbing against my nipples. In between that and the fact that I can feel her breasts pressed against me through the thin cotton of her t-shirt, I'm getting turned on. Lust starts to swirl inside me like a tornado forming. That feeling of connection from the beach yesterday is back in full force.

Her eyes lock with mine and her eyelashes flutter for a second and I swear I hear her breath catch before she jumps back immediately. "Shut. Up. *Please.*"

Her head snaps around toward the kitchen doorway, reminding me Aspen is here. Then she glares at me. "Do you have a shirt you can put on, so we can talk outside?" Terra asks.

"Don't need a shirt. It's Ocean Pines in a fall heatwave," I explain.

"Well, I'm being distracted by your oddly shaped, awkwardly hard nipples."

I glance down. "Oddly shaped?" I rub my fingertips over my nipples and the lust tornado grows bigger inside me, but I don't stop because it's riling her up. "They're shaped just fine, thank you very much. And there's a draft in here. We're standing by the front door, you know."

"Oh my God stop touching yourself!" Terra rants and Aspen's head pops out of the kitchen. She pops back in when she realizes I'm not touching myself *that way*. I focus on Terra again. "Talk, Tink."

She runs her hands through her hair, it's her natural color. When I split three years ago she was in this phase of dying it all kinds of crazy colors. Teal, blue, and she was pink when I left. Now it's that sandy blonde she was born with. "I need to do this in private. Please."

She grabs my hand and yanks me outside, firmly closing the front door behind us. Then she walks down to the other end of the hall by the stairwell, dragging me with her. "I need someone to drive me to my dialysis appointment," she whispers. "The rules are you can't take a cab or Uber and you can't drive yourself. I tried to pass Jay off as family once but my doctor called me out on it because of course everyone knows he's the town Uber driver. So, I can't pull that shit again. Has to be a friend or family member."

"Your what?"

"I'm on dialysis," she says and sighs. "My kidneys stopped working because of the lupus. We fought it with drugs and stuff for a while, but we lost. So now I need my blood cleaned by machines three times a week. It's not a big deal but I can't take myself. Finn and Nova are working. Declan is in Boston for a marketing conference. Dad is on the boat and Mom... I love her but she makes it a stressful experience for me and I'd just rather avoid that."

"How long has this been going on?" I ask and my whole body

starts to tingle with shock, like the news knocked it out and every limb fell asleep at once.

"A little over two months," Terra replies.

"Why didn't anyone tell me?" I ask and my voice does nothing to hide my pain. I'm hurt.

Terra's hard expression softens. "You weren't here."

"That again?" I bark because that's the same excuse they used when Logan went into rehab. I was in Orono doing extra training for work. They know how much that excuse hurt me. How I wanted to know, like a real family member, when it was happening. Even if I couldn't be there. "Did you know that's part of the reason I left Ocean Pines, was you guys leaving me out of the crisis with Logan? I was hurt. I was supposed to be family, you all kept telling me that for years but then you cut me out."

"That wasn't my call and that was also..." she pauses and looks away. "I'm sorry. I wanted to tell you everything. But this is different. You moved away. You weren't just on vacation or whatever. I had no idea you were ever going to move back and so as far as I was concerned, why would you care about my life anymore?"

I reach for her hand. "Terra, I never stopped caring about you or your life."

We stare at each other. It feels like it's a really long time but it's probably only a minute without words. "Can you drive me? I need to go now. Casco Bay Memorial."

"Come back inside while I grab a shirt," I say.

"No thank you. I don't need another glimpse of Aspen's underwear."

Right.

"I'll be back in a sec."

I walk back down the hall and into my apartment. I'm surprised I'm able to do it without tipping over. I'm reeling so hard from this horrible news that I almost feel like I have vertigo.

7

TERRA

HE EMERGES FROM HIS APARTMENT MOMENTS LATER IN A wrinkled forest green t-shirt that he somehow still looks amazing in. We start down the stairs. "Aspen was right there in the front hall, ear pressed to the door trying to eavesdrop, wasn't she?"

"Maybe."

"Jake, if you tell her any of this I swear to God I will—"

"I won't tell her," he cuts me off. "Just like you didn't tell me."

"I'm telling you now."

"As a last resort," he mutters. Wow. He is really hurt. A heavy lump of guilt starts to form in my gut.

"Jake, I was going to tell you when you got back," I tell him. "In my defense you've only been home five seconds. Was I supposed to announce it at your welcome home party? At the beach it didn't feel like the time and I wasn't about to swing by the station on your first shift and say 'Hey have a good first day. By the way, I'm dying."

"You're dying?" He gasps.

"No. I mean, maybe one day if I can't find a kidney, but not imminently. Right now I'm good." I am babbling and he still looks positively stricken. *Great Job, Terra.*

We hit the lobby of his building and he digs his car keys out of the pocket of his jeans. "But this dialysis you do three times a week, it leaves you so incapacitated you can't drive?"

"That's a big word for you," I joke.

"Enough with the snark, okay?" Jake pleads.

"I'm sorry. It's a bad coping mechanism," I admit, my voice softening as we make our way outside. "Everything sucks donkey balls in my life right now, and I'm not handling it well. The no driving thing is just a precaution. I'm always fine. I fainted once, but a couple hours later. At work. But truly, I'm fine. My arms are perpetually bruised and I get these gross lumps sometimes called fistulas which is why I wear long sleeves. It's impressive you noticed, Sherlock. Maybe you should have been a cop instead of a fireman."

"I notice you, Terra. Always have."

His tone is serious and so is his face when I glance up at it, all golden and gleaming in the hot sun. Butterflies flutter through my abdomen and I mentally spray Raid on them by reminding myself that his ex-girlfriend is currently half naked in his apartment. "So Aspen…"

"I was at work all night so that rumpled air mattress you were side-eyeing was all her and Major," Jake tells me bluntly. "We are *not* involved again."

"Sure. Whatever." I open the passenger door and climb inside when he unlocks the Jeep.

"It's the truth, Terra," He says. He starts the engine and as soon as my seatbelt clicks, we're driving out of the parking lot.

"I told them not to tell you," I say as he heads towards the turnpike entrance. "Logan and Finn. When they visited you to go skiing in February, I told them not to mention to you that I was having issues. I threatened to disown them if they did. I just didn't see the point in bringing you into this since you lived so far away. You had just won that medal and gotten promoted to lieutenant and I didn't want to bum you out with bad news."

"You guys love to exclude me and pretend it's for my own good," Jake snaps.

I stare at him. He looks insulted and I know this can't be about just me. "Are you talking about the Logan thing again?"

"To start, yeah." Jake pauses and I can see his jaw tighten as he grinds his teeth, like he's trying not to say whatever it is he's thinking. I learned these cues from my schooling.

"Jake, tell me what you're feeling. No filter." I prompt.

"My best friend hits rock bottom and you guys flew him to rehab out-of-state and handled all the fall-out and didn't even tell me about it," Jake says as we merge onto the turnpike. "You all acted like it was for my own good. I was away in Orono doing training and you didn't want to ruin that for me. But the fact is, it was a family problem, and you don't think I'm family. Because I'm not. But I had been thinking of all of you as family. It was a rude awakening. And FYI I still feel like there's more about that story with Logan getting sober that even years later, no one will tell me."

Wow. This wasn't just a confession, it was a rant, filled with a lot of pent up emotions. I study his face. He is still so hurt, like this happened yesterday instead of three years ago. I hate thinking about the day Logan hit rock bottom and our family found out. No one talks about it much. In fact we purposely talk around it. The guts of it anyway. But looking at the pain on Jake's face I decide I need to rip the band-aid off this.

"You were the first person I wanted to call," I tell him. "But Declan told me not to because there was nothing you could do. Logan would be halfway to rehab in Florida before you got back from Orono. My brothers think of you as a brother, even Deck. And yes, there is more to the story than you know."

His head swivels to take in my expression. My mouth is in a hard line and my eyes are pleading, begging forgiveness for what I'm about to say. "I told you what I could when you got back. What I was allowed to tell. I'm telling you now there is more, but it's not my story, Jake. And Logan… he may not be in a place to talk about it. I'm sorry. I know that's award-winning vagueness, but it's all I can say. And that I'm sorry."

His eyes are staring straight ahead now as we slog through the heavy but steady afternoon traffic and he eases into the right lane for the upcoming off-ramp. "One of the lieutenants leading that training in Orono that week was from King's Rock. He told me they had openings, and I would have a better shot at advancing there than if I stayed in Ocean Pines. I didn't even consider it until I got back and found out Logan was gone. I felt like, after that, maybe I shouldn't be so attached to the idea I had reasons to stay in Ocean Pines."

My jaw drops. "You left town because of that?"

"It was a big part of it. But there were other factors. I wanted… I had stuff to work out, and stuff to prove, and needed space to do it. I wanted people to look at me as more than a fucked up foster kid and the Hawkins twins' sidekick and I didn't think that would happen if I stuck around."

"Why would anyone's opinion matter more than your own? You know you're more than that, don't you?" I ask.

"That is for another time, Tink," he mutters. I can't decipher the expression on his face but I have to admit to myself, I enjoy staring at him while I try. He looks exactly the same as when he left three years ago, tall, dark and perfect. How one man has managed to push all my 'on' buttons since I developed turn-on buttons is insane to me. If there's a Guinness World Record category for longest crush, I'm in the running for the title.

I decide to change the subject because he clearly isn't going to elaborate on this one and his silence is creating anxiety in me, which is the last thing I need before a four hour treatment. "I've actually been incredibly successful at keeping my kidney problems on the down-low. No one in Ocean Pines has figured it out. Only family knows. And Tom."

"Have you heard from that ass wipe since the fight?" Jake says as he pulls out of the parking lot.

Is it wrong that I kind of love how much he hates Tom? Because I do.

"Break-up," I correct. I can feel his eyes on me but I keep staring straight ahead. "Nope. And I won't because I blocked his number."

His chuckle is just a huff of air, with a smile. "I should have known. When you hurt Terra Hawkins, you get the emotional guillotine without hesitation."

"What on earth is an emotional guillotine?"

"You don't push people away. You cut them off. Shut them out. It's actually both terrifying and admirable," Jake tells me. "Also hurts like a bitch."

"You think I cut you off? When? You've been in my life forever," I argue back, kind of annoyed with his description of me, even though I know he's not wrong. "Except when you chose to leave."

"We gonna pretend you didn't treat me like I didn't exist or like you wished I didn't exist from about the time you were fourteen until I left?" Jake says casually, giving me a quick glance. His dark eyes are stern and very, very sexy.

I refuse to speak of what he is referencing. "No deep conversations before dialysis."

He is still staring and my stupid head starts to turn toward him without my consent. If I see pity on his face my heart will break. But it's not pity staring back at me; it's a simple, sweet smile.

"So… can you give me a little more intel on all this kidney stuff?" Jake asks gently. "I can't exactly Google and drive, and I hate to admit my knowledge of dialysis and kidney problems related to lupus are nada."

"Google is not accurate anyway," I tell him and then take a deep breath and give him the Cliff Notes about how lupus can cause nephritis which is inflammation in the kidneys and it affects their ability to filter waste. How I managed it with drugs for years but those stopped working and now my only options are dialysis or a new kidney. I explain how my brothers and parents have been tested, but no one can donate either because of blood types that don't match or because of pre-existing conditions.

"Does the donor have to be family?" Jake asks the question I was hoping he wouldn't.

Tom asked it too, and the answer somehow made him feel obligated. I don't want to pressure Jake for anything. I tried that once in a closet in the Barlowe's basement, and I promised myself I would never do that again. For any reason. But he keeps glancing over at me, waiting for an answer, and I'm not going to lie. "No it doesn't have to be family, they're just usually a stronger match. I'm on the national list to get one from an organ donor. And Nova and Javi are going to be tested. We're waiting on results. After that Ma wants to tell Mrs. Green so she can blog about it in hopes someone in town will want to get tested and donate if they match. Dear God if I have to give that woman a scoop for her gossip blog to get a kidney..."

I roll my eyes in frustration. Jake reaches across the seats and pats my hand. "Nobody hates Mrs. Green's nosiness more than me. Do you know when I was seventeen she came up to me at Illumination Night and told me I had the exact same eyes as the mayor and that he used to frequent my mom's work establishment when he was… how did she say it? On the sauce."

He whispers that last bit in a scratchy voice in a high pitch like he's impersonating Mrs. Green. My mouth falls open at the story. Ugh. Poor Jake. His mother's 'place of employment' for most of his life was the strip club out by the airport. The mayor was far from a drunk, and also a pale, balding, red-headed man that looked nothing like Jake. "But Tink, if her big mouth finds you a match and saves your life I will never slag her again."

"If Aspen heard any of our hallway conversation, Mrs. Green probably already knows," I grumble.

Jake squeezes my hand before returning his to the steering wheel. "She wouldn't tell anyone even if she did hear. In fact she'd want to help you, not hurt you."

"I'd take a kidney from the devil before I took one from Aspen," I say, completely aware the statement is a mix of false bravado and melodramatics.

"You still hate her that much?"

I nod.

Jake shakes his head. "I'm beginning to think this is about more than a prom dress."

I snort. "Please don't say it took you seven years to figure that out."

"You wanna share the truth?" Jake asks as he turns into the parking lot for Casco Bay Memorial

"Ask your roommate." I reply snarkily and then point. "Park over there, please. I need to go in the main entrance, but I don't want your truck in plain sight."

He does what I ask and parks at the far end of the lot under a massive weeping willow then turns off the engine.

"Okay…" I dig in my bag. "Shit. I forgot my blanket."

"Blanket?"

"I get cold sometimes during treatment. They'll give you a blanket but they're always scratchy so I usually bring my own. Anyway, no biggie."

I keep digging in my bag and pull out a baseball cap and my biggest, darkest pair of sunglasses and put them both on. Jake barks out a laugh. "Are we reenacting an episode of *The Ameri-cans* or something?"

I sigh. "Last time I was here I ran into Patti Gordon, from Patti's Parlor, the ice cream place. Who knows who else I'll see today. I don't want to be recognized. The more I'm seen at the hospital, the more people will start speculating and gossiping. And if I'm here with you, the talk will turn secret baby or some-thing equally absurd. So do not get out of this car until I am safely inside the building."

His smile drops like a lead balloon suddenly. "Umm… yeah. Okay. Whatever you want."

"What is it?" I ask, because something about what I just said changed his whole mood in the blink of an eye. "Are you insulted I don't want people to think I'm having your secret baby?"

His mood does not lighten. He shifts in his seat. "So, four hours? And you'll meet me back here?"

I nod. He nods. And then I get out of the car and make my way inside. It's becoming routine now, and that's kind of sad when I think about it. I know all the nurses in the Dialysis Center by name and they know me. I could go through the set-up with my eyes closed. I'm twenty minutes into the treatment when Doug, one of the nurses, walks over with a bag and a smile. "Someone very tall, very dark and very handsome walked up to check-in desk and asked me to give this to you."

"Thank you," I smile and then focus on the bag as he walks away. I use my arm not full of tubes to reach inside and pull out the contents which is a fleece blanket he clearly got in the gift shop by the maternity wing because it's a bold pink and has a giant Tinkerbell on it. *That little fucker. Why can't he just be a jerk so I can stop crushing on him?*

I smile through the rest of my treatment.

8

———

JAKE

I GET TO THE FIREHOUSE AN HOUR BEFORE MY SHIFT STARTS AS Logan requested. He is on the opposite shift today and he asked if I could swing by to see him before everyone else arrives for the shift change. It's been a week since I took Terra to dialysis. The family knows I know about her situation now and none of them seem perturbed. In fact they all seemed relieved, even Declan. But no one has flat-out asked me to get tested. To help her. They asked Nova and Javi and they're talking about asking strangers via Mrs. Green's gossip site, but they haven't asked me. I've been trying to figure out how to not take that personally. Old Jake would have just run away. Literally. I want to be new Jake on this.

Logan's stretched out on the couch in the lounge. The TV in the corner is playing some movie I don't recognize with the sound muted. Despite lying down, he looks anything but relaxed. His jaw is clenched and he's looking at his phone screen, held up in front of him.

"Hey." I say as I lean on the archway that separates the long room from the hall.

He moves the phone from in front of his face at the sound of my voice. "Good to see you. Have you been avoiding us? You haven't been to the restaurant in a few days."

"No. I've been busy setting up my new place. Unpacking." It's a half-lie. I've been purposely occupying myself with unpacking and new apartment chores so I could avoid going to the restaurant.

Logan sits up as I walk farther into the room. "Thanks for coming in early"

"Honestly, I wanted to talk to you about Terra anyway," I say and I drop down on the opposite side of the couch. "Thought you could put on your doctor hat and give me the lowdown."

"It's half a hat," Logan gives me a wry smile. "Only finished two years of med school remember?"

"Well I barely passed high school biology, so you win," I joke. "Why is it the family can't donate?"

"In order to donate a kidney the blood types have to be compatible. I'm AB. Terra is A neg. Finn is obviously AB too. Twin thing," Logan explains. "Ma is B positive. Dad is A though but his age and his diabetes make him a no-go. Too risky for both of them. Deck has A blood type too, and good tissue typing, but … the rules around people with mental health issues donating is left up to individual hospitals and Casco Memorial isn't big on the idea. And then there's the way Declan tried to kill himself."

I grimace at the memory. When Declan was in his senior year of high school and the whole family was out of the house, he went into the garage, got in his mom's car, rolled down the windows, and turned it on with the garbage door closed. He almost succeeded too, but Terra and Aspen decided to skip band practice after school and found him. He spent a month in the hospital and three more in a mental health facility. It was a horrible time for the whole family. Finn and Logan didn't want to talk about it then, so I just tried to be there for them by covering as many shifts as I could for them at the restaurant.

Terra cried when she didn't think I was around. Lucy spent every waking hour she wasn't at church with Declan. Charlie looked just plain tortured. Now, as an adult, I know how complicated mental health is but at the time, I remember being confused that Declan would try and throw away a life I would give anything for.

"The carbon monoxide poisoning caused temporary renal failure as well as liver and lung issues and although he's technically recovered and physically fine, chances are there's lasting changes to his organs that wouldn't work for Terra. Better to leave them in Deck," Logan sighs and scrubs his face with his hand. "We get Nova and Javi's results today. If Javi matches we have to wait a few months because he has to quit smoking first."

"Do they need your family medical history or anything like that after you do the tissue testing thing?" I ask and lean forward on my elbows. My eyes examine the tiles on the floor instead of looking at my best friend because I hate talking about my family. "I have no idea what potential illnesses would be in my history. I did one of those DNA kits while I was in King's Rock. It didn't identify anything too scary or terminal. And I don't know if genetics help, but I'm such an ethnic milkshake that I can probably match with anyone. Found out I'm thirty percent Japanese, twenty-five percent Native American, five percent African American and thirty-seven percent Irish and 3 percent Swedish."

"That thirty-seven percent Irish is probably just from hanging out with us so much," Logan jokes and I finally look up and am comforted by his smiling face. "But seriously, none of that matters for matching. If you wanted to be tested you could be."

"I got tested while I waited for her to finish dialysis last week," I confess. "I'm O blood type—universal donor—so that works. Just waiting on tissue-typing results. I get those any day now but wasn't sure what comes next and if my sketchy background would somehow rule me out."

Logan snaps his head up and opens his eyes. He stares straight at me, his expression awe and relief. "You would do that for her?"

"Yes, you fucking wombat. I'd do anything for any of you," I stand up, annoyed he doesn't know that. "You guys are my family. I've always been all-in, even when I was left out. Your sister means as much to me as you do. Maybe more because she's always tried to be truthful with me."

Logan stands up too and before I realize what's happening, he's hugging me. I've known him since I was fourteen years old and we've hugged—for real like this—twice. Once when he got out of rehab and once when River was born. Logan's voice is thick and low. "Love you, brother. And I've never wanted to lie to you. Never."

"Love you too, bro," I reply and then gently shove him away. "But we both know that's semantics. You may not have wanted to, but you have been lying haven't you?"

Logan looks grim again. Jaw tighter than ever. Blue eyes clouded. "Terra told me what you said to her on the way to dialysis. That I was one of the reasons you left for King's Rock. She wants me to talk to you about it."

"You obviously don't want to, or you would have," I reply and let out a heavy sigh. "You've had ample opportunities when you visited me. You've never tried to tell me anything, trust me I've looked for signs."

"It's not that I haven't wanted to, it's that I haven't been allowed to but..." his sentence trails and his blue eyes move to look at the door to the lounge. He looks back at me. "Wanna head across the street and grab some breakfast? I need to talk to you... away from here."

"Okay."

We make our way to the front of the fire station and out the door to Dunkin'. It's open twenty-four hours, thankfully. We order egg sandwiches and extra-large coffees, mine iced, his hot. When we get our order, we walk toward the firehouse. The sun is starting to rise though and the sky is putting on a color show as Logan stops and sits on the lip of the raised, hip high flower beds that border the driveway. "Don't want anyone in the fire house or in Dunkin' to hear me so let's sit out here while we eat."

I nod and join him. As the puffy clouds start to glow pink and orange and I bite into my sandwich, Logan speaks again. "If you'd been here that weekend my life changed, you would have been right there with the family every step of the way. Hell, you would have probably driven me to the airport."

I nod, and chew. "I know this. What I don't know is why I wasn't given the chance to do that. I would have skipped training and come home."

"Because Declan said it wouldn't be fair to saddle you with this lie," Logan says, his tone tight and heavy, like the words themselves are thick with guilt. "And the family, except for Terra, said he was right. The less people who had to carry this, the better."

I don't know what he's talking about but I want to know even though he's beginning to scare the hell out of me. "Logan, I would do anything, carry any secret, for any of you."

He doesn't react to that or say anything for a long minute. The egg sandwich is in his left hand on his lap. The coffee beside him on the bench and he's staring off into the horizon. I let him, because I know he's just finding the words, not ignoring me.

"I didn't just have some giant epiphany that weekend my friend Bryan died in a drunk driving accident," Logan says. His voice is low, his eyes keep darting around like he's worried someone will walk up on us in the middle of this conversation. He pauses. "You know he killed a man, right?"

"Yeah. He was over in Well Beach, drunk, and he hit a guy and they both died. And when you found out, you confessed to the family you had a drinking problem too, and you were scared you'd end up like him, and they sent you to a rehab in Florida," This was what I was told by Finn when I finally got back from Orono.

He's shaking his head, no, slowly. His face is so twisted with pain it makes my heart constrict and then he says. "Deck is going to kill me if I tell you what I'm about to tell you so you have to promise me that you will never utter a word about this. To anyone. For any reason. Terra says I can trust you, and I know I can, but I have to say that out loud."

"Brother, I would never breach your trust. For any reason."

He takes a deep breath, leaves his half eaten egg sandwich on his lap and scrubs both hands over his face. And then, he looks me right in the eye and starts talking. "I was in the car with Bryan that day. I told him we should drive down to Wells Beach, because there was a great bar there that never cut people off. I knew all the tricks back then. Which bartenders or bars didn't check IDs, didn't monitor your consumption, put up with drunken idiots, all of it. He agreed and we drove down there, drinking beers on the way. We played pool and I moved from beer to rum and Coke. He moved to vodka and Red Bulls, which is why I passed out and he didn't. Apparently, this bar was cool with you getting shitfaced but not sleeping it off at one of their tables, so Bryan dragged my ass to his car, buckled me into the backseat, and decided to drive us home. I woke up in the hospital still drunk with a broken arm and some bruises and cuts. I argued with the doctor for half an hour because I didn't believe what had happened. Then the police showed up, and I realized it wasn't some sick joke. Bryan was dead and we'd killed someone."

The shock of this is so deep my limbs go numb. I put down my sandwich and my coffee and fist my hands, trying to get the feeling back. *Holy shit* is all I can think and my expression must reflect it because Logan looks absolutely tortured as he turns away. I reach out and grab his shoulder. "You didn't kill anyone. You weren't even conscious."

"My heart doesn't care. My heart thinks I should have gone to jail since Bryan couldn't," Logan replies. "And I even told the Wells Beach cops that, much to my family's horror. I begged them to arrest me as I sobbed in that hospital bed. The nurse sedated me, and the cops and my parents left my room to talk. When I woke up again, Declan was there with my parents and they explained they'd gotten me into a great facility in Florida. That they'd talked to the family of the guy who died and they'd offered a settlement to keep me out of the situation. Cops were not going to press any kind of charges because I wasn't conscious, like you said, so I held no responsibility because I hadn't even put myself in the car."

"Settlement?"

"They remortgaged the restaurant, ransacked their retirement fund and gave the family two-hundred grand in medical and funeral expenses," Logan explains. "Declan said we had no choice because if the town found out I was with Bryan they'd cancel me and the restaurant and everyone in the family. And you, if you knew."

I can't say he's wrong. I know how cruel Ocean Pines can be. "I would have taken that chance."

"That's what Terra kept telling us, but I was in no position, mentally or physically, to fight Declan and my parents so I just let it happen," Logan says and the guilt on his face as he meets my eye is visceral. I have never felt more empathy for someone in my life.

"I don't know what to say." I reply.

"It's a lot to take in. You don't have to say anything," Logan replies and picks up his sandwich. He takes a bite and chews but it's mechanical and I doubt he even tastes it. I grab my coffee and take a sip. I don't really taste it either.

I realize his grim expressions, gruff attitude, the way he has become a bit of a hermit who does nothing but work and see River makes sense now. The way, when he used to come to visit me, he never really seemed to fully enjoy our fishing or skiing trips wasn't because he was struggling to stay sober, it was because he was struggling with guilt. He doesn't think he deserves to be happy.

"Actually I do have something to say," I turn to look at him again. "I understand why this still eats at you, and why everyone thought I had to be kept in the dark, but I also think that you've done an incredible job at changing your life around, Logan. You save lives for a living. You're a good dad. You work your ass off to be a better person than most, and you don't have to keep holding onto the guilt as much as you seem to be."

He blinks and a sad smile tugs at his mouth. "You sound like Terra."

"I'm cool with that," I reply and smile.

Logan exhales, hard, and picks up the rest of his sandwich again, but he just stares at it. "So can we change the subject so I can maybe eat this without wanting to throw up?"

"Aspen moved into the Five Seasons," I say because I can't think of anything else.

"Swanky. Abbott's paying for that I guess?" Logan asks and looks over at me as I nod. He squints his eyes. "Anything happen while you two were roommates? Any old feelings come back?"

"Not one. We'll never get back together," I state firmly. "We both moved on a long time ago. In fact she was seeing someone a while ago, but I don't know who. Do you?"

Logan shakes his head. "I haven't seen her with anyone. If you're not interested again, though, why do you care?"

He just trusted me with his biggest secret and I feel like, since I kind of forced him to share it, I should tell him about mine. "Aspen is pregnant. It may or may not be mine."

Logan's eyes grow wide and his mouth starts to fall open but he raises a hand and covers it quickly, scrubbing his beard for a second. "Are you fucking serious?"

I nod.

He drops his hand and blinks. A lot. "Jake. When? How?"

"I came out this way to interview for the OP position," I explain. "I didn't tell any of you because I didn't want the pressure of getting you guys all hopeful and excited in case I didn't get it. I happened to run into her and… we were both lonely, horny, and frustrated with life and… it just happened."

I can't tell him the exact truth on this. *Yeah, well, I got drunk and decided to use Aspen for a little distraction from the pain of realizing I would never get a real shot at dating your sister.*

"What are you going to do?" Logan asked.

"Well, she isn't ready to find out paternity yet," I say. "So I'm just trying to wait patiently in purgatory until I find out my fate."

"Fuck. That sounds like hell," Logan replies. "Is she really not ready to know or is she just not ready to let you go?"

I shake my head. "She doesn't have me to release me. We both know I'm not getting back together with her if it is mine. And she doesn't want me back. She even said I didn't have to be involved."

"But you will be," Logan replies as he takes a sip from his coffee. I nod. "Maybe that's why she's scared to find out for sure. Because she's knows you'll step up and maybe this other guy won't."

"Maybe. But I think she's just getting through some stuff. She has to tell Abbott and deal with her apartment," I reply and take a heavy breath. "I don't know who the other guy is, but if I were her I'd be hoping it was his."

"Why the hell would you say that?"

"Dude, if it's mine you know this town, everyone will be whispering about how his granny used to be a stripper and his dad was a foster failure." I take a sip of my own coffee and then sigh.

"Fuck this town," Logan says. "This kid would be lucky to have you as a dad. And for the record, I wouldn't call any fire-fighter with a medal of valor a failure, Jake. And Aspy… I mean growing up she wasn't my favorite person but she's matured. She's a ball buster and a little eccentric, but she's also kind and smart and she will be a fantastic mom."

I ball up the wrapper from my now eaten sandwich and toss it at the trash can a few feet away. I miss.

A few cars start rolling into the parking lot next to the station. The new shift is arriving. Logan and I stand up, I grab my wrapper off the pavement and put it in the trash can. Logan tosses his from the bench and it sails into the can. He starts to make roaring crowd noises as he lifts his hands in victory. I give him the finger.

As we walk back to the firehouse he seems to get serious again. "I fucking hate lupus."

"We all do." I give his shoulder a squeeze. "But she'll be okay. Someone will match."

He nods. My shift mates start to filter in, yelling greetings at us both and Logan drifts off to strip his bunk and head home. I start my shift.

We actually have a fairly busy morning. A gas leak at one of the restaurants by the pier, a small fire in a backyard—leaves someone tried to burn that got out of control. A cat in a tree. Yeah, we respond to those for Mr. Driftwater who runs an animal rescue partly funded by the town. But despite the grind of a busy day, I feel good because Logan and I have finally cleared the air. The truth was heavy, but knowing that I wasn't shunned by them, makes me lighter. When the day starts to settle and the calls stop coming in, I play cards with the guys, help the probie cook dinner, make a dent in the new Stephen King novel I'm reading and work out, but I keep checking my phone, hoping the doctor will call with some news. And then he does.

"Hi Jake, it's Doctor Kelly Biswell from the transplant team at Casco Bay Memorial," her voice is calm, serene. I don't know her at all but I instantly take her tone as a bad sign. She's going to let me down easy. *Sorry, Jake but you aren't a match. You knew it was a long shot.*

"Do I want to hear this?" I ask and close my eyes.

"Well, you have some decisions to make," he replies. "Because you are in fact a pretty solid match for this patient."

"Are you serious?" I can't move. I can't breathe. I'm in shock.

"Yes. Sometimes long shots pay off," Dr. Biswell tells me. "Now you just have to think about this. Obviously it's a wonderful thing to donate, but it's a serious commitment that shouldn't be taken lightly."

"I'm donating. It's decided," I say and then pause. "If no one else can. She's got some in-laws being tested. I know she would prefer that."

Doctor Biswell chuckles at that. "I think when you're in this young woman's situation, you aren't picky. But before you commit we need you to meet with a hospital social worker and they'll have to approve the match too. Make sure you're in it for the right reasons, so to speak. Can I send you some information via email?"

"Yeah of course," I say but I know I'm donating, no matter what. I give her my email and hang up.

Ten minutes later I get all the information and the results. Dr. Biswell has even scheduled an interview with a social worker for the day after tomorrow. I'm not a big fan of social workers since I spent my childhood being yanked from my home by them, but I will deal with the system one more time if it means I can help Terra. I stand in the hallway outside the kitchen and read all the information the doc sent. Twice. And then I get up and head down the hall to the see the captain. I knock on his open door and he looks up from his desk and smiles. "What's up, Maverick?"

"I have some questions about our medical leave," I say and step inside, closing the door behind me.

"Are you sick?" He is instantly concerned, which is nice. I've always had a great relationship with Captain D'Amato. He has been in charge since I was a probie and he gave me a glowing recommendation when I applied to King's Rock. He also called me personally to tell me when the lieutenant's position opened here.

"No, but I need to have an operation," I say and he motions for me to sit down in one of the two chairs across from his desk. I sit and explain everything, leaving out Terra's name because it feels like I should leave it up to Logan to disclose that if he wants.

"You're the most selfless man I have ever met, Maverick," Captain D'Amato says and leans back in his chair. As he ponders what I just said, he scratches his salt-n-pepper hair at his right temple, staring absently out the window at the dark sky. "You would have to check with the union, because I think medical days are only for unavoidable medical situations, but I will gladly approve you using vacation days for this."

I lean forward, putting my elbows on my knees and resting my chin on my clasped hands. "Thank you. I don't know exactly when it will be scheduled but I'm assuming sooner rather than later. If she needs me. There might be other donors."

"Okay," he nods. He gives me a smile but it's tainted with something that looks like sympathy, which seems weird.

"Is something wrong?" I ask, worried he isn't on board with this.

"No. It's just… I need you to be made aware of something now. I was holding off until you felt more settled in but…" he pauses and sighs. "Simpson, the Battalion chief for Southern Maine, is retiring early next year. They haven't announced it yet but, I've accepted his position. And the reason I was so keen on getting you back here is because when I get promoted to chief, I want you to be the captain here."

I am floored. There is no other way to put it. Not by the news because thanks to Cassidy Green, I'd heard the rumor, but by the fact he has me in mind to take his place. This is my ultimate career goal but I thought it was still out of reach. "I'm honored, sir. It would be my dream come true, but I thought I would be considered too green."

He shakes his head. "You'd be the youngest captain in the history of the Ocean Pines station but you'd also be more qualified than I was at your age. You've written the tests. You've done every single extra training the State has offered. And you've already earned a Medal of Valor for crying out loud." He grins at me, like he still can't believe my accomplishments.

I never actually think about them until someone points them out. Then I have a moment of pride like right now. I smile and sit up, my shoulders pushing back a bit. "I love my job."

"Which is another reason why I want you to succeed me. But if you take a leave for this and then need desk duty when you get back, which you inevitably will for a couple weeks…" He pauses and his smile slips into a look of sympathy again. "I don't think that will help you with the powers that be. The screening process will be taking place during your recovery time. There'll be interviews and tests and they'll send people to watch you work, lead a team. Something you won't be doing if you're on desk duty."

"Oh," I have more to worry about now than the actual operation.

Captain D'Amato suddenly leans forward and smiles again, waving a hand for a minute in the space between us. "Let's not get ahead of ourselves. You said this friend of yours has other options?"

"Maybe. Yes."

"Okay well let's wait to worry about the logistics and impacts until we know for sure," Captain says and I stand up.

"Sounds good. Thanks for your time."

"Always Jake. And I can't tell you how proud I am of you," he replies as I reach the door and pull it open. "I've been working this firehouse and living in Ocean Pines for fifteen years. I know what you've had to… overcome to get where you are now. And this act of kindness you're thinking of doing is above and beyond for anyone."

"It's not. Honestly. The person is like family. It's a no-brainer," I say and leave his office.

I really want that captain's job. It would suck if I get screwed out of it because of this but… what would suck more would be letting Terra suffer. I could never do that.

We get a call. House fire. And I let all these concerns slip away as I rush to the rig to get dressed. The wind is blowing fiercely because a storm is coming in which doesn't help us contain the flames, but then it starts to pour rain and that does help. Luckily, no one is injured.

When I get back to the station, I undress and head to my private bunk room. I had left my phone on my bed and it's flashing with a new message alert. It's Logan.

Nova & Javi = B Neg. No match. Let me know when you hear back.

I don't respond to Logan. Instead, without a second thought, I walk down to the lobby and talk to the probie working the front desk. "Personal issue. Back in ten minutes. I have my cell if we get a call."

I jump in my jeep and start the engine.

9

———

TERRA

"THROW ME A RAG. I'M GONNA WIPE DOWN THE TABLES."

"I can do that. You've worked a double today," Finn says to Nova. He is such a sweetheart sometimes. "Go home, make sure Thelma and Louise's chicken coop hasn't flown away like Dorothy in the Wizard of Oz."

"Really? Finn you're the best, as always," she spontaneously reaches over and kisses his cheek, and he looks instantly uncomfortable like he always does. I will never truly understand my brother Finn. He is so easy-going, fun-loving and the first to get sappy and touchy-feely but crawls out of his skin when someone like Nova hits him with the same attention. Weirdo. Nova heads into the kitchen to go get her coat in the break room, I'm sure.

"You ever going to tell me why Nova freaks you out so much?" I ask with a calm smile on my lips. Finn looks up and quirks an eyebrow.

"You've said that before and I'll give you the same answer," he replies. "You're delusional."

I'm not, but I let it go and Finn and I set about cleaning the restaurant and readying it for tomorrow without a word to each other. It's a comfortable silence. We've both done this more times than either of us can count. He wipes down the bar and counter areas and collects and refills the salt and pepper shakers as I wipe down the tables and stack the chairs on top so I can mop the floors next.

Nova breezes back in, all bundled up in her raincoat and tall rubber boots. She waves to me and Finn but hesitates before leaving. "Terra, you can go home if you want and I can stay with Finn. If you're tired. I know you had treatment today."

She's right. I'm exhausted, but I'm not going to admit it. I smile. "I'm good. If I go home I'll just be alone with my fears, so I don't mind the work."

It's an honest confession. We found out about an hour ago that Nova and Javi don't match. Leave it to me to have a huge family that can't help me. Nova looks at me with love and ferocity. "We *will* figure this out Terra."

I nod. Finn glares at me and points. "Do not do that fake agreement thing you do. Nova is right. We *will* find you a donor. Aren't you the one who always tells us about the power of positive thinking? Do it!"

"Yeah. Yeah. I know, I'm just… having a moment," I sigh. "Go, Nova. It's fine. I promise. If something happens to your chickens in this crazy storm, I will never forgive myself."

"Okay. Love you all," she blows an air kiss and heads out the door.

Finn watches her go and I disappear into the back. When I return with the mop and bucket, I'm out of breath. Finn grabs it from me without a word and I let him. But only until I catch my breath again, which is when he's halfway through the room, and then I insist on taking over. He wants to argue but he doesn't and I continue mopping under his watchful eye.

"Was that just a joke or are you really scared?" Finn asks quietly as I'm wringing out the mop.

"I've been trying not to think about it." I pause and look up at him. "I have the worst luck ever."

"I mean there's still a chance Dad can donate. He's going to his doctor again next week and he's going to push them on it. Declan also found a bunch of medical studies that say that other people with his pre-existing conditions have successfully donated."

"He showed me those studies. I'm not okay with it. The margins are too small," I reply flatly. "I'm going to have to let Mom tell Mrs. Green so she can blab about it to the whole town and pray someone takes pity on me and gets tested. And if that nightmare experience doesn't work out, then I wait. I'm young. Doc says I can go a decade on dialysis, probably."

Finn looks worried. "I'm sorry this sucks so much Terra."

"Me too."

Javi calls out from the back that he's leaving. Finn disappears into the kitchen to lock the back door behind him, and I move behind the counter to mop there. Two seconds later there's a knock on the front door and I jump out of my skin. My eyes fly up and I see Jake standing there, soaking wet, wind blowing his hair across his forehead in wet clumps. I abandon my mop and bucket and rush over to unlock the door.

"Hey," he says casually as he walks in and drips all over everything. The idiot is in nothing but his work t-shirt and pants. No jacket.

"You're soaked!" I say and walk back over to grab my mop. "And you're ruining my freshly mopped floors."

He runs a hand through his drenched, black hair and gives his head a shake at the same time, spraying water everywhere like a wet dog. I yelp and jump back to avoid getting wet. I open my scrunched up eyes and find him grinning sheepishly. "Sorry."

Jake takes the mop from me. I don't let go. It's a small but fierce tug-of-war that he ends up winning. "You shouldn't be doing manual labor."

"I need a new kidney not new arms and legs," I gripe. "I can still mop."

"Listen, Tink, you're doing this all wrong," Jake says sternly. "This is the part where you milk it. If I had a severe illness, I would have the whole damn family waiting on me hand and foot."

"I'm sure there'll be time for that later. When I'm like dying and shit," I mutter and I wish I was joking but I might not be. Only time will tell.

He stops mopping and looks me dead in the eye. "I hate to burst your bubble but that ain't gonna happen, so start milking it now while you can. Because while I'm recuperating from giving you a kidney, I am going to make everyone wait on me hand and foot so they won't have time to baby you too."

My body feels heavy. Like the weight of his words just had turned my blood into cement. I'm unable to move anything but my head and only enough to look up into his dark, endless eyes. "What did you just say?"

He takes one hand off the mop, reaches in his back pocket, and hands me a piece of paper. I don't feel my arms move but suddenly I'm taking it from him and unfolding it as he speaks. "I did the test thing at the hospital. I'm a match, Tink. I'm giving you a kidney."

I read the paper from the hospital. He is a match. A really good one. *Oh my God.*

"Well... that's unbelievable," I whisper.

"You always act like we have absolutely nothing in common, but it turns out our organs have a shit ton in common," he grins. It's his usual, carefree grin and I don't know whether to cry or punch him. This is a serious, incredibly intense, moment and he's acting like he just told me the Red Sox scored or something.

"What the hell is wrong with you?" I ask suddenly and he

blinks like I slapped him. "And also, I can't take your kidney. You need it to save people and crap. I can't."

"You have a really weird way of treating people who have the ability to save your life," Jake says and walks past me toward the counter. He walks behind the bar and puts the mop in the bucket. "And also, I can still be a firefighter with one kidney. I Googled it and double checked with my captain. I will have to take some vacation days. Likely all of them. But it's not like I use them anyway. It's fine."

"No. It's not," I am shaking my head so hard my neck actually starts to hurt. "I can't let you do this."

"You can't *not* let me Terra," Jake says and that grin is slipping. Finally. He leans on the counter on his elbows, looking right at me. "The transplant list could take years. Why suffer that long when you don't have to?"

"I can't ask you to do this," I say in a voice so strangled it sounds like someone else. I run a hand through my hair which I'm sure messes it up. I mean, not that it matters. He walks back out from behind the bar and comes to stand directly in front of me.

"You didn't ask, but I wish you had," Jake replies and I see a flash of pain in his smoldering eyes. "Look, I spend all my time saving people who aren't my family, so you bet your ass I'm going to save the people who are."

Tears suddenly start pouring out of my eyeballs so fast that it actually scares me. And Jake now looks terrified too. "Jesus Terra, don't. It kills me when you cry."

I take a step away from him and frantically wipe at my eyes. "Sorry. I can't help it. I don't mean to. I just… I can't believe this is happening."

"Yeah. Me either," he says and the smile slowly creeps back onto his face. And this time, his smile makes me smile too. "We'll tell your parents tomorrow?"

I nod and he swings open the door and leaves calling "Lock

this behind me!" as he goes. But I don't lock it. I stare at it for almost a minute and then run out into the parking lot after him. He's already in his car, motor running but he jumps out as soon as he sees me.

"Tink! You can't afford to catch a cold. Get back inside!" He hollers as the rain pounds down around us and I throw myself into him. Wrapping him in a hug. He holds me against him, dipping his head down and I swear I feel his lips on my neck, warm and soft, for a heartbeat before I lean back to look in his eyes.

"I'm sorry if I ever made you feel like I don't like you or appreciate you," I blurt out, just about screaming it because the rain is so loud. "I do. I just…"

And then … I kiss him. I press my mouth against his and kiss him with every single ounce of energy and passion and hope and relief in my body. I don't think, I just kiss. My lips parting, my tongue barging its way into his mouth and my hands holding the sides of his head because I'm terrified he'll reject me like he did in high school. But he doesn't. In fact … I think he's kissing me back until…

"What the hell are you two doing?" Finn's voice bellows from behind me and I turn and see him running towards me, holding an open umbrella.

We jump apart and Jake gets into his Jeep and drives away without a word.

"Jake! What the fuck? Terra did he just kiss you? Were you two kissing?" Finn says it like it's the grossest thing he can think of.

"No he didn't kiss me. I kissed him," I reply as Finn holds the umbrella over me with one hand and uses his other to tug me back to the restaurant. I stumble along, my feet not acting like they remember how to walk.

"Why the hell are you trying to make-out with my best friend?" Finn asks inside the restaurant as I watch Jake's car turn and head out of the parking lot. "Is rash, spontaneous and completely stupid decisions some kind of dialysis side effect? You're going to catch a death cold out there too."

"You can't catch a cold virus from rain water," I inform him and press a palm to the glass as the last of Jake's tail lights disappear from view.

"Yeah okay, but you know what I mean," Finn barks. "What the hell is wrong with you?"

"He's giving me his kidney."

"What?"

I turn slowly from the window and look at my brother, who is behind the counter looking for a tea towel or something to give me to dry off with. "Jake did the test. He's a match. He wants to give me his kidney."

Finn's blue eyes widen and his mouth drops. "Are you serious?"

I nod and feel the tears pressing at the back of my eyes again. I blink and then give in and cover my face with my hands as I cry. Suddenly Finn has me in a hug, pressing my face into his wide chest as his arms hold me close. "That crazy son of a bitch. I can't believe it."

"I can," I whisper into Finn's flannel shirt.

I always knew Jake Maverick was something special … I just never thought he thought I was someone special. Someone worth saving. But he does. He may not have kissed me when I was locked in a closet with him at fourteen, but I'll take a kidney over a first kiss any day.

10

JAKE

I HOP OFF THE TRUCK AND SCAN THE CROWD THAT HAS ALREADY started to form. Logan is parking his ambulance a few feet away. Captain climbs down from the front of the rig and claps me on the back. "Big night."

"Illumination Night is a town favorite," I agree.

"Keribo, Murphy, Cartwright stick around the trucks, in case someone comes here for medical attention or an emergency," Captain commands. "The rest of you walk around and mingle. We're here to bond with the community as much as protect it. But keep your radios on."

Logan walks over and joins us. "Hopefully we don't have to respond to anything big tonight."

The Cap holds up his hand and crosses his fingers before he wanders down the parking lot toward the pier, which has a series of booths set up for the night. Illumination Night is an annual event, held the first official day of autumn since the town's inception in eighteen eighty-one. Back then Ocean Pines was a summer town with nothing but uninsulated cottages owned mostly by wealthy Bostonians. This was the weekend they would all come back to close up their places for the winter, and so it was the last time the houses had lights in the windows and lanterns on the porches. Now people purposely decorate their homes as a nod to the past and a symbol of the end of the tourist season since Ocean Pines still gets its fair share of holiday-makers in the summer. People decorate their lawns and porches and put candles in windows or do crazy lights across their roof almost like Christmas and at ten o'clock, people gather on the beach and release sky lanterns in memory of loved ones or in honor of wishes they dream of fulfilling.

"You wanna walk down to the Hawkins booth with me?" Logan asks. "Before things really get going and I end up treating forty kids with scraped knees or a drunken teenager who face-plants?"

I give him side eye. "Is your ma back to normal yet?"

Logan laughs and gives me a shove toward the pier. "Dude, you're saving her baby's life. She will never treat you like a normal person again. Sorry."

I bite back a groan. Lucy Hawkins burst into tears the first time she saw me after she heard the news. And then she grabbed her rosary and held it tightly as she hugged me with more force than any women barely five feet should have and proclaimed me a gift from God. Charlie stood there and watched, his eyes watery but his face stoic and then he clapped me on the back and disappeared down to the dock.

I understand their gratitude, but it still makes me uncomfortable. I don't want to be idolized by this family, just accepted. We walk along the ancient wood pier, past Stan's Seafood booth, past Patti's Parlor booth, past Kurt the Cotton Candy Man's stand. Hawkins' Lobster Shack has the biggest booth, decorated with a string of lobster lights across the top, just under the wooden sign with the business name that Nova created herself. Nova and Declan are the ones manning the booth, and I'm relieved.

"Oh good," Nova exclaims and turns to grab a big cardboard tray with about twelve lobster rolls lined up on it. "This saves me a trip. Bring this to your team will ya?"

Logan nods. "They'll be forever grateful."

"Thanks, Nova," I say.

Her grin broadens. "Those aren't for you. Those are just the standard rolls - toasted bun, mayo, lobster meat. Lucy made two Jake specials for you. And she pre-paid a chocolate peanut butter shake at Patti's just for you. All you have to do is pop over there."

"She did not have to do that!" I argue but I reach across the counter for the bag with my name on it.

Logan knocks my shoulder with his. "Gonna have to learn to live with it, Maverick."

And then out of nowhere, a row of clam shell lights that I hadn't noticed were hanging under the counter pop on and Terra pops up. She must have been under the counter plugging them in. She looks amazing and adorable. Her hair is in two braids and the long sleeved Hawkins Lobster Shack shirt she's wearing is red, which accentuates her perfect, pale skin and the freckles that dot along the bridge of her nose and her cheeks. She's in overalls on top of it, but I can still tell the shirt is clingy, so her svelte figure isn't as hidden as it usually is. "Hey boys, make sure no one burns anything down or drops dead tonight."

She doesn't make eye contact. I swear she hasn't looked me in the eye since that night in the pouring rain. Of course I've only seen her twice since then, once at the restaurant and once at the doctor's office when we met for our first consultation together for the transplant after the social worker gave the go-ahead. At the restaurant she hovered in the background while her family showered me with thanks and then disappeared into the back claiming she had invoices to pay. I had to go into work, so I didn't get to hang around or sneak into the back and confront her. At the doctor's office, Lucy was with her and I wasn't about to bring up anything in front of Mom. Because what I want to talk about with her is that kiss.

"Hey Terra, I got some time before it gets busy, wanna go walk the streets and check out some of the lights?" I ask hoping I sound casual and laid back.

"Sorry, I still have stuff to organize here," she replies as she turns toward the grill at the back of the booth.

"I can handle the rest of the prep," Nova interjects.

"Yeah, and I can help her. I know how much you love the lights," Declan replies.

"You used to make me pay you my allowance money to take me to see them when Mom said I was too young to wander around alone," Terra says giving Declan dagger eyes from over her shoulder.

"You don't let anything go," Declan rolls his eyes. "Well now I'm going to do manual labor so you can go check them out. Consider it an apology."

"Go with Jake, Terra," Nova adds, grinning. "The man is giving you a kidney. The least you can do is give him a walk."

Finally, Terra looks over at me. Her expression is guarded, but why? It's not like I'm the one that kissed *her*. She kissed *me*. Does she regret it? Is she embarrassed? Is she worried I think it means nothing or that it means something? So many questions. But I can't ask them if she stays here. Luckily, after a fairly heavy sigh that feels like an insult, she opens the door on the side of the booth and exits. I hand the bag of lobster rolls back to Nova. "Hold onto these for me until I get back, please? If I leave them on the firetruck they'll get eaten for sure."

Nova takes the bag back with a smile. Terra, on the other hand looks like she's going to the gallows. Great. I turn to Logan before I leave. "Tell Cap I got my radio if he needs me." I pat the radio on the hip of my work pants.

Terra and I walk in silence back down the pier until we get to Dune street. It runs along the beach and has the biggest houses in town. "You wanna check out this street first?"

She shakes her head and points straight ahead to Colby street, which runs away from the beach. "Let's go back to the other side of town, those guys don't get as many people looking at their displays, and they deserve the love."

Another thing that I like about Terra, she is always so sensitive to things like that. We continue down the road, crowds wandering past us in the other direction, keen to be by the pier and the bigger, fancier displays. I know where she's going to turn before she even does it because for more than a couple of years growing up, I tagged along when her brothers chaperoned her at these events. She loves the houses on Free Street. It's a short street with only ten homes and the start of Gold Park, a nature reserve which is thick with pine trees. All the homes are one or two story stone cottages with sunrooms on the side. Every single sunroom is decorated with different kinds of lights. One has pineapple and palm tree shaped lights, one has red, white and blue stars and fairy lights, one has old fashioned lanterns. You can visibly see Terra relax as she takes them all in.

"You still love this street?" I say.

"Always," Terra sighs. She has been obsessed with it since she was little. I remember her telling her mom she wanted to buy one of these stone houses one day. I wonder if that's still a dream of hers.

"I'm hoping to buy in the next year," I say quietly as we wander towards Gold Park. "Been saving up."

The fact that I will likely be passed over for the captain's position may limit my budget and I might end up buying a condo instead of a house, but I still want to own. I'd be the first in my family to do it. My mom has always bounced from rental to rental and my grandparents, who died before I was born, raised my mother in a motorhome.

"Here? You want to buy here? On this street?" she looks positively excited about the possibility.

"If something comes up and I can afford it, of course," I reply with a smile. "Want to rent a room from me? I'll need a roommate. I was going to ask Logan but you're a much better option."

She laughs tilting her head back, the moonlight glinting off her freckles. "How on earth am I a better option than one of your best friends?"

"Because my best friends don't make-out with me when I do nice things for them," I shoot back and she stops laughing so suddenly it's jarring. Like somebody turned off the laugh track on a sitcom.

Her head dips down so now she's looking at the pavement as we walk. "I'm sorry about that. I … it was a mistake. I was just so … overwhelmed. I mean, I lost it. But I swear I won't, like, attack you again."

"So you didn't mean to do it?"

"No. I didn't. It just … happened." She nods her head, eyes still glued to the cracked pavement.

"You regret it?"

"Yes." She says with such conviction that I can't help but feel offended.

I stop walking. We're at the end of the street now anyway. Our only option is to either continue into Gold Park or turn back around and take one of the streets that intersects with Free street and goes back down to the waterfront.

"You used to want to kiss me remember?" I say quietly.

She stops walking too, but a couple feet in front of me. Finally, she lifts her head. Our eyes meet for the briefest second and then she looks away. "No. I wanted you to kiss me. There's a difference."

"Oh?" I consider that. I guess there is, but to me a kiss is a kiss. She clearly isn't a fan of my blasé response because when she looks up at me again her expression is a mix of fire and ice.

"Yeah Jake, believe it or not I didn't want to force myself on you. Not at fourteen and not now." The wind picks up and blows a strand from her braids, and she reaches up and tucks it behind her ear roughly. "You made it clear back then that I wasn't your type, and it hurt. It was awkward and embarrassing but we got through it. I didn't mean to make all those gross feelings come back. So can we just forget what happened?"

She turns and starts to walk way too fast toward another street but I hook her by the elbow and turn her back to face me. "I don't want to forget it happened. In fact, it's all I think about."

She blinks. Repeatedly. And then pulls her arm from my grip. "Jake, don't placate me."

"Why the hell do you think I'm placating you?" I demand and now I'm getting pissed. "Do you think so little of yourself that you honestly don't think I could enjoy a kiss from you?"

"You don't want a kiss from me. You told me. To my face," she replies, hands moving to her tiny hips. "I'll never touch you."

"Are you seriously holding on to a stupid childhood game?" I ask and take a step toward her. "I was a dumb, terrified kid. If I kissed you in that closet, your brothers would have beat the shit out of me and never talked to me again."

"Okay, let me give you the benefit of the doubt on that one," she snaps. "Fine. You were young and scared of my brothers. Needed their friendship. But then you dated my best friend."

"Because you hated me."

"What?"

"After that closet debacle you were a total nightmare to me. For years," I remind her.

"So you date my best friend?"

"You cared?"

"Oh my God, Jake yes! I was…" she stops. "Why the hell do you think Aspen ended up wearing spaghetti?" She turns and bolts. She doesn't head for the street this time, she heads for the park.

Luckily, two of her strides is one of mine—advantage of having a foot of height on her—so I reach her before she can disappear down into the dark woods. "Is this finally the truth?"."

She glares up at me. "I still had a crush on you and she asked you to prom and I wanted to kill her. I knew you'd end up dating, which you did."

"I would never have said yes if I knew that," I confess. If I ever believed Terra still had an inkling of interest in me, I wouldn't have dated Aspen.

"Really?" She whispers in disbelief.

"You seemed to hate me so much, I figured I lost my one and only chance and that you wouldn't care if I dated Aspen or anyone for that matter," I tell her and I can't believe I'm admitting any of this.

"I have a chronic illness. I'm really good at pretending," she replies and the wind rustles the trees around us. A family of four wanders by, too busy looking at the all lit up homes to pay attention to us.

"Aspen and I have been broken up for years," I reply. "And you never—"

"Set myself up to be rejected again?" she interjects, her brown eyes hard. "I know you think it's no big deal, that stupid game from Abbott's sixteenth birthday party, but it was everything to me at the time. I had just found out I had lupus. I felt like damaged goods on top of the regular awkward teenage girl insecurities, and it took every ounce of courage I had to say your name that night. I wanted that perfect, normal kid moment with the hottest guy in school."

She suddenly looks so… young. Almost exactly like I

remember her back then. Vulnerable and delicate, inside and out and for the millionth time in my life I wish I could go back and do that whole moment over. I reach out and take her left hand in mine and without even realizing why, I start to pull her down the trail into the wooded park. I only take her a few feet, until the hundred foot pines towering over head make it dark enough that prying eyes from passersby on the street won't be able to see us clearly.

Then I dip my head. My nose bumps her cheek. I can feel a strand of her hair graze my cheek bone. I inhale, long and slow. She smells like lilacs and ocean breezes. My dick stirs but I ignore it. I slowly turn my head toward her mouth and run my tongue slowly along my lips in anticipation.

"What are you doing?" she whispers.

"Unless you tell me to stop I am going for a do-over," I whisper roughly. "In three... two... one."

I find her lips through the darkness and press mine against them. Her whole body tenses and her hand falls flat against my chest, just next to my left shoulder, but she doesn't push me away. So I press harder, moving my lips, opening them a little. And she fists my work shirt, just above the Ocean Pines Fire Department logo and pulls me closer. My hand on her arm drops and circles her waist, my palm spreads over the small of her back, fingers pressing into the top of her ass. I open my mouth further and she either gasps or sighs, I can't tell, and I slip my tongue into her mouth and I swear to God , this is better than anything that might have happened ten years ago.

An owl hoots loudly in the branches above us and we break apart, both breathing hard and then my radio crackles. "Maverick! You need to get back here ASAP."

"Is that Logan?" Terra says, her voice unsteady.

"Yeah. Shit," I grab her hand and lead her back to the road.

I hit the radio. "On my way. Be there in five."

"Go! Run!" Terra encourages me waving her hands.

I impulsively kiss her again, quick and hard on the lips and then turn and start running. I'm out of breath, but it's not from the exertion. It's from Terra. I don't know what the hell we're doing, but I know it's been a long time coming.

11

JAKE

Turns out it's the most chaotic, crazy night we've had in a while. On the way to our third consecutive call, Murphy points out something we hadn't noticed before—it's a full moon. Now it makes sense. We seriously get way more calls on full moons. It's illogical but true. By midnight I'm exhausted and starving because I never got to consume my milkshakes and lobster rolls, and on my way to a fourth freaking call. This time it's a backyard fire that is licking its way up a couple of trees. The address is on Free street, where Terra and I were earlier tonight. The last house on the street, the one directly next to Gold Park where Terra and I kissed.

Because it's Ocean Pines, I know who owns it, so I have a strong suspicion who caused the fire. And my suspicion is proven right when we get there. Mr. and Mrs. Ellis are standing in front of their little stone cottage in their bathrobes. Mr. Ellis looks furious. Mrs. Ellis looks stricken. She runs towards us as we jump off the truck. "Robbie is hurt! My son burned himself. Can you help?"

Mason and Logan jump out of their ambulance and run over to her. "Take us to him," Logan says calmly.

Forty minutes later, the fire is completely out and we managed to contain it to only two trees and half their lawn. Robbie Ellis isn't so lucky. He's got first degree burns on his right forearm, and on his forehead and is missing one eyebrow. He's sitting on a gurney behind the ambulance, getting treated by Logan and Mason as we pack up the hose.

"Robbie, what have we told you about using your deep fryer drunk?" Logan says in a voice that sounds so much like his dad I can't help but smile despite the seriousness of the situation.

"I wasn't drunk. I was tipsy," Robbie Ellis argues. He went to school with us. Was captain of the varsity soccer team and homecoming king two years in a row. Now he lives in a converted garage on his parents' property after two failed marriages and works as a part-time caddie at the golf course in Old Orchard. I grew up listening to Springsteen because Mr. Hawkins played his stuff all the time at the Shack, and Robbie Ellis is exactly the type of working class, small town dude who won't grow up that Bruce Springsteen sings about in "Glory Days."

Logan hits him with a scowl as he coats Robbie's forehead in burn gel. "We have to run you to the hospital Robbie. This is pretty serious."

"The torched trees are gonna have to come down too, Robbie," I explain "They're dead as a doorknob and if you leave 'em up, the first good winter storm will knock them onto the house."

"Great! Fabulous. Rob you're gonna cut those bastards yourself. I ain't gonna be killed by a tree in my sleep because of you, and I sure as hell ain't paying for someone to clean up your mess," Mr. Ellis barks from a few feet away, angrily tightening the belt on his faded purple bathrobe. Next to him, Mrs. Ellis, her hair in curlers, puts a palm over her heart.

"Maurice, it was an accident," she insists. Ah, the enabler. I've seen this before in a lot of relationships when I respond to emergencies. "I'll get it removed, Robbie honey. You just heal up and promise Mommy you won't do it again."

Logan's jaw visibly clenches. I turn to face the parents with a sympathetic smile and walk over to them. "Ya'll can go to bed now. I promise it's all fine for tonight."

"Thank you so much," Mr. Ellis says to me and shakes my hand. "Jake Grady, right? You went to school with Robbie. You played soccer too."

I nod. "Yes sir. But it's Maverick now. I changed my last name at eighteen."

I hate what comes next.

Mrs. Ellis pats my hand. "Fresh start. I understand why you'd want that."

"Actually it was my middle name," I shrug. "My mom picked it from a character in her favorite movie growing up, *Top Gun*. She was sixteen when she had me, and I guess it seemed like a good idea to name your kid after a Tom Cruise movie. Anyway, I always thought it sounded cooler than Grady so I changed it."

She looks confused. Mr. Ellis looks like a lightbulb has gone off in his head. "Oh right. Your mom was … well, look at you now though. You're a responsible young man with a respectable job. I bet you know how to use a deep fryer and don't just drop in an entire frozen turkey all at once."

I don't answer that. Instead, I hand them one of the pamphlets I keep in the truck. Mr. Ellis looks at it. "This is a very good program for adults who might need a little help with their drinking or other substances. It's day patient, and you don't need insurance. It's free, covered by public donations and therapists who donate their time."

Mrs. Ellis lets out a huff and shakes her head. "Whatever would we need that for?"

Mr. Ellis shakes my hand again. "Myrtle, this is exactly what the damn kid needs and you know it. Thanks, Jake."

I nod and leave them on the porch to fight, which is exactly what they do. Logan is still treating Robbie, who is suddenly concerned. "Will my eyebrow grow back?"

Logan shrugs. I try not to laugh. "Usually, but people who abuse alcohol sometimes have a harder time healing."

"Shit." Robbie mutters.

I slap Logan's shoulder. "See you back at the firehouse."

"Hey… Maverick!" Robbie calls out in a slurred voice. I turn around and see him pointing at me with the arm Mason isn't bandaging. "Were you here earlier tonight? In the woods, sucking face with some chick?"

How the hell is he so drunk he murdered his own eyebrow but somehow still has the ability to recognize me while I was making out with Terra? Shit. I shake my head and shrug. "I've been work- ing, Robbie."

"Yeah but I swear…" his eyes scan the firefighters who are all starting to climb back into their trucks. "I mean I saw the crest on the uniform and the guy was tall, and you're the tallest … the girl was not tall at all. Like teeny weeny itsy bitsy and I—"

"Robbie, did you fall when the deep fryer exploded? Maybe hit your head?" I interrupt. Logan has gone back to help Mason get the stretcher Robbie is lying on into the ambulance.

"I dunno," Robbie mutters and tries to scrunch his brow while he ponders the thought but it makes him wince. "Oww! Don't make me think, Maverick. It hurts."

I smirk. "Okay Robbie, don't think about anything then. Or talk. Just chill while they get you to the hospital."

Mason stays in the back with Robbie as Logan hops out, shuts the doors and walks around to the driver's seat. "See you later at the station."

I nod and walk back to the fire truck. I try not to freak out that Robbie saw Terra and me. He doesn't know for sure and he didn't recognize her so if I'm lucky, he'll forget it completely or everyone will chalk it up to him being drunk and getting confused.

We roll into the truck bay at the station and I jump out and start peeling off my protective gear. Logan and his partner went to an ambulance-only call so they aren't here yet. The captain walks up to me, smiling. "You know what you did back there, talking to that guy's family about the addiction program, that's why you're definitely the best candidate to replace me."

I smile, grateful he's in my corner. "I applied. They start the interview process next week, so that might be an issue. The donation process is really rolling forward now. I could be in the hospital."

He nods and looks conflicted. "I'll do everything I can to champion you and push them to make exceptions and give you more time if you need it. But Green also wants this, bad, and he is older and been local this whole time. Plus with you being so young, they might just move ahead without waiting for you because they know you'll have another shot at the position later on in your career."

I hate that because it's not necessarily true. If Ronan Green or any of the other lieutenants applying from other stations get the spot, it won't become available again for a long time. I'll have to switch houses to grab a captain's spot anytime soon and I don't want to leave Ocean Pines again.

"Thank you, sir."

"It would help if you let me tell them why you're off work," he suggests for the third time this week.

I shake my head like I have all the other times. "Not right now. I'll tell them if I need to."

"Okay," he nods.

I don't want to use this as some kind of way to get respect because my work ethic and performance should do that. After we're all done most of the guys go into the lounge to watch TV or gather in the kitchen to play cards at the table. I head out into the driveway to call Aspen. It's more private to be outside than it would be calling her anywhere in the station itself.

She answers on the first ring. "Barlowe Investigations."

"You know it's me, Aspy. You don't have to answer like that." I say.

"Sorry, Jake. Force of habit." She says with a giggle, but both her voice and laugh are muffled and low. "Can I call you later? This is not a good time."

"I'm at work," I explain. "Until seven tomorrow night."

"So am I," Aspen whispers. "In Ogunquit until late tomorrow night."

"What are you doing?" I ask as I pace the huge driveway.

"Surveillance on a dude who claims his back is so messed up from a fender bender he can't possibly work," Aspen explains. "I'm in my van outside his brother's house. I got a tip the two of them do CrossFit in the garage late at night when they think everyone is asleep. On warmer nights they even open the garage door. Tonight is seventy-one, Jake. My camera is poised and ready."

I worry about her line of work now. As if she's sensing that, she says. "Everything is fine. I'm good. Baby is good. I've been eating balanced meals, even when I'm hiding in the van all day and taking vitamins. Doc says I can continue to work until at least the last trimester if I'm smart about it."

"You went to the doctor?"

She laughs again. "Yes, Jake. I went to the doctor. Even got my first sonogram. That thing with the jelly on your belly and the wand that shows you the blob that will turn into a kid."

"Alone?"

"Well yeah, I forgot to plan a viewing party," she retorts with level ten sarcasm. "FYI I haven't told Abbott yet and he's the only one who would be at appointments with me."

"If it's my kid I'd like to be there. I mean, if you need someone to be there," I tell her. "And I want to be at the birth."

"No one - I repeat no one - is going to be in the room with me, looking at my hoo hoo being torn apart, Jake. Sorry," she replies bluntly and I wince at the description. "I mean if it's yours and you want to be at the hospital, fine. In the waiting room with Abbott if he isn't in the playoffs. This kid is due right around then."

"So … can we find out if it's mine so I can pencil you into my day planner?" I ask lightly, but I'm dead fucking serious. I don't just want to know now, I need to know.

"I'm not ready," Aspen replies flatly. "Soon. I'm almost there. I mean, before I start showing I guess I should know who the dad is because lord knows everyone in the damn town will want to know."

"Here's the thing Aspen…" I pause and figure out how to word this delicately but bluntly. "I need to know. There's some stuff going on in my life that would be impacted by this. So … can we go next week? Please? It's a simple blood test."

"I have to go! There's a light on in the garage," she says suddenly.

"Can we meet when you're back?" I beg. "Talk in person."

"Yeah, fine. Text me later." She hangs up.

That did not go as smoothly as I had hoped. I head back into the house and I'm wandering around the kitchen, trying to figure out what I want to eat, when my phone buzzes. It's a text from Terra. *I'm at the fire station. Can you meet me in the parking lot?*

What the hell? I head straight down the hall, down the stairs and out the front doors. I'm worried something may be wrong but she's standing there grinning, so I sigh in relief. She holds up a Hawkins Lobster Shack bag and a milkshake container from Patti's Parlor. "You never came back for your free food, so I thought I would bring it to you."

"Oh my God you are a saint," I say and walk over, taking the bag and the shake from her tiny hands. She stares up at me grinning happily at my reaction. "You're also fucking gorgeous, you know that?"

The skin under the freckles that decorate her cheeks turns pink. "I've waited my whole damn life for you to say something like that to me."

"I've waited my whole damn life to find the guts to say it," I tell her and she steps closer puts a hand on my chest, over my heart.

"I sent a lantern up at the beach tonight. Want to know what I wished for?"

I put a hand on her shoulder and let it slide slowly toward her delicate, long neck. "World peace?"

"That you kiss me again," she whispers.

"That's not something you have to wish for." I slip my hand behind her neck and tip her head back, dip my head down and give her a kiss that gets interrupted by the flash of headlights cutting across our bodies. I pull away and step back, way back. My head snaps around and I watch Logan's ambulance drive right past us into the bay. "Shit. That was your brother."

"You think he saw?"

"I think so."

"Okay well… I'm going to let you go and handle that," Terra walks backwards towards her truck. Grinning, not even the slightest bit remorseful. "Just please remind him that you need to be in great physical shape in order to have an organ harvested so he shouldn't try to kill you or anything."

"Solid advice, Tink," I reply and can't help but laugh even though this is not a laughing matter. I wait until she drives away and then walk back into the station. Logan is leaning against the front desk, staring right at me as I walk in. I suck back a big mouthful of the chocolate peanut butter shake because if he does intend to kill me, I want that as my last meal.

I decide to play dumb. "Terra brought me the food I never got to eat. I'm starving so I'm just gonna go to the kitchen and—"

"Can we talk for a minute?"

"Sure," I say hoping I sound casual and not as frantic as I feel. Logan walks over to the stairs that lead up to the bunk rooms. He sits on the third step and I sit beside him, sucking back even more of the shake as I wait for him to say something.

He looks solemn but that's Logan's face ninety percent of the time, so I don't take it as a sign. He tells me about his last call, an overly drunk girl they had to bring to the hospital to get her stomach pumped. And then he says. "So Robbie was leaving the hospital when I dropped the girl off. He was out by the emergency bay waiting for Uber Jay to pick him up because his dad refused."

I nod. "I really hope they convince him to try treatment. He's gonna lose more than his eyebrow next time."

"Yeah. I hope so too," Logan agrees absently and turns to face me now, his pale eyes boring down on me. "He was chatting away with me as I loaded the stretcher back into my rig, and the thing is, he swears he saw you kissing someone in Gold Park. And I told him it was impossible because you weren't with anyone but Terra. And you wouldn't be making out with my sister ... would you?"

"Robbie is also the guy who almost got arrested for drunkenly pretending to be a lifeguard at the beach last summer and yelling shark every ten minutes."

"Yeah, he's a bit nuts, but you kind of didn't answer the question," Logan replies pointedly and his laser focus on me is making me antsy. "Were you kissing my sister in the woods, or was your first kiss ten seconds ago in the parking lot?"

I swallow. The milkshake is curdling in my belly thanks to adrenaline and nerves. "Actually our first kiss was in the pouring rain outside the lobster shack. The night I told her I could be her donor."

Judging by the way his jaw drops, he didn't see that answer coming. "So what the fuck are you two doing?"

"I don't know, if I'm being honest, but I know that I like her. And I've liked her for a long time," I confess.

Logan takes a minute to process that information. I watch his jaw as it clenches and unclenches. "Any news on Aspen?"

Fuck.

"I'm meeting her as soon as I can. Going to make her understand why I need to find out the truth sooner rather than later," I tell him.

"Okay…" Logan has so much more he wants to say so I wait, but he just stares. So I stare back and will my face to not give anything away. "So I guess maybe you should figure that out. I mean, I would figure that out before getting involved with someone new."

He doesn't say anything else, just stands up and walks away.

12

———

TERRA

"Hey! Perfect timing!" Nova Hawkins calls out in a cheery voice from behind the counter. "The milkshake machine limped through the lunch rush but now it's flatlining. Help?"

I smile and walk over, surveying the dining area to my right. It's calm, which is to be expected at half an hour before close on a weekday with school back in session and vacationers gone back to their regularly scheduled lives. There are only two tables occupied and one booth. Mr. Hobbs, a regular who consumes more lobster chowder weekly than all our other customers combined, is sitting at the counter. I smile at him and he grins back in-between mouthfuls of chowder.

I slip in behind the counter and join Nova, who hands me the screwdriver in her hand. I am a wiz at mechanical issues around here. I'm not even sure why, but I am. Nova's full mouth with its trademark glossy lips grins. *"Gracias, hermana."*

Nova kisses my cheek and walks away to the other side of the counter. Nova is the same age as me, twenty-five, and started as a server here when she was seventeen. She was a shy, quiet person I barely knew anything about despite working more than a few shifts with her. She kept to herself and never hung out with the staff for the first four years she worked here, so it was a big surprise to everyone when my brother Declan showed up to Thanksgiving dinner four years ago holding her hand and announced that they had eloped. But seriously, as shocking as it was, it's gotta be the best decision he's ever made. Nova is a perfect addition to the family.

"How was the dinner rush?" I ask as I tinker with the machine, unscrewing the stainless steel side panel.

"Not bad," Nova replies with a shrug. "Steady stream but we weren't slammed. There was this one guy…"

She keeps talking about the customers and how the day has gone so far and I keep tinkering with the milkshake machine but, my brain is picturing that moment when Jake tugged me into the woods. It's been twenty-five hours since Jake Maverick *freaking kissed me*. This is how I measure time now, by how long it's been since my lifelong fantasy became my reality.

"Earth to Terra?" Nova says and snaps her fingers in front of me.

I blink. "What's up?"

"You tell me," Nova replies, her smile soft and curious. "You're not hearing a word I say."

"Miss Nova, dear, I think I need to get the check now," Mr. Hobbs calls out in his wobbly voice. "If I don't stop eating now, I'll have to undo the button on my trousers."

Nova smiles at the kind old man. "Coming right up, Mr. Hobbs."

I glance over my shoulder at Mr. Hobbs as Nova brings him the check and he hands her a ten dollar bill. I notice the small bundle of daisies wrapped in brown paper on the counter beside him. "Off to see your wife now?"

Mr. Hobbs raises his pale blue eyes to me, and they crinkle like tissue paper in the corners when he smiles. "You know my schedule as well as I do. Hoping to watch the sunset with her."

Mr. Hobbs and his wife used to come in here every Wednesday because the special is unlimited lobster chowder with fresh baked garlic rolls and they both adored it. Two years ago Mrs. Hobbs was moved into a care facility because of her rapidly progressing bone cancer. He then came in for take-out so he could bring it to her. That went on for almost three months until she passed. And now, he comes in alone once a week, flowers in hand to take to her grave after he's finished his meal.

"Be careful on your walk, Mr. Hobbs," Nova says as she brings him his change.

The cemetery is two blocks from here and it's all uphill. He gives her a grateful smile and leaves his change on the polished countertop with a wink.

"He is the sweetest man on the planet. And I miss seeing him help Mrs. Hobbs on with her coat and hold her hand while they walked in. And how he used to sit on the same side of the booth as her," Nova gushes and sighs with a hand on her heart once Mr. Hobbs is out the door. She is a romantic. Like a Hallmark-movie-marathoning, Valentine's-Day-celebrating, mistletoe-kissing, romance-novel-reading, hardcore romantic. And she married Declan, who I don't even think can spell romance. So odd.

The swinging door that leads to the kitchen and separates the counter from the bar moves and Declan emerges from it. He's wearing a crisp, navy suit with a light blue shirt and a checkered tie. He sticks out in his surroundings like a sore thumb. He glances at me. "Do I need to order a new one?"

"Nope," I assure him and hold my breath while I flip a switch. The machine swirls to life and I grin, victorious once again. "There's a little screw in the turning mechanism on the arm that's end-of-life. I'll text Dad and he can grab one at the hardware store."

"Awesome," Declan doesn't grin so much as grimace and then he rubs his smooth, wide forehead again. "Now back to trying to teach Finn how to do the schedule. Do we know if Mom dropped him on his head as a kid? Or like if Logan accidentally absorbed his brain in the womb?"

"Be nice!" Nova commands.

"Do you want my help?" I ask because Declan and Finn fight like cats and dogs at the best of times.

"Didn't Dad just drop you off after dialysis?" Declan asks and when I nod he replies, "Just chill. I can handle it."

I give him a grateful smile and go back to working on the milkshake machine. I think about the way Jake looked at me in the fire station parking lot. Like I was perfect. No one has ever looked at me like that. Ever. I've always been the kid/girl/woman that was imperfect and I certainly never felt perfect. Lupus never lets you feel perfect. My senior year of high school I had hair loss so bad I took Rogaine and wore a wig to prom. Meds fixed that and it grew back. Sure it's thin, but there are no bald spots anymore. I've had random rashes pop up on my face or hands since I was a pre-teen. They were hard to hide at times. The aches and internal pains no one could see kept me from feeling normal let alone perfect. So did the steroids I occasionally get prescribed that turn my face into a puffy pumpkin. And now the battered arms from the dialysis. Jake's known me through all of that and he still looked at me like I was perfect last night.

A hand whips by my eyes. I blink and turn to find Nova right there again, laughing at me. "You left the building again mentally? What the hell has you so flighty?"

"I… Illumination Night… He…" With every stuttering word Nova's thick, dark eyebrows inch higher and higher. I haven't told a soul what happened but I suddenly need to desperately. So I put down the screw driver, walk over to the kitchen door and peek through the porthole type window in it. The kitchen staff is busy. Finn and Declan are nowhere in sight. "Jake kissed me."

The second the words leave my lips I can actually feel the

shock like a sonic boom emanating off Nova. "I'm sorry… what?"

"He kissed me," I whisper it even lower than the first time and nervously tuck my hair behind my ears. "I mean, technically I kissed him first—accidentally—when he told me he was going to be my donor. But I didn't mean it. Then he wanted this do-over for the time in high school he refused to kiss me and … *he* kissed *me*. And then we kissed each other again, later in the fire station parking lot."

Nova's eyes are enormous. "So was this like a peck on the cheek? Peck on the lips? Was there tongue? Every time?"

"No. No, and holy shit yes," I whisper back and Nova gasps so loud I turn red and panic. My eyes dart to the kitchen door but no one rushes through it wondering what is going on. When I turn back around, Nova is standing there with both hands clamped over her gaping mouth. I shush her even though she's not speaking.

"I'm still so confused, Sis," Nova says after she finally unclamps the hands over her mouth. "What the heck is he trying to make up for? And how, exactly, does a person accidentally kiss someone?"

I explain what happened in the parking lot when he told me he was a match and then give her the details of that party oh so long ago. Nova has this frown on her face when I finish talking.

"Oh honey, You're still the smartest Hawkins just not when it comes to your own heart," Nova cups my face in her hands and grins. "Everyone thinks you two are like cats and dogs, oil and water, fire and ice, whatever silly analogy you can think of for opposites," Nova says as she grabs the keys to the front door from under the cash register and walks over to lock it. "But I've always believed the other saying, where there is fighting there is fire. Opposites attract. Jake likes you. And you like Jake."

"The expression is where there is smoke there is fire. Not

where there is fighting," I correct her. Nova always gets metaphors slightly wrong. It's kind of her thing. The family calls them Nova-isms. She once told Declan, before he did the Boston marathon, to go at it balls to the wind instead of balls to the wall. Dad almost died laughing.

"Nah. I meant it the way I said it this time," she says confidently, walking around the counter to flip the sign to closed on the restaurant door. "Look, if Jake didn't find you attractive, he wouldn't have kissed you. He would have just apologized. And you made out with him, not because he told you he was your match kidney-wise but because you know in your heart he's always been your match on every other level too."

My heart is racing and my skin feels hot because she's right. Nova is one hundred percent right. "I do think that, but I always thought I had no chance."

"You have a chance," Nova replies with simple, solid confidence in her tone.

"I think I do now."

She smiles but her eyes leave my face and dart to the plate glass window at the front of the store. "Speak of the devil!"

Jake steps through the front door. His eyes land on mine immediately. "I was just about to lock it. Kitchen is closed but luckily for you, I kept you some food," Nova says and disappears into the kitchen to get it.

"Thanks," he calls out as he saunters toward the counter. He looks extra fine today in my totally skewed opinion. It's hard not to be biased when I can still recall the way it felt to have his tongue in my mouth. His eyes never leave mine. "How are you Terra?"

"Good. How are you?"

"Better now," he says with a slow smile starting to pull at the corners of his perfect mouth.

"I said I need a break!" Finn's voice bellows from the kitchen.

"Fifteen minute breaks are mandated by the state of Maine. Don't make me call the goddamn government on you."

The door swings open forcefully and Finn marches into the restaurant. He smiles at the sight of his best friend. "Hey! You just get off work?"

Jake nods. "Craving a little Hawkins… lobster roll."

He said that with a pregnant pause on purpose but Finn has no idea what double entendre he just pulled. I do though, and my cheeks pink as I bite back a smile. "Well I'm craving a DNA test to prove that we're actually related to that robot man in the suit back there. Because if we aren't then I don't have to deal with his anal retentive ass trying to teach me the scheduling system."

"You still don't have to," I remind him. "I can do it from home with remote access to the system."

"You have to rest after this op," Finn argues.

Nova sails back in with a plate with two lobster rolls and a generous serving of fries. She places it in front of Jake. "I'm messing around with new roll ideas. The one on your left is my Asian fusion one. It's got wasabi mayo and kimchi instead of lettuce. The other one is your standard lobster roll."

"I'll let you know my thoughts," Jake says as Nova grabs a tray and heads toward the tables to collect the salt and pepper shakers as the last customers walk out the door. Fall hours mean we close by eight every night, which will be a blessing when they're short-staffed because I'm off recovering.

"I was not a fan," Finn shudders. Jake chuckles.

Declan bursts through the kitchen door. He looks panicked. "I can't fix it. Finn fucked up next week's schedule. He deleted Mary's shifts and when I went to restore them, it wiped out every-one's shifts for the entire month. The month!"

"Deep breaths. I'll take a look," I say calmly because I know the system like the back of my hand and I'm confident I can un-do whatever they did.

"Guess I'm not the only one who isn't great with scheduling," Finn remarks.

"I was fixing your mistake!" Declan barks but I take him by the arm and drag him through the kitchen and into my office. It takes me four whole minutes to get the schedule back and show Deck what happened to make sure he doesn't do it again.

I head back into the restaurant, eager to see Jake's face again. Nova is mopping now while Finn wipes down the counter. He's still talking to Jake and his conversation stops me dead.

"How the hell do you forget to ask about sex? It would be the first question out of my mouth," Finn is saying to Jake, his voice thick with shock. "Hell, I would have Googled that shit on the way to the test."

"What difference does it make?" Jake says, his eyes drifting toward me for a second before focusing back on my brother. "If they say I can't have sex for a week or a year, I'm still going through with the operation."

Nova stops mopping and cocks her head. "Why are you talking about sex?"

Finn pulls his phone from his back pocket and dips his head as he types something. "Because we're dudes, Nova, and sex is important. And this saint of a man is prepared to give it up. For a freaking year."

Say what now?

My eyes dart to Jake, who doesn't look the least bit concerned. He finishes chewing the last of Nova's new creation. "Finn is being dramatic. In other news, that roll was pretty damn good, Nova."

"I'm so confused," I mutter. "Why are you giving up sex for a year?"

"I'm sure that I'm not," Jake says and his eyes linger on me, making my skin heat.

"Four to six weeks," Finn announces, sighing in relief. "That's still a long time, but at least it's not a year. I would fucking implode if it was a year."

"I'm sure you would," Jake replies popping some fries into his mouth. He chews, swallows and then shrugs. "I can handle it. I haven't had sex since early June anyway."

My jaw drops before I can stop it. I'm not shocked he's been celibate for four months. But that also means he had someone in his life in King's Rock. I'm mildly and completely inappropriately jealous. Who cares? He's not with her now… right? Plus, I had Tom.

"You had a girlfriend in King's Rock?" Nova asks, what I'm thinking. "How come no one mentioned this?"

"There was no girlfriend in King's Rock," Jake replied and shifts on his stool. He is not comfortable with the questions and that makes *me* uncomfortable.

"Well then how did you have sex with someone?"

Jake and Finn hit Nova with flat, blank-faced stares and you can tell by the blush that hits her cheeks that she regrets the question immediately. Nova has never confirmed it, but I'm almost a hundred percent positive she has only ever been with Declan. The concept of one night stands or bed buddies is foreign to her. She knows they exist but they're an abstract concept, one she forgot to think about before she spoke a second ago.

Finn smacks a hand down on the countertop and leans forward and says, with the seriousness of a mortician. "You've been dry for months and now you're not going to have sex for another four weeks, at least. That's pure torture."

Something flickers in Jake's eyes, a moment of sheer panic followed by a few seconds of despair, maybe? But he seems to suppress it quickly and he shrugs again. "I won't die."

"I fucking would," Finn retorts as he lifts a hand to his blue work shirt like he's checking to make sure his heart is still beating at just the thought of celibacy. My brother glances at me like he just remembered I was in the room. "That goes for you too Ter, maybe warn Tom."

"First of all you need a hobby other than boning," I tell him, and his face scrunches in disgust that his baby sister is talking sex with him even though he brought it up. "And second, Tom and I broke up."

"What?" he looks distraught. It's amusing.

"Oh please, like you care," I say and push the swinging gate open and head into the main part of the restaurant to start lifting the chairs on the part of the dining area Nova hasn't mopped yet.

"He was an okay guy," Finn says, and I can't help but laugh. Nova joins me.

"Is that what you want for your sister, Finn?" Nova questions him. "An okay guy? Don't you think Terra deserves more than okay?"

"Well yeah, she deserves fabulous and charming and traffic-stopping handsome," Finn says in a serious tone but then he grins and lift his arms in the air. "But she can't date her brother so … you know Tom was an acceptable alternative. Seriously, he was nice and chill. He vibed with the family well, which we all know isn't always easy."

"I vibe with you all just fine," Nova retorts and leans on her mop, her curvy hip cocked as she places a hand on it. "And Jake vibes perfectly too."

I'm lifting a chair directly behind Nova and as I place it on the table, I give her a subtle little mule kick to the back of her shin. She doesn't act like she notices, but I know she does. Finn laughs. "Well, yeah you both are honorary Hawkins so technically she can't date either of you either."

I turn around and look at Jake but he's looking down at his now empty plate. I know he clearly heard what Finn said but he isn't reacting. I'm getting angry. It's irrational and I hate being irrational, but yet here I am.

"Well obviously I'm not going to date Nova," I say and roll my eyes as I place the last chair on the table and walk back toward the counter. "She's married to Deck and last time I checked, neither of us were into girls. But I could date Jake if I wanted to. Unless he is still involved with Miss June."

Now Jake turns and looks at me. His angular features are hard, like he's *really* annoyed. "Of course I'm not."

Finn is oblivious to the sub-texts floating all around him. "Aspen? Hell no. That was just a Britney Spears moment, right Jake?"

Did he just say...

"What's a Britney Spears moment?" Nova asks.

"When you hook up with an ex out of boredom or desperation," Finn explains as I stare at Jake and he refuses to stare back. His eyes are back to being glued to his empty plate, his head tipped down. "You know, "Oops I Did It Again" sex. Like her song title."

Nova rolls her eyes. "I'll have to remember that. So Jake was with Aspen in June?"

"Yeah but whatever, ex sex is harmless. Doesn't count as real sex," Finn answers for him.

He hooked up with Aspen. Just a few months ago. Logically I know I have no right to care, but emotionally ... it's *Aspen*. She's still an open wound and Jake is the perpetual salt.

"I'm not feeling well," I announce and it's like sucking the lighthearted energy out of the room with a vacuum. Every set of eyes turns to me with a serious glint. "Nothing major. Just tired from treatment today. I'm just going to head home, if you guys don't mind finishing close duties by yourselves."

"Of course not, go," Nova says and Finn nods his agreement.

Jake gets off the stool. "Can I drive you home?"

I shake my head. "Nope. I'd prefer if you just help them. I'm better off alone."

Nova's bright expression darkens and Jake looks like I just kneed him in the nuts. I leave without another word, heading into the kitchen to grab my stuff out of my office. Javi is back there, just taking off his hairnet and apron after cleaning the kitchen. "You good Ter?"

"Yep. Just tired. Heading home. See you tomorrow, Javi," I say casually as I grab my coat and purse. I decide to head out the back door, the one that leads to the alley off the break room instead of walking back through the restaurant where I'll have to see Jake again.

13

———

JAKE

I SHOULD HAVE GONE TO HER LAST NIGHT AFTER SHE STORMED out of the Shack. I should have driven straight to her house and talked to her like a fucking adult, but I didn't. Because when I do talk, I want to be able to tell Terra exactly what happened with Aspen, and I don't know that yet. If there's going to be lasting repercussions from that night, she needs to know. I don't want to hide it, but I don't know the answer myself.

So I sent her a bunch of texts instead, telling her I was thinking of her and if she needed anything to call, even if it was the middle of the night. And then one last text a little after one in the morning that said; *Aspen was a one-time thing, Terra. I swear. Never again.*

I stopped short of calling it a mistake because if that child is mine, I don't ever want that word used in anything pertaining to his or her existence. Ever. Not even now. Terra didn't answer any of my texts, but she saw them and she didn't tell me to fuck off, so … it was not the worst thing, I guess.

Now I'm bobbing up and down in the ocean, watching Finn ride a wave I was too tired to catch myself because I barely slept

147

last night. I give up and paddle in. I have to go meet Aspen soon anyway.

"You forget how to surf while you were in the mountains, buddy?" Finn says ten minutes later as he walks up the beach to join me by our cars. I could surf on the beach in front of my new apartment. That was part of the draw when I picked it, but it's windy today and the best waves on a blustery fall day are at Goosefare Rocks clear at the other end of the seven-mile beach that lines Ocean Pines.

There's a little, concrete public bathroom there too for changing in and out of wetsuits, although it's mostly used by women, not men. We tend to just change at our cars. Finn runs a hand over his soaked hair, sending ocean droplets everywhere then he pops the trunk on his SUV and grabs a towel and rubs it over his face and scrubs his beard with it. There's another car parked beside us but I don't see anyone in the water.

"Hey listen," I say as I shove my board into the back of my Jeep and grab my own towel. "I really wish you hadn't told Terra and Nova about the Aspen thing."

Finn stops unzipping his wetsuit and looks over at me. I yank the cord on the zipper of my own wet suit, pulling it down to my waist. "It's just maybe Aspen doesn't want everyone to know. I really don't. I'm not ashamed of her or what happened, but it's not something I need advertised."

"I'm sorry man, I didn't know it was this huge secret. I mean, not from Terra and Nova, they're family," Finn says. He peels out of the top of his wetsuit, exposing his naked torso, which is the only way anyone would know for sure it's Finn and not Logan. He's got zero tattoos whereas Logan's got three. "And you know, if you wanted to get back together with Aspen, no one would judge you."

I shake my head. "Why do you think I would want that?"

"Well, because you slept with her," Finn reminds me and

smiles. "And because despite your words, you seem to be spending a lot of time with her. She stayed at your house, you're hanging out with her today, your last day before you go in for surgery. Your very last day for sexual contact."

"That's a lot of my business you just commented on," I quip. "What are you, Mrs. Green?"

"Did I just hear my name?"

Finn has a towel loosely wrapped around his waist and is in the process of tugging down the rest of his wetsuit underneath that towel when, like a sea monster in a really bad horror movie, Nellie Green's head pops up from the other side of the enormous rocks that line the left side of the parking lot. We both jump. Finn thankfully makes sure to hold onto his towel, or Mrs. Green would really have something to gossip about.

"Oh hi there, Mrs. Green," I say trying to sound casual. "Do you always hide in the rocks out here?"

She lets out a loud giggle that is far too loud and, well, giggly. She looks down beside her. "Cassidy, honey, help me won't you?"

The head of her daughter now pops into sight too. She's not in her Dunkin' uniform today. Instead, she's wearing a pair of very short jean cutoffs and a tiny, cherry red, triangular bikini top. Finn's eyes nearly bulge out of his head. Cassidy takes her mom's arm and helps her up the rocks. "Hey boys! Long time no see, Jake. Are you trying to cut down on caffeine?"

I shake my head. "Nope. Just been busy."

"Cassie honey, there was a full moon the other night. You know I told you the police scanner was buzzing all night." Of course Mrs. Green owns a police scanner. I fight the urge to roll my eyes at that as she and Cassidy walk around the side of the rocks to stand on the paved parking lot. Her eyes are filled with concern under the brim of her very wide sunhat. "How is Robbie Ellis? Heard he burned himself pretty darn good. Poor Myrtle. She's such a good woman. Comes to church every Sunday. Don't know where they went wrong with that boy, but I thank the good lord I got blessed with the well-behaved, god-fearing babies I did."

Cassidy smiles brightly but then when her mom goes back to adjusting her hat, which is fighting to stay on her head in the wind, Cassidy's god-fearing eyes sweep over Finn's mostly naked body with a look that is not exactly pure. "How are your sons, Mrs. Green? Eddie still in the pot business?"

Ouch. Finn just went straight for the jugular.

"He still works at a cannabis dispensary, yes. You know it's perfectly legal for medicinal purposes, and he helps so many people with their health issues," Mrs. Green says, her smile turning acidic instead of saccharine. Sure, Eddie works for a legal company now, but he still deals on the side just like in high school.. "Jake, perhaps Eddie can help you find something to help with pain management after your operation. What is it for?"

Her green eyes are like little daggers pointed straight at me, and my stomach rolls with anxiety. *Shit*. She overheard Finn talking. "It's a personal matter. Private."

"Privates?" Cassidy says as the wind whips her dark brown hair around her face and she struggles to pull it back. "Did you say privates?"

Oh great. The town gossip is now going to think I'm getting penis enlargement or something. "No. I said it *is* private!"

"Jake, you know that this town has always been here for you," Mrs. Green steps a little closer and gives me a sincere smile. "Whenever your mama had … her episodes and couldn't take care of you, people watched out for you. You can count on us again if you need something. And they've let you become a fire-fighter even with your criminal record."

"Two petty theft arrests under the age of eighteen is *not* a criminal record," I remind her through gritted teeth. Before I can add that the first arrest was at nine, because my mom made me steal cigarettes, and the second was at fourteen when I stole from the grocery store because I was starving, Finn interrupts. "He's donating a kidney to my sister, who is in kidney failure from her lupus."

My head snaps around to glare at Finn. He shrugs. "What? Everyone was going to find out eventually."

"Oh my lord," Mrs. Green puts both hands to her chest. "How did I not know Terra was sick?"

"Because she didn't want people to know," I say to her as the wind picks up again and Mrs. Green's hat goes airborne. Cassidy and I chase after it. Finn tries too but almost loses his towel, so he stops, much to Cassidy's dismay.

I fetch the hat as it lands on a rock and carry it back to her. She smiles up at me gratefully and actually reaches up and pats my shoulder. "You are a special child Jake Maverick. You defied all the odds, had nothing stacked in your favor, but yet you made something of yourself. You should be very proud."

Oh God, I'm going to end up on her damn blog again.

"It's such a shame your mom doesn't know what a good boy you've become," Mrs. Green goes on. "Have you even seen her since you got back? She's living in that trailer park off of Cascade Road. The one the golf course put up a huge line of hedges to block from sight because it was such an eye sore."

"You never told us why you are hiding out in the rocks, Mrs. G." I say to get the topic off my mother.

"Hiding out?" She lets loose one of those jarring giggles again. "We were exploring tide pools, just beyond the rocks. It's where you can find sea glass at low tide. I collect it and make jewelry out of it. I have a booth booked at the Christmas Market. Be sure to come by and check it out in December. You can pick up a little something for Aspen, since you two are still… hanging out."

Oh hell no. She heard us.

"You boys have a blessed day," She and Cassidy walk over to the other car in the lot, get in and drive off.

Finn finishes pulling off his wetsuit. I stand there numb from panic and fighting the urge to puke. "She heard you say I slept with Aspen."

"Maybe not," Finn replies, tugging on some sweats under his towel. Nausea rolls through my belly like the waves on the ocean a few feet away. "Maybe she just heard me saying you were hanging out with her on your last day for sex."

"I'm gonna puke," I announce and bolt to the garbage can by the restroom entrance, making it just in time.

"Shit, you still do that?" Finn remarks, surprised. I don't have much in my stomach so it doesn't take long to empty it. When I stand up, Finn is fully clothed now in a hoodie and sweats and he reaches into his car and tosses me a pack of gum. "I didn't know you still had that nervous stomach thing."

"It comes and goes," I mutter and unwrap a stick of gum.

I toss the pack back to him and walk back to the car and finish changing too. I pull on some black sweats with the OPFD logo on them and a charcoal Henley and shove my feet into some sneakers.

"Listen, even if she heard the Aspy part, she's got a bigger scoop now. Hawkins kid gets kidney transplant from award-winning firefighter. That's the real scoop."

"Terra is going to kill you for telling her," I remind him.

Finn doesn't look the least bit worried. "Let's be honest, in this town, it's a miracle no one found out she was sick before now. And when both of you are wandering around town all stitched up and stuff, people are gonna talk. Now we're controlling the message. It's a PR move."

"I'm sorry, but who are you? You look like Finn and Logan but you sound like Declan," I ask cocking my head to the side and squinting like I truly don't recognize him.

He gives me a shove and laughs. "Don't tell Deck but some-times I listen when he talks."

"I gotta go meet Aspen," I tell him. "You better tell Terra Mrs. Green knows before it ends up on the blog." He nods and waves as he jumps into his SUV and I slide into the Jeep. Ten minutes later, I'm back on the beach but at the other end in front of the Five Seasons hotel. It's the newest building in Ocean Pines, and the tallest at ten stories. It was built to blend with the historic town so on the outside it's wood shingles and wrap-around verandas like a mansion more than a hotel, but inside it's all modern rooms with gleaming marble and posh furnishings. Aspen is beside me and Major is bouncing like a lunatic in front of us as I hold up a tennis ball.

"Just a couple throws, Jake. Major is an old boy now and he will start limping if we throw it too much," Aspen explains. Her curly hair is plopped up haphazardly on top of her head. She's not wearing makeup and there are shadows under her eyes.

I toss the ball and Major takes off like a rocket. "How long until you can get into your old place again?"

"Still fighting with the insurance companies, mine and the building's," Aspen sighs. "I'm looking at other options now. Get a whole new place."

"And working a lot I see?" I say and nod toward the circles under her eyes.

She gives me a wry smile. "Always know how to make a girl feel special, Jake."

"Sorry," I mutter. "You need to take extra care of yourself now."

"I know. I am, I promise. But you've got me worried about you now," she counters and pulls her phone from her pocket and shows me the screen. "You text me last night to confirm the meeting today and added something crazy about needing me to be your emergency contact. Isn't that what the twins are for?"

"They can't be my person for this," I reply vaguely and take a deep breath. "But before we get into that I wanted to talk to you about a paternity test again."

"Fuck, Jake. You're a broken record," Aspen complains as Major drops his tennis ball a few feet ahead of us and charges at the crashing surf. He loves trying to bite the waves as they roll in. "I've been busy trying to salvage what's left of my apartment and find a new place and battle corrupt insurance companies while also working for them, catching the people that defraud them and make them leery of genuine claimants like myself. Oh and barfing and feeling like I've been run over by a parade of Mack trucks. I've been busy doing that too."

"I'm sorry but I need to know sooner rather than later," I say, trying to sound firm but not like an asshole. "I have a lot of big things happening in my life right now and how and what I decide to do hinges on knowing if this is part of my future."

Aspen stops too and bends to pick up the tennis ball that is now at our feet. Major leaves the waves alone and dances expectantly on his paws waiting for her to throw it. She does and he bolts after it. "I'll get the blood test with you."

"Really?"

She nods curtly.

"Thanks. I really appreciate it."

"Now explain this whole emergency contact stuff and why it isn't the twins, or Mr. and Mrs. Hawkins."

"Finn is my emergency contact for work. Has been for years," I explain as Major runs up the beach to the drier sand and starts to dig. There's a couple of women up there on one of the benches by the dunes. Aspen squints to get a better look and make sure Major isn't giving them a sand bath. Luckily, he's not.

"But this is for the hospital because I need an operation and Terra is having an operation at the same time. Every member of the Hawkins family will be concerned with her, so I can't … won't ask them to be there for me, too."

Aspen puts two fingers in her mouth and whistles and Major stops digging and runs right back. We continue walking and he's glued to her side, tennis ball in his mouth, tail wagging. "What the hell do you need an operation for? And what does Terra need one for? And how the hell is it at the same time?"

"I'm donating a kidney. To Terra"

Aspen stops walking. "Holy shit, Jake. Terra needs a kidney?"

"Not for long. In forty-eight hours she'll have mine," I reply and brace for impact because Aspen is going to blow.

"Are you insane? That's a major surgery! And what if you damage the one they leave in you at your highly dangerous job?" Aspen rants at me, her arms flailing to accentuate her words. "If you only have one, you can't take risks. And all you ever do, Jake, is take risks. You have always put everyone else's needs before your own. It's like you don't believe you're as valuable as everyone else, especially the Hawkins."

"Take a breath, Aspen," I say and try not to be offended by her words.. "Tell me you wouldn't give her one if you could. Tell me you'd let her suffer, even now, with your seemingly endless grudge match. Tell me to my face you wouldn't give Terra a kidney if you could."

Aspen's lips form a flat line and she looks up at the pale blue sky above us. "Of course I would. I still love her like a sister even if I hate her."

She starts walking again, the frown on her face turning into a bit of a smile. A wry one. "So I get a baby and she gets a kidney. Aren't you a generous boy, Jake?"

"Not funny."

"A little funny," she argues and then pauses, tiling her head to the side. "So I have contacts at the hospital. Chatty nurses who love to gossip if I buy them some Dunkin'. I use them for cases, but I sometimes get info I don't need. One of them told me Robbie Ellis burned his eyebrows off and when he was being treated, he mentioned seeing you making out with some girl in the woods by his house."

"He was drunk."

"He said the girl was, and I quote, 'some tiny, little thing.'" Aspen cocks an eyebrow. "He said he thought you two were gonna go at it like bears in mating season."

I rub the back of my neck with my hand and focus on Major. "You and I are not together, Aspen. I'm allowed to kiss anyone I want."

"You kissed Terra."

"Yes." I reply, my voice calm, but hard.

She frowns. "Her brothers didn't want you going anywhere near her, remember?"

"We were kids when they threatened to disown me. I'm sure that's changed, and if it hasn't, I don't care." I stare back at her, confident. I won't be bullied or talked out of my feelings for Terra now like I was as a kid.

"Speaking of those brothers, can't they donate? Or can't another one of her loving, supportive family members do it instead of you?" Aspen asks and there's definitely pain in her voice. She won't look at me now, her eyes focused ahead on Major who is attacking the waves again.

"None are a viable option, but I am."

"I've always been jealous of that, you know?" Aspen says quietly, eyes on the sand in front of us. "The way she has so many people who love her unconditionally. That, by the way, is part of what ruined our friendship."

This is more than I've ever gotten out of Aspen. "I know your senior year food fight that turned your friendship to rubble wasn't about a prom dress."

"Nope. It was about a prom date," Aspen admits freely now

like she hasn't been hiding it from me for a decade. "Terra had parents who loved her unconditionally, brothers who supported and protected her, a town that seemed to know who she was everywhere she went and adored her. The only person to ever not love Terra Hawkins was you. When you turned her down in that closet. Jealous, infantile me wanted the one thing she couldn't have. So I asked you to prom and I sunk my claws in."

"So you were using me to hurt her?"

"No. You were hot and sweet and I was totally, honestly into you," Aspen clarifies. "But I knew she was still into you despite the fact that she pretended she hated you, and I went for you anyway. Broke the girl code. Obliterated a twelve-year friendship. And in the end, I didn't even get the guy."

She stops walking and turns back to me. I think she might cry, and I start to feel guilty but I shouldn't. She's hurt herself and she knows it. I was just kind of an unwitting pawn. Man, I was stupid. "Aspen, it's never too late to try and mend fences."

"So back to this emergency contact stuff," she changes the subject without blinking. "I'm supposed to find out if you're the dad of my baby and then pull the plug on you?"

"There won't be any plug-pulling. It's honestly just a precaution," I reply but suddenly asking her feels selfish. "I swear. The doctor called it a formality."

"Nope. Can't do it." She starts to march back up the beach to the boardwalk, Major following dutifully.

I panic and blurt out the cold hard truth. "Aspen, if it isn't you then it has to be my mom. I don't have anyone else."

She stops dead in her tracks, swears, and turns to face me. She wants to tell me off. I can feel it as strong as the wind blowing around us, but she doesn't. God bless her, she doesn't. "I'll do it but only if you let me wait until after the op for the blood test. I can't ... I won't be able to do it if I know one hundred percent this kid is ours. It will be impossible, and you would be a heartless asshole to put me in that spot. So pick it. Paternity test now or emergency contact-slash-potential-plug-puller?"

I want to push her to do both but I know Aspen can't be pushed. When she sets boundaries, they're as solid as cement walls. "Plug puller."

"Email me whatever the hell I have to sign, then. Goddamnit."

She turns and I stand and watch her until she disappears down off the beach. Major looks back at me with sympathy, I swear, but stays with Aspen.

I exhale loudly and stare at the surf.

14

JAKE

I'VE BEEN STANDING IN MY KITCHEN STARING AT THE CONTENTS OF my fridge without really seeing anything for a good ten minutes. We check into the hospital tomorrow at four in the afternoon. The operation is scheduled for the following morning. I've been poked, prodded, evaluated, and have peed in more cups than I can count for over a month, but we're finally here.

I grab a beer from the fridge, twist off the top and then stare at it. Am I allowed to drink right now? Is it too close to surgery? I walk into the dining room and start to check the pre-op papers the transplant coordinator gave me. I think I would have remembered a no alcohol rule, but I riffle through them anyway. I can drink, moderately, tonight … but the sex thing is right there in black and white, mocking me. No sex for four weeks post-op or longer if the doctor advises it.

My doorbell rings.

I'm not expecting anyone. But I figure maybe it's Logan or Aspen, so I swing open the door without hesitation and Terra barges right into my apartment. I watch her tiny, little butt wiggle as she marches past me into the living room. She looks around. "You're alone?"

"Yes."

"Okay. Well, Mrs. Green just told the world on her stupid blog that you're giving me a kidney," Terra declares.

"Yeah … I knew that was coming."

Her eyes flare. "And you didn't tell me?"

"I've been sorting through some shit. I had a few things to settle before the operation. And besides, I thought you were ignoring me because of the whole thing Finn told you the other night," I tell her. "And just for the record, Mrs. Green finding out was also Finn's big mouth, not mine."

"Oh I know. He owned up to it and she named her sources on the blog, like the good fake journalist she thinks she is," Terra replies and starts to fold her arms across her chest but winces and drops them to her sides, hands in fists. "I hate that everyone knows."

"So … are we talking again? Are you going to let me explain?" I ask and watch as she starts pacing back and forth beside my couch. I still have a couple of boxes I haven't bothered to unpack, so she has to dodge them.

"Explain that you got together with Aspen somehow even though you lived over seven hours away?" She stops pacing and starts bouncing on her Ugg covered feet just a little bit.

"I didn't get together with her. I had sex with her," I correct but her frown just deepens. "It wasn't emotional. It was physical. She agrees. This isn't anything more, no matter what."

"How did it happen? Like over Zoom or something?" Terra wants to know. "Did she go visit you?"

"I came back here. Very end of June for twenty-four hours for the interview," I explain and with every word that falls from my mouth she looks sadder and sadder. "I didn't tell anyone. I was worried it would jinx it."

"And you decided to add in a little sex with the ex?" Terra

interrupts. "That seemed more appealing to you than seeing your best friends, the family that basically took you in?"

"I accidentally ran into Aspen. Nowhere near Ocean Pines and she was getting over someone. I was … in a mood," I swallow and heave out a loud breath. "King's Rock was great for work, and for finding myself and figuring out what I really wanted but … what I really wanted wasn't any of the women there."

"It was Aspen?"

"Hell no," I bark back. "But she was there and she wanted me and I wanted to be wanted. And we fucked. Two consenting adults using each other to get off. That's all it was, no matter what."

"You keep saying no matter what," Terra notes and tilts her head in confusion. "What the hell does that mean? Is that like a 'even if she was the last person on earth I would not date her again' type of thing?"

"Yeah, even if she was the last person on earth, Aspen and I would never be a couple again." My heart starts to beat faster and I pause, preparing myself for what I have to tell her next. Because I have to tell her… Aspen will kill me but… "Even if—"

"But you'd sleep with her if she was the last person on earth," Terra interrupts and runs her hands through her hair as she starts to pace my living room again. "Because you did. You picked her for that need, even in a world full of other people. She's your go-to for sex even after all this time. You picked her."

"I didn't pick her," I argue back. "I went to find you. That night I drove to the Shack but you were kissing a dude I now know was Tom. You were *with* Tom. Aspen was with no one."

I can see her try to decipher the meaning of my words, looking for some hidden message, scared to take them at face value. So I clarify. "I said King's Rock was great for figuring stuff out. Well, you know what three years there made me realize? I want you. I wanted you for years, and I was finally in a place where I thought I had something to offer you and at a time in our lives where I didn't live in fear of losing your brothers. So I came back, but you were taken."

She's this tiny little statue, in the middle of my living room. Staring ahead, eyes glued to my face, chest barely moving because she's hardly breathing. "You wanted *me*?"

"I *want* you," I repeat. "Do you want a beer? I feel like you need one right about now."

"Yes," she says, and so I walk over to the dining room table and grab the open beer and hand it to her. She takes it and puts it to her lips, taking a long sip. "Well, I can't drink alone. That's sad."

I take the bottle from her, slowly, letting all my fingers brush all of hers. I raise it to my lips and watch her watching me. It's hot. It's making me hard. I take a long slow sip and hand it back to her. "Now you're not drinking alone."

"Are you like a closeted nudist or something?" She asks and motions towards my naked chest with the beer bottle. "Every time I come by you're half naked."

"That would make me a half-nudist," I reply and run my fingers along the waistband of the sweats I changed into when I got home. Her eyes follow my fingers as they skim the space between my belly button and the waistband with the intensity of a cat tracking a laser pointer. "You want to focus on my affinity for going topless instead of the fact I just told you I want you?"

"It's easier," Terra replies softly.

I cock a smile at her. "When have you ever done anything the easy way, Tink?"

She blinks and shakes her head, and takes another sip of beer, more of a gulp this time. She speaks but her eyes stay on the bottle in her hand. "I came over to clarify what Finn told you. About sex after the op. You *can* have physical activity as soon as you want to after the operation, just not actual intercourse."

"Really?" I heard what she said, but my brain can't seem to process it.

"You can do stuff, just not… *that*," she says and I watch her cheeks start to turn pink as her knuckles around the beer bottle go white. I reach out and slowly peel the bottle from her vice-like grip, worried she'll accidentally break it.

"I'm confused. Can you elaborate?"

I am far from confused but she is smokin' hot when she squirms. "You can mess around with yourself or someone else. Or both. You don't have to be celibate is what I'm saying. You're the king of Google, put those fingers to work and find out for yourself."

Her breathing is shallow, I note as my eyes skim over her chest. How the hell does she look so good in a plain black T-shirt? "My fingers are good for more the Googling. In case you're interested."

I notice her arm. The inside of her left forearm has a few long, large swollen lumps from her forearm to her biceps, to the point where it looks visibly deformed. It's from the dialysis, I know. She catches me staring.

"It looks worse than it feels. But this is why I usually wear long sleeves when it's like this as you know," she explains, her voice barely above a whisper. "I don't want pity."

She pivots and takes two steps towards the hall that leads to the front door but I grab her by the shoulders. I step up right behind her, half a foot between us and lower my head so it's hovering next to the side of hers. I squeeze her shoulders. "So let's get back to the post-op sexual contact stuff. You're saying, no sex for six weeks but I can… touch myself? Jerk off?"

Her breath audibly hitches. My dick feels the sound like a warm caress. She nods her head and her soft hair brushes my cheek. "Sure. Or other stuff."

"Like what?"

I use my hands on her shoulders to gently turn her to face me. She surprises me by tipping her head up and meeting my eye. I thought she'd be too timid. "You could… kiss someone."

"Like you?"

"Like me."

I dip my head down and capture her lips. It's not slow or cautious. It's hard and deep, because I'm so fucking hot for her right now, it's unbearable. She doesn't seem to mind the force with which I sweep into her mouth or the hard press of my lips against hers. A few minutes later I pull back and we're both breathing heavy.

"What about you? Are you allowed to do stuff?" I ask when I catch my breath and she nods. So I let a hand slip from her neck, down over her breast and I stop and cup one firmly so she knows it's not a mistake. I mean to touch her. "So this is allowed?"

She gasps a little as my thumb, rubs her nipple through her T-shirt and I feel it pebble. "Yeah and so is stuff like this…"

She palms my hard-on.

Holy shit.

I actually feel my knees weaken. I can't stop staring at her face. She's beautiful and confident, not a bit timid about what she's just done, and I swear I get harder because of that. I push my hips out, pressing myself into her hand, and lean in to ghost the column of her neck with my lips. "It's good to know what the rules are. So to be clear I could, in those first six weeks, put my lips here?"

I kiss the shell of her ear and gently bite her earlobe. She shivers and my hands move under the hem of her shirt. "Yes. And I can put mine here."

She presses her mouth to my left nipple, which is at eye level for her, and when I feel her tongue circle it I grunt. We need to stop this or I am going to fuck her and I can't fuck her. Can I?

She nips my nipple and a current of lust as strong as an electrical current shoots down my spine and into my balls. I push my hands up the soft skin of her torso, lifting her shirt with it and she lifts her arms so I can remove it completely and throw it to the ground. Her skin is perfect - alabaster with a peppering of pale freckles on her shoulders and I want to kiss each one, like the ones on her nose. But that urge is replaced by the need to put my mouth on the swell of her breasts, pushing up from her bra. So I do. She shivers again.

I pull both straps from her shoulders at the same time and bend my knees a little so when I dip my head, I have her right breast in my mouth as soon as it's exposed from the bra that I've tugged down. I hear the faintest, breathiest "Oh my God."

Her skin tastes faintly of strawberries and smells of vanilla. Her hands move to my hair, nails scraping against my scalp, creating a tingle that rushes down my spine. "Still allowed?"

"Mmm hmm," she moans and I move to her other breast. Her hands move to my sweatpants and before I can even fathom what she's about to do, I feel her palm, soft and warm, wrap around my bare cock. "This is allowed too. If you want."

"You're all I want," I confess, my voice thick. She strokes me. I groan against her breasts, then move my hand to the front of her jeans.

She's lost a lot of weight. The dialysis is screwing with her appetite, so the top of her jeans is stretchy and loose. I pop the button but don't have to get the fly undone to make my way into her underwear. I feel a soft thatch of hair and then … wetness. She whimpers.

"Is this allowed after the operation… just so we're clear?"

She nods. My middle fingers traces her slit. "Terra… is it allowed now?"

She nods.

"Look at me."

Slowly her eyes raise. "Yes."

I slip a finger into her and she gasps, her hand around my shaft tightening. I attack her mouth as I slide in and out of her with two fingers now, my thumb rubbing her clit. This is everything my bumbling younger self wanted to do with her for years, but was too terrified to admit. She pulls back from the kiss abruptly and I freeze. We look at each other, the weight of what we're doing, our hands all over each other, is heavy but in a good way. "You know what we can do right now? Before the op?"

"What?"

"Have actual sex."

"With each other?" I sound like a complete imbecile, but the idea has been so completely off limits my entire life that it feels taboo even now that she's half naked in my arms.

"With whoever you want," she replies softly.

"Terra…" I take my hand out of her pants. I have to tell her about Aspen, but she won't let me speak.

Terra covers my mouth with her hand. "Look, right now I want you and you want me, right?"

I nod.

"And after tomorrow we aren't going to be able to act on it, or anything with anyone, for six weeks so … why are we over-thinking this? What if something goes wrong and we never get to act on this or anything ever again?"

It's a dark, sobering thought that kind of sucks the heat between us right out of the room. The timing is horrible. I have so much I need to say to her, but she's right. This operation could go wrong and one of us might not be here in seventy-two hours. And I've wanted her my whole life. So I cup her ass and scoop her up. She lets out a little squeak and holds onto the back of my head, wrapping her legs around my waist.

The sun has set outside and the apartment is inky as I walk her toward the bedroom. She's kissing my neck, tracing her tongue up the side to my ear, which is making my cock throb.

I reach my bedroom and ease her back onto the bed, tugging off her Uggs and dropping them on the floor before lying down on top of her. As soon as I feel her soft, warm bare torso against mine every hormone in my body sparks to life. I have never felt this turned on, this needy and horny at the same time, in my entire life.

I grind into her and she grinds right back. Her bra has a front clasp and I pop it open with one hand and put my mouth back to worship her breasts again. She's using her feet to push my sweatpants down my legs, and I lift a little to help her. When they reach my ankles I kick them off and move my hand to her jeans. But she starts to push me away. Her hands are on my shoulders, trying to get me to lift off of her so I do, sitting back on my knees in between her legs. She reaches for the lamp on the night table and turns it on. I have a horrible feeling she's changing her mind.

"I…" she pauses, bites her lips and her eyes shamelessly sweep my naked body. "I wanted to see you. I have dreamed of this for too long to not see you."

I feel a surge of warmth, something softer and more soothing than the need that's been coursing through me, but I don't bother to analyze it. I grab my cock and give it a stroke. "You don't look disappointed, so that's a bonus."

"Definitely not disappointed." She gets up on her knees too, facing me and moves my hand, wrapping her own around my length. "God, Jake, you're a work of art."

I hold her chin, tilting her head. "That's my line."

I capture her mouth, my other hand returning to her jeans, making quick work of the fly since the button is already undone. She's pumping me in long slow strokes but they falter when my hand slips past her underwear. The kiss slows and I pull back just enough to watch her eye lashes flutter and her breath hitch as I slip a finger into her again. She's somehow wetter than before and my ability to think evaporates again. I flip her onto her back and start to yank her jeans and underwear right off her body in two urgent tugs.

She reaches for the light, but I lean over her and grab her wrist before she can flip it off. "You wanted to see me, and now I want to see you. You're not the only one fulfilling a fantasy here, Tink."

She looks nervous, but drops her hand back to the bed and lets me sit back and devour her bare body with my eyes, and then my mouth. I kiss her everywhere, her lips, neck, collarbones, breasts, bellybutton, hip.

"You're a dream come true," I whisper as I position myself over her, and reach for a condom in the night table drawer.

As soon as I'm sheathed, she wraps her legs around my waist and uses them to pull me forward. Sexually aggressive Terra is mind-blowingly hot. I slide into her easily, and every inch of it is pure heaven. I want to come immediately.

"My God."

"I know."

She rocks her hips and tightens around me.

"Terra, baby, don't. Oh God…" I freeze and bury my face in her neck, leaning my whole body on hers to keep her still. But she has a trick I can't stop. She clenches her pussy around me again. "I'm going to fuck you hard if you keep that up."

"You're the only one who never treated me like I was breakable, so don't start now," she whispers against my ear and kisses my neck again.

Fuuuuck.

Well, she asked for it.

I start to move my hips in long, hard strokes. Her back arches immediately and she moans my name loud and holy fuck I need to make this good for her fast because I am not going to last. I roll my hips, keeping our bodies tight so I can touch her clit with every push and she rocks her hips up to meet me. It's a perfect match. We're a perfect match. And then she swears like I've never heard her swear before and wraps her arms around my neck pulling me down flat on top of her and I feel her come apart around me and damn if she doesn't take me with her.

I come so hard I swear I have to fight to stay conscious.

15

TERRA

I want to enjoy this moment, but turns out that when an unre-quited crush is suddenly requited, my logical, levelheaded brain goes into full-on flight-mode. He's still collapsed on top of me, warm and heavy, and I should be drowning in bliss, but instead I'm fighting a panic attack. I hate my body more right now than I ever did for having lupus.

I close my eyes and do what I have been learning to teach others to do in my therapy program, focus on my breathing, remind myself I am safe in this moment, everything is actually perfect right this minute … don't spiral.

"Are you asleep, Tink?' He whispers a few minutes later against my shoulder. I feel him slip out of me and roll away, and get off the bed but not before pulling up the duvet bunched at the bottom to cover me and keep me warm.

"Uh-uh," I mumble. "Just floating back to reality."

Crashing would be a more appropriate description.

His deep chuckle actually helps calm me a little. "I'll be back in a second."

The wooden floorboards creek as he makes his way down the

hall to the bathroom and I sit up and find my underwear, pull them on and then dart into the living room to retrieve my T-shirt and yank it on. Where is my bra? I tip toe back into the bedroom, still can't see my bra. I thought I would stop there, with just the t-shirt and undies but then suddenly I am completely clothed. Everything including my Uggs but not my bra because I can't find that. Why am I fully dressed when he is going to walk out of the bathroom naked? What if he wants to snuggle or go again? I have spent countless hours begging the universe for this exact thing, so why do I want to run to the front door, pull it open and keep running?

He appears in the bedroom door, every naked, sweaty inch of him. And there are *so many* inches. He looks so perfect it hurts. Except for the look on his face which is nothing but shock. No euphoria, no post-orgasmic bliss, no contented cocky smirk. Just shock. "Are you leaving?"

"I… I don't know…" I confess and run my fingers through my hair. "I should, right? I mean I've never had a bed buddy but—"

"I'm your bed buddy?" He looks offended. Oops.

"One night stand?"

"I'm a one night stand?"

"Jake I don't know what you are," I blurt out. "I mean… what *we* are. Do you?"

"I guess not," he says and starts walking toward me. "But we can't figure it out if you go and run away, now can we?"

He takes me by the shoulders and pulls me to him and presses his lips to the top of my head. I relax against his warm, bare body and close my eyes and for the first time… I absorb this moment. I'm in Jake Maverick's arms. He's naked and at this very moment, he is mine.

And then someone pounds on his front door.

"What the actual fuck," he hisses, annoyed.

I jump out of his embrace. He doesn't move. "I don't want to answer that. Whoever it is will go away."

There's more pounding.

"That sounds like a Hawkins fist doing the knocking and we never go away," I tell him and he grins.

"This from the girl who was about to orgasm and run."

Okay, now I'm grinning too. But mine is one hundred percent sheepish.

More pounding. "Jake! You in there?"

It's Logan. I know because although he sounds like Finn as much as he looks like him, which is completely, Finn is at hockey so it's got to be Logan. Jake pulls on his sweats and I grab a t-shirt from a pile of discarded clothes on a wicker chair in the corner of his room and toss it at him. He looks confused. "Well you live on the fourth floor and I'm not climbing out a damn window, so put on all the clothes while I think of an excuse for being here."

"And you might wanna smooth your hair. You look like you've just been pounded into the headboard," Jake says proudly.

"Never touched the headboard," I reply as I follow him out of the bedroom.

"We'll have to work on that, Tink," he murmurs and throws a wink to me over his broad shoulder before he swings open the front door.

Logan is standing there with the biggest, cutest ball of fur I have ever seen in my entire twenty-five years of life. It's cappuccino brown and fluffy with a dollop of white between its blue eyes and on its chest. Logan is grinning like I don't ever think I've seen before and that makes me just as joyful as the puppy. I squeal! The puppy wiggles in his arms.

"Is that a baby bear?" Jake asks as Logan puts it down and it lumbers, like only a puppy can, into Jake's front hall.

"What's its name?" I ask and drop to my knees in front of it.

"I don't have a name yet, but I'm working on it," Logan confesses.

Jake squats down too as Logan steps across the threshold and shuts the door behind him. "I was going to surprise you tomorrow, Terra. I didn't think you'd be here."

The puppy is the perfect reason not to look him in the eye as I lie. "Wanted to go over some pre-op stuff with Jake so I swung by after work."

"We were going to order Chinese. You in?" Jake says and I'm too busy burying my face in the puppy's neck to make a startled face.

"I'm starving," Logan admits, pulling the beanie he's wearing off his head. His hair is all over the place. "I drove all the way to Gray to get him."

"Is it a puppy? Because it's already the size of some grown dogs," Jake notes and the puppy flops down on his back offering us his belly for scratches. "What breed is he?"

"Newfoundland," Logan says as he smoothes his sandy brown hair. "I wanted a big dog and these guys used to pull in the nets for fisherman in Newfoundland, Canada, which seemed fitting for a Hawkins family dog. And then Mason told me about his aunt in Grady who has a Newfie who accidentally got knocked up before she could get her fixed. Anyway, she was giving away the puppies to a good home."

"Sounds like fate," I say softly as the puppy jumps to his feet and starts showering me in kisses. I giggle like a maniac. "Oh my God, I'm already falling in love."

"Me too," Jake says.

I tumble backward, the dog climbs on top of me, but my eyes are on Jake who is staring at me, not the dog. I smile and fight a blush. Logan walks up after toeing off his shoes by the door and scoops up the dog. "So Jake you gonna order the grub or what?"

"I should go," I say as panic sets in again. I'm worried if I stick around Logan will somehow figure out what we just did.

"Nope," Logan says flatly and pushes the dog into my chest. I hold him and am shocked at how heavy he is. "You're gonna stay, eat crispy beef and chicken fried rice, and help me name him."

TWO HOURS later and two bottles of beer, which is a lot for me, I put down the container of crispy beef on the coffee table and grab my water glass. After a big sip, which I definitely need, I dip my fingers in the water and flick the droplets on top of the puppy's head. "I officially christen you Chewbacca Hawkins. Welcome to the family, Chewie!"

"It's perfect," Logan says smiling and leaning back in the leather recliner across from me. Jake is on the old wooden rocker by the window, so Chewie and I have the couch to ourselves. "I can't believe I didn't think of it. River is obsessed with Star Wars. He'll love it."

"The dog does look like Chewbacca," Jake says and sips his beer. "Good job, Terra."

I smile at him, but make sure it's brief because Logan has definitely been staring at us harder than normal. I'm sure he doesn't believe my story about why I'm here. Jake starts to clean up the remnants of the Chinese food and refills my water glass. Logan stands as Chewie circles twice and curls up on my lap. He's like a furry, weighted blanket. "I know the timing is a little crazy. The family is gonna have a lot to manage in the coming weeks as you and Jake recover, so I'm sure Declan will call my timing selfish."

"He won't," I reply but I'm not exactly sure about that. Deck loves to judge Logan's life choices. It's like a full-time hobby. "And even if he does, he's wrong. It's the perfect time to add this guy to the clan. We need something happy and light … figuratively speaking."

Logan laughs. "Yeah he's going to weigh more than you by the time he's full grown."

"Great, we get a dog and I'm still the runt in the family," I snark.

Logan looks at his watch and stands up. "Want a lift home tonight? You can't drive after drinking."

"I walked."

"Still. It's late. Let me drive you," Logan insists so I nod, reluctantly.

Jake reappears from the kitchen. "You heading out?"

Logan and I nod simultaneously. Jake's dark eyes linger on me longer than Logan. I know he wants to finish our conversation from earlier, but we can't. If I don't catch a ride with Logan, he'll know something is up and I'm not ready for Logan's two cents on my love life. Or anyone's for that matter.

Logan scoops sleepy Chewie from my lap and holds him like he holds River. Chewie's fluffy head on Logan's shoulder. I pull my phone from my pocket and snap a picture. "This is going on your dating profile."

"I don't have a dating profile," Logan replies with a frown.

"A girl can dream," I mutter back. Jake chuckles.

"Okay… drive safe," Jake says as he follows us to the front door. Logan shoves his feet in his shoes and I let Jake drape one of his hoodies over my shoulders because I came here without a coat and the temperature outside has dropped. "See you … later?"

I nod and smile. He winks.

Outside, Logan puts a leash on Chewie, hooking it to the red collar around his neck and lets him walk to the car, biting at the leash the whole way and stopping to pee on the back tire of Logan's SUV before he gets loaded into a massive crate in the back. I give him one last kiss on the head before Logan closes the crate door.

I climb into the passenger seat and as soon as we're buckled up, Logan pulls out of the parking stall. "Beth is bringing River by the restaurant on her way to work tomorrow morning. I'm introducing him and the rest of the family to Chewie. Can you be there?"

"Wouldn't miss it."

"What were you and Jake talking about?" Logan asks.

"Pre-op stuff," I mutter and look out the window. "Don't want to bore you."

"There's nothing you two need to discuss about the op," Logan replies firmly in that tone he gets which always makes me think he would have made a great doctor. It's so authoritative and confident. "In fact, a huge percentage of kidney transplant patients and donors never even meet."

"Yeah well, we're friends and so we're discussing stuff. Why do you care?" I dare to steal a sideways glance at him. It's dark in the car, but I can see he's not scowling. Not smiling either, though.

"Because I'm worried your childhood crush is back full force and it was a bad idea then, and it's a bad idea now," Logan tells me. "You're both in a really vulnerable space and Jake doesn't make great decisions when he's vulnerable."

I glare over at him. "Did you just call me a bad decision?"

"No. I mean … that's not what I meant," Logan sighs. He tightens his jaw, I can see the muscle in it bulge. He's literally fighting to keep his mouth shut about something. "He makes rash decisions. Really big ones. He changed his middle name to his last name. He moved clear across the state because he made up some big personal attack in his head."

"He doesn't exactly have the proud family history we do, Logan." I can't believe I have to remind him of this. "He's probably better off without his mom's last name. And we hurt him by not including him in your crisis. He has abandonment issues, rightfully so, and we added to it. Did you tell him the truth?"

Logan nods tersely. "Yeah. We're good. He understands and won't even tell anyone else in the family I told him."

I nod. That's probably a good thing because Declan would blow a gasket if he knew we were talking about this again. Even with Jake.

"My point stands. Jake's just a guy who doesn't really think things through. Aspen's apartment burned down and he automatically invites her to live with him. You know how bad they are together. That's another bad decision," Logan turns onto my street.

"And I dated Tom for half a year and ignored all the warning signs he wasn't the one or even worthy of consideration for the title," I reply and tip my head back against the seat. "We all make rash decisions at some point, Logan. That doesn't mean *every* decision is rash."

"Why were you dating Tom if you didn't see a future with him?" Logan asks as he stops at a red light and looks over at me with curious blue eyes.

"Because I was lonely. And Tom was a great guy. On paper," I sigh, put my elbow up on the door and start to twist a lock of my hair. "There just wasn't that rush, you know? That feeling like you can't focus when they're in the room and the constant excitement at the possibility of seeing them again when they aren't in the room."

Logan nods but then shrugs. "I've never had that either."

"Not even with Bethany?" I ask of River's mom.

He pauses a second and I can see the guilt take over his face. "I was stupid-drunk the first time we hooked up and I figured it was a one-night stand, but she kept hanging around and showing up and calling and she liked to party as much as I did, so I kept seeing her. I asked her to marry me when she got pregnant because Ma would have murdered me if I didn't."

"Shit, Logan, I never knew that." We didn't realize how bad Logan's drinking was until that car accident, but I still didn't realize that he never had real feelings for Bethany.

He shakes his head now as the light turns green and he continues driving. "Don't get me wrong, I would do it all again if it meant I got to have River exactly the way he is, which means having him with Bethany. But I would have not let Ma's Catholic guilt get the better of my decision-making."

I think back to what just happened with Jake and wonder if it could have happened earlier if I hadn't been dating Tom. "I probably wouldn't have dated Tom knowing what I know now."

Logan nods. "Makes sense. But Terra, you gotta promise me that you won't let this—Tom or the lupus—cloud your opinion of yourself and what you deserve."

"I don't think I deserve less because I have lupus," I reply and close my eyes. "I just think the disease has taken away some of my options. And don't tell me it hasn't, Logan, because it has. Part of the biggest battle with this disease is trying to convince other people you're sick. Don't make me convince you."

"I know you're sick, Terra. I was almost a doctor and also, I grew up with you. I saw the struggle, the exhaustion, the fevers, the pain, the hair loss, but that doesn't make you unworthy of love."

"This from a guy who refuses to even attempt to date because he made one mistake in his life," I can't help but say. Logan frowns.

"Not the same thing. I made a massive mistake, you have an illness you didn't cause."

"Technically, alcoholism is an illness you didn't cause either, and it's responsible for your mistake," I argue back.

"I am responsible for my mistakes," Logan replies firmly. "And stop trying to turn this around on me, please."

"Okay let's talk about Jake instead," I say casually. At least I hope it sounds casual because as soon as I say his name, my heart skips a beat and I feel warmer all over. "Why do you think he's still single?"

"Because he wants to be," Logan turns into my apartment complex. "He, like you, thinks he's not good enough for the whole white picket fence and passionate, undying love crap. And that's why I worried too, Ter. You want that perfect love story and Jake doesn't think he's that guy for anyone. The man has a fucking medal and still won't call himself a hero of anything let alone a love story."

"He's grown a lot and I don't think you give him enough credit," I reply as he pulls to a stop in front of my apartment complex. "He's no longer worried about what other people think. And you can't scare him into not dating me… if he did want to date me."

"So threatening to fire him from the Shack then tie his ankle to the boat anchor and sink him with the lobster traps if he touches you isn't going to work this time?" Logan asks and I glare at him. "What? Finn and I were stupid teens who didn't want you to be touched by anyone, let alone our buddies."

"Why couldn't I have sisters?" I sigh. "Look, don't bug Jake. I like him. Not again but still. I've always liked him. He gives me that rush that Tom didn't and he's also kind of saving my life. Remember that."

Logan turns off the engine and twists his torso to star at me more easily. "Just go slow. There's a lot going on—for both of you right now. And when it comes to the tough stuff, you both have a go-to defense system that shuts other people out. And there's gonna be tough stuff in the next few weeks, not just regarding the kidney situation."

"Yeah, I'm sure the whole town knowing our business won't

make it easier. Thank you Nellie Green," I frown. "Sometimes I hate this fucking town."

I dig in my coat pocket for my keys and act like it's really hard to find them. "I should get going. I have to pack for the hospital and get my stuff in order."

"See you tomorrow," Logan says and reaches out to squeeze my hand. I squeeze back and then twist to blow an air kiss to the perfect giant fur ball in the back who is whining in his crate.

I jump out of the SUV and into my building. As I climb the stairs to my apartment, my phone pings in my pocket and I pull it out to see a text from Jake. It's a picture of my bra and the words: *Found this behind the couch. If you left this as a reminder, I don't need one. You're all I can think about.*

I open my front door and kick it closed behind me as I type back.

I'm going to sleep in your hoodie... and nothing else.

And then I lean against my door grinning like a complete idiot.

16

JAKE

I SHOW UP AT THE RESTAURANT AT A LITTLE AFTER NINE IN THE morning like Logan's text demanded. And it was a demand. He wasn't 'Hey buddy, come see River meet Chewie.' It was 'Be at the Shack at nine.' So I know as I get out of my Jeep and walk toward the building, this is about more than the new dog. Logan and Finn are both out in the parking lot playing with Chewie, who is zooming back and forth between the two of them while they toss a stuffed toy back and forth. Finally Logan sees me and waves. At least I think it's Logan but can't be a hundred percent sure from this distance. He tosses the toy up in the air and Chewie jumps for it but it hits his snout and bounces off. He picks it up off the ground and does a victory lap through the empty lot. Finn jogs after him, to make sure he doesn't escape.

"Thanks for coming," Logan says rubbing the back of his neck, which is a horrible sign. He does that when he's stressed.

Finn scoops up Chewie and walks right over. "I'm gonna step in here, because my twin didn't get the confrontation gene and we don't have time for all his roundabout blabbering. Dad's boat will be back soon and Mom and Nova will be here in a sec to open up, and Terra is already inside making coffee for everyone."

I stiffen, but Finn gives me a smile. It's probably supposed to ease my worries, but it doesn't reach his eyes. "Terra has had a crush on you since middle school and although we're so happy to have you home and beyond grateful you're giving her a kidney, it's made that crush start up again, and we're worried you don't see it."

"I see it and I welcome it," I admit and reach out to give Chewie a scratch under his chin. "I saw it when we were kids too. I'm not a moron."

"Okay…." Logan swallows hard. "So I guess this is the part where we warn you that she's obviously really vulnerable right now and you probably have a lot of your own shit you're dealing with, coming back to town and everything, so maybe boundaries are a good idea for now."

Oh boy. Here we go… "You guys really don't give your sister enough credit. She's a smart girl. Emotionally and intellectually. Smarter than you two put together. And you must not think much of me if you think I would ever hurt her."

"You dated her best friend." Leave it to Finn to state the obvious. "And hooked up with her. Recently."

Logan's eyes lock with mine. Finn doesn't look nearly as intense as his twin so I know Logan has kept my secret.

"If you two are against this, I'm sorry to say, I don't care," I counter. "She's an adult. I'm an adult. I've been nothing but a loyal friend to you two and if she can get over the Aspen thing and give me a shot, it's not your place to hold it against me."

"Can she?" Logan challenges. His gaze darkens like a storm cloud. "Handle the Aspen thing? *All* the Aspen things?"

"Look, forget the Aspen thing. That's in the past, but right now you guys are both about to go through a lot physically and it will likely bring you closer, but that might make you both … I don't know, like, get confused," Finn says and his smile is less forced and more honest. "I'm not the fucking Brainiac and empath in the family, obviously, and I would be thrilled if she ended up with you one day, Jake. Truly. I just worry about things starting right now. I know she kissed you and I know she's vulnerable. I worry."

Chewie drops the toy and barks impatiently for someone to pick it up. Finn reaches for it and Chewie snatches it and runs. Finn runs after him leaving me alone with Logan. Logan rubs the back of his neck again. "Does Terra know everything?"

"No. Aspen promised to do the paternity test after my operation, though," I swear and I hope he can see how serious I am. "I didn't plan for things to progress with Terra before I found out, but it kind of did."

He is fighting a grimace. Typical guy shit. He doesn't want to think about what progressing means when his only sister is involved. "Yeah, okay. I've been there, but Jake, if this kid is yours and you don't tell her … she won't be the only one not talking to you."

"If there's a reason to tell her," I explain and inhale deeply. The air is thick with the salty smell of the ocean just behind the restaurant. He looks skeptical, which hurts, but he nods. Finn walks back over to us, holding Chewie. Logan pulls a leash out of the pocket of his jacket and hooks it to Chewie's collar. "You said Tink is inside?"

They nod simultaneously and without another word, I head inside. Terra has her back to me, facing the coffeemaker, filling several mugs on a tray. They don't open the actual restaurant until eleven, so I figure she's the only one here. I walk behind the counter and she turns because the bell on the door announced my presence. But there's a moment of shock on her face followed by a big smile. "Hey."

I glance out the window. Logan and Finn aren't paying attention to us because Nova and Lucy have arrived and are out there fawning all over the new furry family member. "Hey yourself."

I bend and give her a kiss, short, sweet, and not at all what I need. What I need is to throw her up on the counter, wedge myself between her legs and kiss her breathless, but that's out of the question right now. In fact, I guess the little kiss is too because she steps back as soon as it's over. "I think we need to wait until after the op to tell everyone this is a thing."

"Finn and Logan kind of already figured it out," I say. "They just had a talk with me."

She cringes. "Ugh. I'm sorry. Was it horrible? Were they jerks?"

"It was fine. Better than when I was seventeen and they told me they would break my nose, shove me in a locker naked, and let me bleed to death if I touched you." I smile but she looks positively horrified.

"They said that to you?"

"No. They said it to Kevin Ritchman when he made some comment about how hot you were at lunch," I explain. "To me they just said don't do it. It will ruin our friendship forever."

"Kevin Ritchman liked me?" she blinks. I nod. Now she grins, it lights up her whole face and the whole room suddenly looks brighter. "Wow. I wonder how many other potential boyfriends I've lost because of those dickheads."

"Would you like me to write you a list?"

Her smile turns cheeky. "Yeah, I mean maybe I have options I didn't know about."

Her hair is in two braids, then ends of which sit on her collarbones and I want to reach out and grab them both and tug her to my mouth again to show her exactly why she doesn't need to revisit anyone else. But Declan blows through the kitchen door. He's in a charcoal suit with a burgundy tie and pocket square. I step back from Terra. "Hey *Succession* extra."

Declan smirks. "Hey *Chicago Fire* extra. You here to see River meet the fur ball?"

I nod. Declan grabs a full cup off Terra's tray without so much as a thank you and takes a sip. "You guys still allowed to eat and drink?"

"Until noon," Terra replies. "Then it's pre-op fasting time."

"You should order everything on the menu for breakfast," Declan jokes and smiles at me, but then he sighs, staring out the window as Nova squeals in delight as Chewie licks her cheek. "This is the last thing we need right now. Another problem."

He turns and walks back into the kitchen. Terra scowls after him. "He's never happy for anyone."

A car pulls into the parking lot. "Bethany is here. It's go time."

"Oh!" Terra reaches into the front pocket of the overalls she's wearing and pulls out her phone as she charges toward the door. "I don't want to miss this!"

I follow her outside. Bethany's gotten out of her red Toyota and is walking around the car to open the back passenger door and let River out of his car seat. Her eyes are glued to Chewie who is biting at his leash at Logan's feet. "Logan... what's going on?"

"I got a dog," Logan replies and she freezes. "Let him out of the car, Beth."

She looks like she's furious but she does lift River out. River looks across the parking lot and sees his dad and Chewie and gasps in the overdramatic, adorable way only kids can. He starts to run. "Slow down!" Bethany yells, but of course he doesn't.

"River. Stop!" Logan commands when the little guy is a couple feet away. River listens despite his excitement. "What have I told you about approaching dogs you don't know?"

River's nose and forehead scrunch as he thinks really hard. Then he starts walking toward Chewie, his little hand out. He takes one little step at a time. Chewie is yanking on the leash to get closer too. Logan commands him to calm down, which the puppy sort of does. He sniffs River's hand and immediately licks it and River squeals and pulls it back, and Chewie's tail starts wagging.

Terra is filming the whole thing beside me on her phone and it's almost impossible to not pay attention to her over this Hallmark moment. I just love the glee on her face. It rivals River's when Logan says. "He's ours buddy. You and me. His name is Chewbacca."

"Really? He is mine?" Logan nods and River moves closer and pets Chewie softly on the head. Chewie licks him again and River squeals. "I love him, Daddy!"

Lucy sniffs. She's crying happy tears, and I realize Logan's timing on this is perfect. Everyone needs a happy distraction from what comes next with Terra and me. Bethany, on the other hand, doesn't see it that way. "Logan, can I talk to you? In private."

Logan glances over at her. She still hasn't really approached the family, standing closer to her car than us. He hands me the leash and walks over to Bethany like he's walking a plank on a pirate ship. "That woman…" Terra hisses. Luckily, River is too busy playing with Chewie to hear her. "He's tied to her for life. Ugh."

Aspen pops into my brain but I push her out. It's not the same thing. Aspen is a good, kind person who isn't expecting a ring from me. Bethany was. She had a truck load of expectations Logan never met so she's bitter.

A few minutes later, Logan and Bethany are still arguing by her car. No one can hear what's being said, but arms are flailing and expressions are grim.

"Who is this?"

We all turn and see Charlie lumbering up from the dock. He's in a pair of rubber fisherman pants, pulling off his gloves, just off the boat from emptying the lobster traps. River wraps his arms around Chewie's neck. "This is my dog, Grampy!"

Charlie makes the most exaggerated shocked face I have ever seen and Terra giggles beside me. "Are you sure?"

"Yes! Yes! He's mine and his name is Chewbacca, and I love him with my whole heart." Okay, now the kid has me wanting to tear up. Charlie smiles down at his grandson and ruffles his hair before doing the same to the top of Chewie's head. He takes the leash from my hand.

"Okay then, let's go walk your dog, River," Charlie says loudly, and Bethany and Logan stop bickering and look over. Charlie's expression turns hard, and his eyes laser in on Bethany. "Beth, Logan , I'm going to walk Chewbacca with River, teach him how to do it. He just told me he loves Chewie with his whole heart, so we should teach him how to care for him, right? Unless…"

Bethany glares at Charlie but then River pipes up again. "I promise to learn. I promise to take care of him. I promise! I cross my heart and everything."

Bethany's shoulders drop two inches. "I'll be back to pick you up after work, Riv. Be good and careful. That's a big puppy."

River nods vigorously. Bethany blows him an air kiss, glares at Logan, and gets in her car and drives off. Logan jogs back over. "Let's walk him down on the beach and see how he does with waves."

Charlie peels out of his rubber pants and hands them to Lucy along with his gloves and walks down to toward the water with Logan and River. Once they're all out of ear shot, Lucy Hawkins swears. I think it's only the second time in my life I've heard that. "That woman is the fucking devil."

She storms into the restaurant and we all follow. Lucy disappears into the kitchen while I sit at the bar with Finn, and Terra starts handing out the coffee mugs. Nova grabs the little packs of Half-n-Half, which are put on the counter in bowls for the customers during business hours, and slides it toward me and

Finn. "Was she really going to try and make Logan get rid of Chewie?"

Declan and Lucy come back into the restaurant. Declan slides past Terra and grabs what's left in the coffee carafe to refill his mug.

"I wouldn't put it past her," Nova says and frowns. "Lucy isn't far off in her description. Bethany lives to make Logan's life hell."

"To be fair, co-parenting means telling each other about big decisions before you make them," Declan interjects and Finn rolls his eyes. "What? Now River is going to beg to come over to Logan's all the time so he can be with the damn dog. It's emotional blackmail."

"Excuse me?" Nova says, and her offended tone gets all of our attention. "She's the one using emotional blackmail by thinking up every excuse in the book to keep River's time with Logan to a bare minimum."

"Yeah well, Logan supplied the evidence when it comes to blackmail," Declan mutters.

"Declan do not go there. I swear to—" Terra gets cut off by Lucy who slams her mug down so hard it echoes and coffee slops over the side leaving a big brown blob on the pristine white counter. Everyone falls silent.

She turns and looks up at her eldest. "Declan don't you have some marketing thing to do?"

He looks annoyed and turns to his wife for support, but Nova immediately looks away. She's had it with him too. Declan has always been the black sheep, and I really can't feel bad for him because he goes out of his way to own that title sometimes. At least now I finally understand why everyone gets so tense over the subject of Logan.

Declan slinks off into the kitchen. Terra lets out a heavy sigh. As soon as the door swings behind Declan, Lucy turns back to us, reaching for a wet cloth from under the counter to wipe up her mess. "I was thinking that you two need to recover at our place."

"What?" we say in unison.

"Jake's apartment is on the fourth floor. Terra's is on the third. It's a lot of stairs if you want to come and go," Lucy explains. "And what if you need help at night? Or if you don't feel well?"

"We can call you, Mom. Or call the doctor," Terra says. "And if we don't feel like climbing the stairs and want fresh air, we both have balconies."

"What if there's a fire at either of your buildings? You two won't be able to evacuate easily at all," she counters, and I smile.

"You've got about a hundred more excuses don't you?" I ask, and she nods. "Lucy, I'll be fine at home."

"That place you're in isn't your home. You've been in it for, what? A few weeks? Have you even hung up a picture yet?" she cocks an eyebrow and then smiles triumphantly when I turn sheepish. I still have boxes to unpack and not a thing on the walls. "You know my house like the back of your hand. You practically lived there yourself. You can stay in Finn and Logan's old room and Terra can stay in her old room and I would just feel better about it."

"I don't know…" Terra says and I can almost see her brain spinning trying to find a valid excuse not to humor her mom.

"Look, you know Mom is going to be checking on both of you every day," Nova adds and I can tell they've pre-planned this ambush. "If you don't want to do it for yourselves, do it for Ma. So she doesn't have to keep driving back and forth across town carrying food up and down all the stairs to your apartments because you know she's going to want to feed you."

"I'm just going to go ahead and accept on both their behalves," Finn says standing up. "Because let's face it guys, fighting is futile."

"Ugh. You're right," Terra drops her head onto her arms on the countertop. "Fine. We'll do it."

"We will?" I appreciate the sentiment, but I am failing to see how Terra and I can have some alone time in Charlie and Lucy's house. And that's what I know I'll want after this. I want it now, for crying out loud. I was hoping we could both just stay at my place, just Terra and I. But Finn is right; resistance is futile. I sigh. "Okay, cool."

Lucy claps her hands and smiles. "Oh good. I promise to be the best nurse you've ever had."

Finn slaps my shoulder as he walks by to head behind the counter. "Milk it, buddy. You're her new favorite son, so get her to make you buttermilk blueberry pancakes every day and lobster bombs and double batter fried chicken."

"Yeah, I have to fit into a firetruck after all this," I remind him and he laughs.

The Hawkins family moves all around me now, getting the Lobster Shack ready to open. Terra disappears into the back, announcing she has to finish the scheduling. She's planning it out for eight weeks and pre-paid certain vendors so no one has to carry too much of her workload. I sit at the counter a while and have a second cup of coffee then I announce I'll bring my cup to the dishwasher and slip into the back. Javi smiles and nods as he chops claw meat. I wave, hand my cup to Manny the dishwasher, and slip into Terra's office.

"Hey!" I say loudly so everyone who might be listening can hear. "Did the surgeon call you about that thing…"

She looks up from her computer and I close the door behind me. There's no lock. Damnit. She starts grinning as she sees my hand fumbling to find one. "I like what I think you're thinking. But the door doesn't lock, and now we have even more reason to keep this on the down-low."

"What?"

"Lucy Hawkins, my uber-religious, cross-wearing, Bible-quoting mother," Terra says, pushing her chair back and walking around her desk so she's on the same side as I am. "She said she was going to give you Finn and Logan's old room and I would be in my room."

"Yeah. So?" I honestly don't know where she is going with this, but she's grinning at me deviously so I think I'm going to like it.

"Finn and Logan's room is connected to mine through the shared bathroom, remember?" She comes to stand in front of me, and places her hands lightly on my hips. The feel of her touch makes my dick stir. "Which means, I can sneak into your room and you can sneak into mine without ever stepping foot in the hallway."

Bingo.

"She finds out we're into each other in *that* way and she will stick you in Declan's old room," Terra says. Declan's old room is in the attic and the stairwell up to it is directly beside Lucy and Charlie's room and if I remember correctly, creaks like hell.

"Then you need to get your hands off me, Tink," I reply but dip my head down and skim my lips over the curve of her neck, inhaling deeply that perfect Terra smell. "Because I'm all for conjugal visits."

She steps back, her hands falling to her sides, but she purposely brushes one against the front of my jeans as she turns back to her desk and I groan. She giggles.

"I'm going to go home and pack up for the hospital. Well, maybe take care of what you just created in my pants and then pack."

Her eyes drop to my groin as I adjust myself and she grins proud of her accomplishment. "I'm just finishing up here and then I'm doing the same."

"Cool. So I'll see you later, when Lucy and Charlie drive us to the hospital?"

She nods. She bites her bottom lip and her dark eyes grow serious. "I don't even know how to thank you, Jake," she whispers.

Before I can answer, the door opens, smacking me in the back. It's Declan. "Hey. I… oh. Jake."

"I'm just heading out."

Declan nods, but his ice colored eyes are inquisitive. I ignore it and wave good-bye as casually as possible to Terra, who purposely barely registers my exit. Because that's how we were with each other before we got naked together so it raises no suspicion.

I walk back to my Jeep in the parking lot and make a promise to myself. Whether Aspen does the damn blood test or not, I'm going to let her know. I'm telling Terra about this potential child whether Aspen likes it or not. If I have a shot at a real relationship with Terra, she has to know.

17

TERRA

"OH! I THINK SHE'S COMING TO, DOCTOR," I HEAR AS MY EYES water and flutter open. There's a nurse beside me, staring down with a smile. Then suddenly the surgeon, Dr. Leclerc, is there. "Welcome back, Terra."

"Where's Jake?" I croak out. "How… is… he?"

The doctor's smile deepens. "He's right beside you, as requested."

The nurse takes a step closer to the foot of my bed and I turn my head and see him lying there, eyes closed, chest rising and falling evenly. "Is he okay?"

"The men, especially the big ones, sometimes take longer to wake up but I promise you he's fine," the surgeon smiles down at me. "Would you like to know how *you* are doing?"

Oh. Right. I nod.

"As I've informed the fan club in the waiting room, every-thing went perfectly," she explains. "No hiccups or complications in the procedure. Time will tell how we do with rejection and healing, but I'm optimistic."

I turn my head again and stare at Jake. I wish he would wake up. I just want to hear his voice. The nurse checks my IV and asks me my pain levels. I don't feel much of anything right now, just a dry throat and a dull ache in my middle.

"Can I get you anything?"

"Water, please?" I croak. "And him."

She smiles and walks around my bed, rolling it sideways gently so it's closer to Jake. Yesterday when we checked in they put us in different rooms beside each other, but I requested in post-op that we be placed together because I read they can do that with donors and recipients who are known to each other.

As the nurse walks away to get me some water, I carefully slip my hand through the rails on the side of my bed and lay it on top of his where it rests above the covers. He feels warm but his hand is limp, and I don't like it. I have this overwhelming irrational need for him to wake up.

"Jake… can you hear me?" I say, my voice still raw. "Can you wake up please before I freak out and pop my stitches or something?"

Nothing.

"I assure you, he's good," the nurse promises as she arrives back at my side and hands me the teeniest cup of water I've ever seen. "You can only have it in little doses because after anesthesia too much liquid or anything at once can make you vomit."

I swallow down the shooter-sized amount of room temperature water. Better than nothing, I guess. I thank her and hand her back the cup and my eyes go to Jake. "Do you have a rough idea of when he will wake up?"

"Should be any time now," she replies. "Don't worry. Your boyfriend is in good hands."

"He's not my boyfriend," I say softly and then I feel his hand move undermine. I snap my head around to face him and instantly regret the fast motion.

"Tink…" his voice is just as hoarse and rough as mine, but the sound of it makes me cry.

"Jake. Welcome back," The nurse turns toward his bed and walks over to the other side, so as not to disrupt our hands, which are now joined because he's turned his around and laced our fingers.

"How do you feel?" I whisper.

"Okay. How are you?" Jake asks. "Did it work? Is everything good?"

"They say yes," I reply and he blinks away his grogginess a little more and notices my wet cheeks. His dark eyes fill with concern. "Are you in pain? What's wrong?"

"I'm just so relieved you're awake," I whisper.

"I'm not going anywhere, Tink," he promises, and a drowsy smile pulls at his lips. "I have to stick around and convince you to let people think I'm your boyfriend."

My heartbeat suddenly gets stronger. "Is that what you want people to think?"

"That's what I want the truth to be."

The surgeon comes over and asks Jake the same questions she asked me and then she says, "Your family is anxious to see you both, so we'll call some orderlies and move you back into your own rooms."

I feel instantly disappointed. I want to stay here holding Jake's hand until they send us home. Jake must feel the same way because he replies. "Can we take our time on that part? I kind of like it here."

He squeezes my hand. I close my eyes, a smile on my lips, and revel in the feel of our intertwined hands. I must have dozed off because the next thing I know, my arm is tucked under the sheets on my gurney and I'm being wheeled into my own room. Damnit.

My mother, Declan and Nova are there to greet me, all smiling but on the verge of tears. I know it's from relief. I feel it too. Although, my battle is far from over. There's anti-rejection meds and a risk of infection and a whole bunch of other things to deal with now. My mom pushes my hair off my forehead and places a kiss there. "Dad and the twins are in Jake's room. We will switch after half an hour."

I smile and nod, relieved they aren't all in here with me. And then I see someone in the corner of the room that makes me think maybe the Tramadol drip is a little too generous and I'm hallucinating. Is that… Tom?

"The doc says everything went really well," Declan tells me. "And Jake is doing great too."

"I know. I was with him in recovery," I reply and Tom stands up and walks over. Now he's standing next to Nova, and I swear I would think I'm imagining it except my mom acknowledges his existence.

"Tom wanted to see how you were doing," she explains. "He called me last night to see if he could come and sit with us while the operation went on, and of course we said yes."

She leans over the side of my bed to glance over at him and smile. He smiles back but his eyes dart back to me. "Terra, I… I know you need rest right now but hopefully we can talk maybe in a couple of days?"

"Maybe," I reply my tone flat and noncommittal because I don't want to talk to him about anything. "I am really tired right now and would like to rest."

"Of course. I just had to know you were through everything," Tom says and pats my hand. I'm irrationally angry for a moment that he touched the hand that was laced with Jake's earlier. "I left you some flowers over there." He points to the vase of carnations on the window ledge.

I muster a smile. He pats my hand again and heads out. Nova scowls at his back as he goes, but Ma looks absolutely dreamy-eyed. Oh great. This is the last thing I need. My mom loves Tom more than anyone because he goes to church. Every now and then he would get up early when he was spending the weekend and go with her, and I would meet them later for brunch. Much to mom's dismay, none of her kids kept up the church thing—or religion for that matter—once we turned eighteen and couldn't be forced to go. I never told Ma that Tom ran like a bitch over the kidney problems, but now I realize I should have. She wouldn't have forgiven him that, but she thinks we just had a tiff or something and she is all about the second chance romance. That's what my dad was for her.

Once Tom is gone Declan says, "Do you want us to leave you alone to sleep too?"

"You can stay but I may drift in and out," I say.

And I do just that. Every time I wake, the light in the room is different. It goes from full sun to evening light to no light but there's always a different family member there by my side. And every time, I ask them if someone is still with Jake. Thankfully they always say yes.

By the next day, I feel much better. Tender as all hell but more alert and they've moved me onto a lower dose of pain meds. Doctor Leclerc pops in to check on me and clears me for more movement, not just the two feet I've been walking to the bathroom. Nova is with me when I get the news, having convinced my parents to go home and get some actual rest. They'd been here in the hospital for almost twenty-four straight hours. Declan and Finn are back at the restaurant ,and Logan is with River and is going to bring him by later this afternoon if I'm up for it.

"Can I walk with Jake? Is he allowed to walk yet?" I ask the nurse.

I carefully pull myself out of the bed and onto my feet. Nova hands me my robe so that the stupid hospital gown doesn't flash my ass at people as I go on this journey. The nurse nods his head. "You can walk over to his room and ask him if he wants to join."

Nova takes my arm gently at the elbow and I let her because

I'm a little nervous about this. Jake's surgery was done laparo-scopically, but I had to be opened right up and the incision area is super tender. The nurse follows behind as I slowly but steadily make my way out of the room and turn left.

I'm smiling, excited to see Jake, and I can show it around Nova because she's kind of in on this. I haven't told her about anything more than the first two kisses, but still. I've seen Jake since the recovery room only once. He snuck into my room last night after midnight. I was in that weightless pain-killer induced place between sleep and awake. I could barely open my eyes, but I knew it was him who kissed my cheek and whispered my name. I could tell by the scrub of his stubble and the feel of his lips. My Mom was asleep in a reclining vinyl chair by the window when I finally opened my eyes completely and I saw him slip out of the room.

The expectant smile on my lips disappears the second I walk through the wide-open door to his room. He's sitting on the edge of his bed with Aspen standing in front of him. I know it's her even from behind because those wild, wheat blond curls are one of a kind in Ocean Pines. If it wasn't for the hair I might not have known straight away because she isn't dressed like Aspen. She's in leggings and Converse and a very oversized, chunky knit sweater that almost hits her knees. Aspen's style is usually tight, clingy stuff.

Jake sees me in the doorway and the color drains from his face, which makes me feel like he's guilty of something. I turn abruptly. "Sorry. I'll see you later."

"No!" Jake calls out. "Stop!"

"Terra, wait!" Aspen adds, her voice desperate. I want to keep walking but Nova has stopped and is still holding onto my elbow. I begrudgingly turn back around. Aspen looks nervous and some-thing else. Sad? Depressed, maybe? She says, "I hope you're doing okay. You look good."

I tip my head down and look at my pale green hospital gown and the unicorn slippers on my feet that my mom brought me from home along with my fuzzy blue robe I'm wearing. I also know my hair hasn't been brushed in forty-eight hours and I don't have a lick of make-up on, and my lips are slightly chapped. I cock an eyebrow at her. "I look good, do I?"

"Well, I mean… you look healthy. Like you have a hunky new kidney." She attempts a smile but it's awkward. "I mean… his insides have gotta be as hot as his outsides, right?"

Her voice raises nervously, like she's terrified I won't be able to joke with her. Suddenly, I am reminded of the good times we had together growing up and how her voice would get like that any time we were on the verge of trouble. Like the time we got caught trying to break into the teachers' lounge because we found out they had Crispy Kremes delivered every Friday. I have to force myself not to smile. Remembering she slept with Jake just three short months ago does the trick. "It's probably a good-looking organ, you're right. And so far it's happy in its new home, thankfully."

"Good. I'm glad, Terra. Honestly. Happy everything is working out for you. All of it," she says softly and then grabs her purse from the chair by his bed. "I've got to go. See you around when you're home and stuff. I hope."

"Bye," I follow her with my eyes as she walks down the hall and turns the corner to the elevator bank. Something is weird with her. I shouldn't care but I do for some reason.

"You're walking? That's good," Jake says getting up off his bed. He's in a pair of gray T-shirt material pajama bottoms and a black T-shirt, both clearly not hospital issued like most of my outfit. His feet are clad in hospital socks with the little grips on the bottom. "Do you want company?"

"That's exactly why we came," Nova says before I can answer. She motions for him to come forward. "Why don't you go with her and I'll go downstairs and get a coffee. I'm suddenly feeling rundown, like I need a pick-me-up."

"You don't drink coffee, Nova." I remind her flatly.

She grins. "Today is the day I've decided to start. See you soon. Don't overdo it."

"I hate you," I mutter but not loud enough for anyone to hear because I don't really mean it. Jake is now beside me. Instead of taking my elbow, he takes my hand in his.

"This good?" he asks.

"I can manage without help," I reply and realize the chill in my voice so I pause and take a deep breath. "But yeah, it is good. To feel you again."

He smiles. "Feels good to feel you too."

I feel energized by that. Stronger. I start walking with more confidence than I had on my way to Jake's room, but I still keep the arm rail attached to the wall within grabbing distance. The ache in my side doesn't get worse, but it doesn't get better either. He looks like he's not in much discomfort.

"You seem good," I say.

"A little achey and all the laparoscopy holes on my stomach make me look like I have gun shots wounds which is weird, but I'm better than I thought I would be," Jake replies, his thumb is absently skimming back and forth across my wrist.

We reach the end of the hall and turn around to start back.

"She was just here checking on me as a friend," Jake tells me, clearly not afraid to tackle the elephant in the hallway with us.

"I didn't know you'd told her about the operation is all," I reply and slow a little bit. How is this so exhausting? I'm on my feet running around a restaurant all day every day. My steps tracker has me averaging ten thousand steps every work day, but I'm almost out of breath from half a hallway.

"I had to tell her because I needed a next of kin AKA medical proxy," Jake tells me and I snap my head up to look him in the eyes. I'm shocked he picked her. "Terra, I couldn't put the twins down or your parents like I've been doing since I was a kid because I didn't want to pull their focus from you if something went wrong. And how guilty would they be if they had to… you know pull my plug because of this? It had to be someone independent and it was her or Kelsey."

His mom. Wow. He hasn't brought her up since he got back to town. "You know Kelsey isn't the right person to contact in an emergency so it had to be Aspen."

I try to take my heart out of this equation. It's hard, but I do it, and realize that Aspen, unfortunately, makes sense. But I still say "You could have put down Nova."

"Are you kidding me? That bleeding heart would have kept me alive at all costs, even if all hope was lost. She's too much of an optimist," Jake says with a smile. "I thought about making it Declan for like two seconds."

"Yeah he would totally pull your plug without batting an eyelash," I reply. "Unless there was a way to monetize your coma or whatever. Like if it could help sell lobster rolls."

We both laugh, because we know we're kidding. Mostly. But laughing makes my guts ache right now so I force myself to stop. He squeezes my hand. "I want to kiss you right now."

"So do it."

He looks around. "Is there a closet somewhere we could borrow?"

I open my mouth to laugh but he covers it with his own. The kiss is gentle, tame and short but absolutely perfect. When we break apart, we continue to walk.

As we get closer to my room, for some reason, I think about the conversation I had with Logan the night he drove me home from Jake's, about our defense mechanisms. "I'm sorry Aspen just makes me irrational. I always saw her as perfect in all the ways I wasn't. She was gorgeous and ballsy and an extrovert and healthy. For a long time I just felt grateful she would even be friends with someone like me. When she went after you and you actually started dating her, it reconfirmed she was better than me."

"She never should have done that. And if I knew any of that history I never would have gone to prom with her let alone date her. But the girl I really had a thing for was off-limits and I'd pissed her off so she refused to even acknowledge my existence," he reminds me and he's grinning that easy, lazy smile that's always turned my heart into a gold medal gymnast on a set of uneven bars flipping around like her life depended on it.

I take a deep breath. "A part of you lives inside my body, so ignoring your existence is an impossibility now," I say as we reach my room.

We walk inside and I head straight for the bed. I'm tired and hot. He sits in the chair in the corner. "I didn't give you a kidney to make you like me."

"I know. But I was actually talking about the part of you that lives in my heart now," I reply and study his face.

Yeah, I'm telling him I love him without telling him I love him. I'm still too scared to throw it right out there.

He looks me straight in the eye. He looks vulnerable, and it takes my breath away more than the walk did. "I was a damn fool for waiting this long."

"Yeah, we both were," I smile and he laughs for a second but then winces.

Nova appears behind him in the doorway. She waltzes in and perches on the window sill, a paper cup of what's probably an herbal tea in her hands. Her brown eyes slide back and forth from Jake to me and her smile is smug. "Good walk?"

The surgeon appears in my doorway before either of us can answer Nova. "So I've got good news and bad news."

The light, calm feeling that had filled me disappears

completely. Jake pulls himself out of the chair and walks over to my bed, sitting beside me. "Okay… shoot."

I reach for Jake's hand as the surgeon explains. "Jake, you're going home this afternoon."

"Just me?"

She nods. "Terra, you've still got a fever."

Oh no.

Jake reaches up and presses a palm to my forehead. His eyes lock with mine and he knows I know. "Why didn't you say something?"

"I was hoping it was nothing."

"It might be," Dr. Leclerc explains. "It's not ideal but it's not uncommon."

"But it's also a sign of rejection according to Google," Jake says.

"Google says a lot of things," Dr. Leclerc gives us a smile. "It's like a drunk uncle at thanksgiving. Spews advice on everything whether it's facts or not."

"So it's not a sign?" Nova interjects and I already see her hand slip into her bag, no doubt looking for her phone so she can update my family.

"It's not necessarily a sign," the doctor replies. "Most of the time it's just the body working overtime to help the organ settle in, for lack of a better word."

Jake frowns.

I squeeze his hand. "Hey. Believe her. She has no reason to lie."

He nods, but I'm not sure he's taking my words to heart. I really wish he would because then maybe I'd believe them more myself. Nova gets up, leaving her tea on the window sill, her phone now clutched in her hand. "I'm gonna make a call."

"Don't let them freak out!" I yell as she slips out of the room, knowing she is about to update my parents.

"Jake, I need to take one last look at your laparoscopy incisions and talk about that extra blood work you requested."

"Extra blood work?" I repeat and frown.

"Yeah. For work. No big deal," Jake says and gets up. "See you later?"

"I'll have to check my schedule, but I should be able to pencil you in."

"Good to see the snark wasn't accidentally removed with your bum kidney," he quips.

The doctor chuckles and leaves, but Jake doesn't follow right away. He bends down and kisses the top of my head and then he gingerly squats right in from of me as I sit on the bed, he puts his head close to my torso and says. "Hey kidney. I'm not taking you back so might as well get used to it in there and make yourself at home."

He stands and leaves, giving me a wink as I giggle at his antics.

A couple minutes later, as I settle in my bed, Nova walks back in. She smiles but it doesn't reach her eyes, so I know how the conversation went. "Ma is freaking out?"

"Yep," she admits. "But I called Logan too and he is on the way to her place to talk her off the ledge with all his doctor-speak. He assured me the surgeon is right and this means nothing. Yet."

Nova leans against the window ledge and picks up the cup she abandoned earlier. "So, Aspen. What was that about?"

"She was checking in on him," I explain. "She was listed as his next of kin because he didn't want to put one of us and can't put his mom."

"Kelsey Grady is still … around?"

"Maybe," I reply and Nova looks as shocked as I was. "Anyway … I trust him when he says it's over with her."

"I trust him too," Nova replies without a moment's hesitation. Then her expression darkens a little. "I happened to notice Aspen on my way back from my little cafeteria jaunt. She looked sad. Like she'd been crying."

"Over Jake?" I ask and Nova shrugs because she has no idea.

"She was coming out of the obstetrics ward so maybe visiting a friend who had a baby?" Nova says with another shrug. "But definitely sad. Puffy eyes, blotchy cheeks, sad face. Maybe she thought her and Jake would get back together?"

I ponder that. I was so filled with jealousy and rage when Aspen asked Jake to prom and he said yes and then they started dating. I used to lie awake at night and fantasize that somehow, some way, he'd change his mind and leave her and be with me and it would make her cry. At the time, my eighteen year-old heart was filled with joy at the prospect. But now … the idea that it might be happening is not joyful. I don't feel guilt or remorse. I want Jake and I feel I deserve this happiness. But I don't take joy in the idea that it might be hurting her, even after what she did to me a million years ago.

18

JAKE

I'VE BEEN OUT OF THE HOSPITAL WITHOUT TERRA FOR FORTY-eight hours. It's been great being at Lucy and Charlie's. Lucy is waiting on me hand and foot and Charlie is a hoot. He yells at the TV during the Eagles hockey games like he's the coach on the bench barking orders. But we're all worried about Terra.

At night I lie awake in Finn and Logan's childhood bedroom trying to convince myself her body won't reject my kidney, that the universe won't be that cruel, but another part of my brain keeps listing all the ways the universe has been a total bitch in the past. Reminding me there's no reason it won't be again.

They had also asked us to limit our visits and told me specifically that I should stay home and rest, so I haven't seen her since I left the hospital. So this morning, when we got the call Terra's allowed to come home, I insisted on going to pick her up. Now I'm in the back seat of Declan's car as he drives to the hospital. Lucy is chattering away excitedly in the seat next to him as I watch the Southern Maine scenery whirl by. I want to see her so badly my skin is tingling.

We get there and I'm almost ready to run to her room and offer to carry her out instead of them wheeling her out in a wheelchair, but of course I can't do that because I'm still healing. And more importantly, that would cause everyone to ask questions we don't want to answer right now. I smirk to myself as we enter the lobby and I think about how long I forced myself to ignore my feelings for her. A fucking decade. It wasn't easy then but now that I've given into them, pretending they don't exist again is absolute torture.

"I'll go get her," Lucy says. "Declan can you head to billing and see what we need to do there."

Declan nods, his expression grim. He heads in one direction and Lucy heads in the other. I stay in the lobby and wait impatiently. A couple minutes later Declan appears from the hall he disappeared down, but he's not alone. Tom is with him.

"Tom you remember Jake," Declan points as they stop in front of me. "He's Terra's donor."

"Right. Of course," Tom extends his hand and I reluctantly shake it. "Dude, thanks so much for everything."

"Terra's my… she's my family. I'd do anything for her." I say, staring him straight in the eye. "You don't need to thank me for helping your ex."

He blinks and stands a little straighter. I don't know if it's because of the purposeful pregnant pause in my first statement that gets his back up or the use of the word ex. I'm good with either reason. Declan feels the tension building and seems confused, his pale eyebrows knitting. "Tom just did the most amazing thing. He paid Terra's insurance deductible on the op."

"What?"

Tom shrugs, my shocked reaction making him more relaxed as he lets go of my hand. "It was nothing. She has really good insurance it was just a few grand. I couldn't be her donor, but I could do this."

"And it's an amazing help, Tom, honestly," Declan tells him, grasping his shoulder and squeezing it in gratitude. "We had to remortgage the restaurant a few years ago due to a financial crisis. And of course we'd pay anything to get Terra healthy again, but you just saved us having to dig out from under even more debt. Really, thank you."

"Seriously, Deck. I don't want to be thanked," Tom replies as I start to feel bile swirl in my stomach. "I'd do anything I can for Terra. I love her."

Declan's cell buzzes and he pulls it from the pocket of his suit and double-takes at the number. "I'll be outside. I have to take this." He walks towards the door, smiling again at Tom.

Tom nods and stays right there next to me as Declan heads out. We stare at each other. Neither of us are holding onto pretenses and our smiles evaporate. He knows I don't like him. He might even know I like Terra. I give zero fucks. "You waiting for a receipt or something?"

"I'm waiting to see Terra," Tom explains. "I'm hoping she lets me drive her home."

"She won't."

Tom blinks again, shoulders pushing back ever so slightly. "You think you know her so well, don't you?"

"I know I know her," I reply, my voice is oozing confidence. "She's over you."

"With all due respect, I'm not going to take your word for it," Tom replies.

"That's cool," I say like I don't care when inside I'm actually trying to figure out if I'll do any damage to my healing body if I punch him in the face. It's irrational but I'm seething that he's here and that he wants her back.

Terra and Lucy appear at the end of the hall, with an orderly pushing her as she sits in the wheelchair. Her eyes land on me, and her smile is brighter than an August sun. And then they see the guy beside me is Tom and not Declan and her expression clouds over immediately, which makes the tension in my body slip down a few notches. She's got this.

Lucy looks thrilled at the sight of him and she opens her arms and pulls him into a hug. "Tom, you sweet thing! We timed it perfectly."

Timed it?

Tom grins down at her as she lets him go. "Thanks for helping me out, Lucy." He turns to Terra. "You look good, T. I've missed you but I've tried to give you the time you needed to heal."

"I'm not done healing, Tom," Terra replies, her tone cold and eyes flat. I smile and cover it with my hand when Lucy notices.

"Terra, sweetie, Tom is trying to make amends," Lucy pats her daughter's shoulder. "Tom gave you a gift sweetheart. Let him tell you."

"Let me drive you home and we can talk about it," Tom smiles confidently which makes Terra's frown deepen.

She looks up at the orderly and then at me and Lucy. "Can you guys all give us a minute?"

Terra's chocolate eyes land on me. Now she doesn't look so stern. She looks conflicted. Does she *want* to go with him? I must look as worried as I feel because she shakes her head and asks again. "Just a couple seconds?"

I motion for Lucy to join me. "Declan is outside. Let's go wait with him."

Lucy nods hesitantly and follows me to the main doors. I hold the door open for her and as soon as we're both outside she lets out a sigh that's heavy with frustration. "That girl of mine is more stubborn than a mule. I get that Tom isn't perfect but no man is and he's trying to make amends."

"I don't think he's a good fit."

Lucy looks shocked for a second and then she smiles and reaches out and squeezes my arm. "That's because you don't know him. He treats her really well, Jake. He's a good boy. He's got a good job and his family really loves her. They've got this lovely lake house on Sebago and we all went up there for a weekend and it was so great. I could literally see her getting married up there one day. It would be so lovely. And I know something went wrong between them but he must realize he made a mistake because he's back and he's trying to make up for it."

"What if Terra wants someone else?"

Lucy chuckles softly at that. "Terra doesn't know what's best for her. She gets hurt and shuts down. I don't fault her that. I was the Queen of cutting people off for their mistakes. Ask Charlie. I wasted years holding a grudge against him."

Declan hangs up on the call he was on and walks over. "Did Jake tell you? Tom paid all her medical bills."

"I already knew. He called me last week to ask if he could," Lucy explains. "I'm the one who told him when to be here so he could meet up with her when she was discharged."

They're all conspiring against me but I can't even hold it against them because they don't know it. And I also can't explain it to them. I'm suddenly really agitated. My life feels like a web of secrets and I'm not the spider who built it but the fly stuck in the middle of it, unable to break free.

"I don't like him," I declare. "Not for Terra or in general."

They both stare at me, stunned. But before they can say anything more the hospital doors open and Tom is wheeling Terra out of the building. When he stops, she stands and, to my horror, she hugs him. Well, he hugs her and she lets him. I guess she's not able to slug him without pulling her stitches. At least I hope that's her reason.

If she walks toward his car, I am going to stop her. In front of everyone. Even if it means I get banished to Declan's room in the attic or get sent to my own place to recuperate alone, I don't care. I'll deal with that better than watching her drive away with him. But thankfully, they part there on the sidewalk and Terra walks over to us.

"I'm tired and don't want to go home with Tom," Terra says calmly as she approaches. "I told him we'll talk later."

Lucy looks so disappointed it wounds me. Declan just shakes his head. "You know Ter, it's just as easy to fall in love with a rich college professor from New Hampshire as it is a poor dude from Ocean Pines."

"I'm going to fall in love with someone who doesn't make me feel like I'm a worthless burden," Terra snaps as Declan pulls out of the parking lot. "And that's exactly what Tom did. He volunteered to get tested to donate a kidney, then chickened out and tried to make me feel like I'd pinned him down. I didn't."

No one says anything at that information. Lucy gasps though, which I take as a good sign. Terra throws her hoodie on the back seat between us, over my hand resting there, and slips her hand under it to hold mine. I glance over at her and smile but it feels forced. She turns back to her family in the front seat. "And I do not want to talk about Tom ever again, okay? I need to get better and talking about him doesn't help me."

They honor her wishes, and I do too, and Tom's name never comes up again for the rest of the day or night. Later, I still have a gnawing uneasiness I can't shake. Even after everyone has gone to bed and the bathroom door creeks open and she crawls under the covers with me.

"So… Tom," I say after she lays a long, hot kiss on me.

"Are you serious?" she whispers back. "We're talking about this now?"

"He paid for your medical expenses because he's trying to win you back," I say. "I'm pretty sure no matter when we talk about it, it's going to be awkward."

"He could pay my medical bills, my college loans, and my parents' mortgage and he's still not getting me back," Terra replies flatly. She falls back beside me, and gingerly rolls onto her side, her head in the crook of my arm. Her hair feels silky on my bicep. "Do I look like someone who can be won by a wallet?"

I shake my head but then I find myself saying. "You know I have some savings. I can lend it to you if you want to pay him back."

She sits up abruptly and then winces. I sit up too and flick on the bedside lamp, worried she hurt her incision somehow. I reach out to touch the hem of the t-shirt she's wearing but she pushes my hands away. "So I do look like someone who can be won by a wallet."

"No. Of course not," I sigh and lean back against the headboard which is hard wood shaped like a ship's wheel. Logan and Finn have had the same bedroom furniture in here since they were twelve. "Fuck, Terra, I don't like that he's still around and that your family thinks he's such a good fucking match."

"Well I don't think it," Terra leans forward and kisses me again, her tiny hand cupping my jaw. "And they won't either when they find out about us."

Is she right? I don't know. I mean he didn't realize it when he said it, but I'm that poor guy in Declan's analogy earlier, not the rich college professor. She tilts her head to the side, her golden hair glinting in the dim moonlight filtering in from the window. As she leans even closer. "I mean I will wake them up right now and tell my parents about us. About how much you mean to me and have always meant to me if it will make you feel better. Or I can do this…"

I feel her other hand slip under the covers and curl around the half hard-on I've had since she snuck into my room. She presses down on my length and gives it a firm rub. My eyelids flutter. "Maybe we should wait to tell them."

She lets out a breathy giggle. But then I place my hand on hers and stop her. Our eyes meet in the dark room. "Did he take the hint?"

"No. He says he's not ready to give up on us," Terra admits after a second. Then she lifts my hand off of hers so she can rub me again. "But trust me, my mind and heart are made up."

She kisses me and I tangle my hands in her hair and kiss her back, my heart clenching as my brain tries fruitlessly to convince me that Terra won't reconsider her choice if that paternity test I took the day I left the hospital comes back positive.

19

JAKE

Charlie's snoring. Loudly. That's our cue! I peel back the covers, get out of Logan's childhood bed, and make my way across the room. I had left the curtains open so the moonlight could guide me. Last night I hit the desk chair with my foot and almost broke my baby toe. It was worth it, though.

It's been three days since Terra came home. She had a check-up today and her blood and urine work is great. She's definitely on the mend. The first night, after she snuck through the bathroom that joins our rooms and had the Tom talk, we just held each other and made out like horny teenagers. Last night started the same but she rubbed my hard-on through my pajama pants and I slipped a hand into hers. She came around my fingers and I had to bury my face in my pillow as I came into my pajama bottoms.

I'm about to open the door to the bathroom to see what amazing sexual adventure tonight brings us when Terra opens it from the other side. She's wearing a loose, soft pink T-shirt and matching pajama bottoms. It's turned cold this week, finally, with the temperatures dipping drastically at night. Lucy and Charlie keep the house warm enough, but her nipples are still hard. I can see them in the pale light. She smiles up at me. "I thought I would save your toes and come to you tonight."

"How are you feeling?" I ask her reaching out and taking her hands in mine as I take a step closer. We're almost touching. The soft cotton of her shirt brushes my tank top.

"I'm ready to go home," Terra replies. "I love my mom, you know I do, but I need less hovering and more time to myself."

I start to take a step back. "I can give you space."

She scurries right up to me, wrapping her arms around my neck, rising up on her tip toes, and pressing her whole, perfect little body against mine. "You know I'm not talking about you."

She's pulls my face down to hers and I'm not about to stop her. My mouth grazes hers, teasingly, before committing to the kiss. It doesn't take long for it to get heated and within minutes we're tangled together on the bed. This whole no sex thing is becoming ridiculously hard, and we are only a little over a week post-op. I'm so hard right now I feel like I could break boards with my dick.

Terra must feel the same. "I'm pretty sure I'll die if I can't have actual sex with you soon."

"You can't do that," I murmur back, my lips tracing their way down the column of her neck while my hand is sliding up, under her shirt. I'm careful to not touch her stitches. "It would be a waste of an incredibly good-looking, hard-working kidney."

"Wow. Donor life has made you an egomaniac," she whispers and giggles. It makes her whole body shake, and it's adorable. Terra is adorable. Always has been, in that incredibly hot way.

"Do you remember how you used to turn on that horrible boy band music and dance around with the mop during close at the restaurant?" I say suddenly. She looks at me and nods. "And how when you had cleared the last table of the night and brought me the dishes you'd do that little butt-wiggle thing with your arms up and your elbows tucked in."

"Yeah…" she sounds nervous.

"Why did you stop doing that?"

"I grew up, I guess?" She pauses and bites her lower lip for a second as she thinks and then her eyes move to me.

"You stopped almost instantly after the party. Abbott's party and the whole closet thing," I tell her. "I noticed."

"That was a part of what felt like a rude awakening," she says and reaches up and runs her fingers from my temple into my hair, brushing at it absently. It feels like heaven. "I had just found out I had this disease that would never go away, I was going to have to take meds for God knows how long. My hair had started thinning at that point, and the boy I'd been insanely, madly crushing on for years wouldn't kiss me. It felt like the universe was telling me this was it—my life was now a series of disappointments and rejections. So, I don't know … goofing off seemed less fun. And goofing off around you was a giant no. I was already so humiliated I just wanted to limit my contact with you to the bare minimum."

"I'm sorry. I wish I could have explained myself better then. I wish I'd also told you that all your dorky dancing and the way you would sing those songs and hug that mop was hot as hell," I say and then I pause, kiss her chastely and give her a big, sheepish grin. "I know some guys think lingerie and tight skirts and grinding at nightclubs is hot but … you being you and loving every minute of it was the most gorgeous fucking thing I had ever seen in my life back then. I'm sorry I ruined that for you and for me."

She stares at me, wordlessly. The smile on her lips is vulnerable. Then she pulls me in for a scorching kiss, her lips crashing against mine, her tongue owning my mouth and her hands yanking my tank top up. "Please can we get naked and just lie here making out like we should have done back then?"

"Your wish is my command."

And we do just that, touching, exploring, teasing. She brings me to the brink with her hand over and over as I kiss her everywhere and my own hand slides between her legs. Before either of us lose the battle with our orgasms. I pull away from her, slide down the bed and between her legs. I have a need to bring her there with my mouth. Feel her come against my lips, taste her as she breaks apart.

She writhes against me the second my tongue makes contact and her sigh is shaky and heavy. I grab my cock and jerk myself off while I make her come on my tongue. It's so fucking hot to watch her. I've had sex enough in my lifetime and none of it has been bad, but none of it has been *this*. I've never wanted to come just from watching someone else do it. I lean back, fisting myself, on the verge and in desperate need of release. I look for my tank top in the dark so I have something to come into. But Terra, still panting from her orgasm slips off the bed and onto her knees in front of me. She grabs my wrist forcing my hand away from my cock and I look down at her in confusion. "Use my mouth instead," she whispers and her tongue slides out and licks my tip.

And then she takes the rest of me into her hot, wet mouth. I come with only the third slide of her mouth down my shaft. It takes every ounce of my willpower not to grunt—roar—in pleasure. As I stand there shuddering she raises to her feet, smiling proudly. "I liked that."

"Clearly so did I," I smile and pull her naked body against mine, holding her to me in the moonlight.

"Jacob?"

At first I think it's her who just said my name. But Terra has never called me that. No one does. I won't allow it.

"Jacob!" And then I realize with horror it's coming from outside.

"What the hell?" I whisper and let Terra go. I walk over to the window in a daze of confusion made worse by the fuzz of my orgasm. Who the hell is yelling that name outside the Hawkins' house after midnight?

Terra darts to the bed and gets dressed quickly. She throws me my clothes but I'm not expecting them and they hit my elbow and fall to the ground while I look out the window.

My mother is standing in the Hawkins's driveway.

"JACOB! ARE YOU OKAY? JACOB GRADY!"

"Get dressed! Whoever is yelling is going to wake up my parents!" Terra hisses and she walks up behind me and glances out the window. "Who is that?"

"Kelsey," I reply flatly and bend to grab my clothes. But I don't get them on before the door to my bedroom swings open and someone flips the light switch on the wall.

Charlie Hawkins gets a full, unobstructed view of my bare ass. Our eyes connect and he immediately looks away right at his daughter standing right next to me but thankfully now fully clothed.

"Dad!" Terra squeaks and jumps to stand between her dad's eyeballs and my ass. Sweet girl, protecting my honor.

He shuts the door with a loud thud and through it he calls. "Your mom is outside, Jake. Can you come handle it or do you want me to?"

"I'm on my way! Thank you!" I call back. I turn and look at Terra, while I yank my pants all the way up. "I just need to die first."

"It's not the end of the world," Terra says as she follows me to the bedroom door, down the hall and down the stairs. "We're adults and we were going to tell them eventually anyway. And better that Dad walked in than my mom who would be driving directly to church right now."

When we reach the front hall, Lucy is standing in the open front door in her housecoat. "Kelsey, if you do not stop yelling, someone is going to call the police. Plain and simple."

"I want to see my baby boy! I heard he was in the hospital," Kelsey replies, not quite yelling but still way too loud for sleepy Ocean Pines after midnight. "I need to know he's okay."

Everything inside of me turns to lead. I know this feeling all too well but I haven't experienced it in almost fifteen years and I would have given more than a kidney to avoid feeling it ever again. But here we are.

Terra puts a hand on my back just under my shoulder blade as I walk up behind Lucy. Charlie is on the porch to the side. His arms are crossed and he looks infuriated but he isn't saying a word, just scowling at my mom. Kelsey is on the driveway. She's in a pair of gray sweatpants which are stained and saggy like they're two sizes too big. On top she's got on a pale pink sweatshirt with an airbrushed kitten and tulips on it and a ratty beige cardigan over that. There is a lit cigarette dangling from her left hand.

"I'll handle this Lucy," I say and she glances up at me, her brown eyes full of concern. I give her a reassuring smile. "It's okay. Go back to sleep. I promise she won't wake the neighbors."

Lucy gives me a small nod and turns to Charlie. "Let's go, honey."

Charlie hesitates. His eyes laser-focused on Kelsey. Kelsey doesn't notice because she's spotted me as I step out onto the porch. If her eyes could light up they would, but there hasn't been light in Kelsey Grady's eyes for probably two decades now. Maybe there never was. Charlie finally backs up and retreats from the porch, joining his wife inside. "I'll be in the kitchen until I know this is settled."

I nod.

"Jacob baby? Oh my gosh, it's so good to see you." My mother gushes.

"Terra go with him, please," I ask and she shakes her head.

"I have training in dealing with people with substance abuse and mental health issues," she whispers to me.

I give her a wry smile. "And I have training in dealing with Kelsey. Besides, you'll just agitate her. You know how she feels."

Terra frowns but steps inside with her dad. I close the front door and turn back to my mom. She's left the driveway now and is stumbling across their front lawn. Luckily, it's fall so she doesn't crush the flowers that usually line the path from the driveway to the front door. I walk off the porch to meet her halfway. "Hi Kel … Mom."

"Jacob, what's this I hear that you had an operation?" Kelsey asks and reaches out with her right hand, the one not holding the smoke, and touches my abdomen. I step back, she tries to cling to my tank top but doesn't have a good enough grip, thankfully. "Why do I need to hear this from other people?"

"I didn't want to bother you," I lie and try to give her a smile. There's a faint odor wafting off of her. Stale cigarette smoke, maybe a sweet booze and definitely a lack of deodorant.

" Still at the park on Cascade," she says. "The third trailer on the left from the gate. You can come by anytime."

I nod. "Okay. I'm back now, so we have tons of time to catch up. Don't need to do it in the middle of the night in the Hawkins' driveway."

"Back from the hospital?" she asks. Oh, right. Apparently whoever told her I had been in the hospital didn't tell her I moved away for almost three years. Or she forgot. I sigh and she notices. "Are you in pain? What happened to you?"

"I'm good. I just…" Lie or the truth? Lie would be easier but I'm not big on lies. "I donated a kidney to someone who needed it."

Her face contorts, making all the deep lines and wrinkles even deeper. Life has not been kind to Kelsey. My mother was a beauty at one point before I was born. Her hair was jet black, glossy, and wavy. Her eyes, a caramel color, were wide-set and fringed with naturally thick lashes. Her nose petite and straight. Her smile bright and bold. I still have her high school year book photo somewhere in a drawer at my place. It used to be framed on her dresser when we lived together when I was a kid. I took it the first time they hauled me out of her custody and into foster care when I was nine. I never gave it back, and if she noticed, she never said anything. Now she looks at me, the lustrous hair thinning and gray before its time, her lashes sparse, her eyes bloodshot. "Why would you give someone a kidney?"

"Because I care about them and they needed one."

She doesn't understand that at all, and it's so apparent on her face that I almost smirk. How in the world does this woman not understand the concept? She takes a long, deep pull on that cigarette of hers and slowly lets out the smoke as she tries to understand an act of kindness like she's figuring out Pythagorean theorem. "But you need 'em."

"I need one. I had two," I explain. "Anyway, I am perfectly fine. Doing great. Going back to work soon."

She frowns. "But why are you living here with these lobster people if you're fine?"

I used to get annoyed about how she always called the Hawkins family "lobster people" until I told Finn and he'd laughed and said, "It makes us sound like we are literally people sized lobsters waddling around." If he can make light of her ire, so can I.

"They're taking care of me."

"You should have come and stayed with me," Kelsey suggests as she also blows cigarette smoke out of her mouth and into my face. "I would have kicked my roommate off the couch he rents from me and given it to you. He ain't pulling his weight anymore anyway."

That's Kelsey Grady code for the junkie she is letting crash at her place isn't sharing his drugs anymore.

"Who did ya give the liver to?" she wants to know.

"Kidney," I correct. "A friend."

She scowls. I have a nauseating moment of panic because if she gets angry instead of placated then she will wake up the whole block screaming and carrying on. I don't want to get her angry. I have to diffuse this.

"Who did you give it to, Jacob?" Her words are slow and clipped, like there's a period in between each one.

I swallow. "Terra."

Her face turns more sour than milk a month after its expiry date. "Of course. I knew it'd be one of the lobster people or that rich bitch you date."

"I haven't dated Aspen in years, Mother, and if you call her that or insult the Hawkins again tonight, I will call the police on you myself," I warn, my voice even and calm but dead fucking serious. "I'm tired. It's late, and if you want to discuss this more I can swing by your place later this week."

"Okay fine. I'm sorry." Wow. I wasn't expecting that. And she almost looks like she means it. She sucks on the cigarette again. "I'd like it if you come by."

"Okay. I will. In a couple of days," I promise. I'm not looking forward to it, but I'll do it.

She nods and smiles. Her teeth are yellow and she's missing her left eye tooth. That's new… and horrifying. And a sign her battles with meth might be back. She was relatively clean when I left for King's Rock. She was off the hard stuff thanks to a court ordered detox and was sticking to weed and booze. "Must have been pretty painful. Your operation."

"It wasn't bad," I say and walk her toward the curb because I don't want to continue this. "Do you have a ride home? Can I call Uber Jay for you or I can drive you back myself?"

She tips her head back and to the side. My gaze follows, and I see an ancient hatchback parked across the street that used to be white before but is now mostly rust.

"My friend Clarence let me borrow his ride."

"And you're okay to drive?" I have to ask even though I know she is going to get pissed off.

She stops walking and frowns. "You always have to play the saint. Nothing ever changes. I'm fine, Jacob. I may not be all high and mighty like that family you're obsessed with, but I'm able to drive a fucking car. I haven't had a drink."

"Okay."

"What about you?" she asks and her expression changes to curious from annoyed, but it's off. Like too curious. Eager. "They must have you on some strong painkillers. I bet taking out an organ hurts a lot."

Oh. Now I know why she's actually here. I feel disappointment. Of course she wasn't concerned about me. I should have known. I put my hand on her bony shoulders and walk her across the street to the car. "Not really. I was on some stuff at the hospital but now it's just ibuprofen."

"What?" She looks devastated. "I thought for sure they'd send you home with some Oxy or something."

"Nope."

"What about the lobster girl?" Kelsey asks. "She must have some good stuff. She's tiny and sick with that other thing … leprosy?"

"Lupus," I correct but I don't know why I'm bothering. "Mom, it's late. Time to go. I'll visit you soon."

"If she doesn't finish her prescription maybe you can bring me some?" she asks. "I got an awful pain in my back that just won't go away." All of a sudden she's clutching her lower back and hunching over.

"You should see a doctor about that, Mom. The free clinic on Tunis will take you without coverage."

"They don't believe me. Incompetent assholes," she scowls and gives me her version of puppy dog eyes. "But if your friend has some Oxy she won't even miss a couple tablets. And her doctor would give her more anyway. You want to help your mama don't you, Jacob?"

Her favorite line. She used to say that to me to coax me to steal her cigarettes when I was young. I was good at it too but on the off occasion I got caught, they didn't always call the cops. Sometimes they just chastised me and called my mother who promised to punished me, and she did. For getting caught.

"You know there's a program over in Old Orchard Beach. An outpatient thing you can go to and it won't cost a cent," I tell her, my tone calm, firm, and quiet.

"You and your fucking programs. I'm not allowed to wanna fix an ache or pain without being called an addict," she sneers and flicks the end of her lit cigarette onto the lawn of the house next door.

"Mom, it's been a dry fall. That's a fire hazard," I walk over and pick it up then grind it out on the sidewalk.

"You know what, Jacob Maverick Grady? You aren't fooling those people," she says way too loudly and points to the Hawkins's house. "They are doing what they've always done. Using you. Just like that rich bitch girlfriend you used to have. She used you to upset her high and mighty parents, and these ones are using you for body parts. They'll turn on you first chance they get. You're just like me, kiddo. Not good enough and no one really wants you."

She swings open the door to the shitty, little hatchback and slams it shut. A light comes on in the house across from the Hawkins. I cringe as Kelsey squeals the tires and takes off down the street.

"What the heck is going on out there?" Mr. Pattison calls from his bedroom window across the street.

"Sorry sir. It's taken care of," I call back. "Sorry!"

When I get back into the house, the light is on in the kitchen. Lucy and Terra are sitting at the round oak table. Charlie is by the stove, arms crossed over his plaid pajama top. Terra jumps to her feet as I enter.

"I'm so sorry," I say and try to not let them see the humiliation that is consuming me right now. Terra hugs me but I don't hug her back. I give her back a little pat and step away.

"She's a mom," Lucy says softly and gives me that smile I used to see all the time when I was a kid. It's kind—too kind. She doesn't know it, but it makes me feel worse. "She was worried about you."

"She wanted me to give her any painkillers they'd given me," I reply flatly and Lucy's smile drops like a lead balloon.

"Jake, I'm so sorry."

I nod at Terra, but don't make eye contact. I just want to go bed. "I hope you guys can fall asleep again. I'm really sorry, but don't worry. She won't be back."

Charlie nods. "You got nothing to apologize for."

Lucy stands and smiles up at me. She reaches out and rubs my arm. "Terra here was just telling us that you're her boyfriend."

I turn my gaze to Terra who smiles. "It felt like it was time."

I look up at Charlie who looks away, but he's not scowling so he's not mad just embarrassed. Welcome to my world, Charlie. I focus back on Lucy. "Yes. Sorry we didn't tell you sooner."

"Good news is good news even when it's delayed," Lucy says her eyes crinkling with her broad smile. "I couldn't be happier, Jake. For both of you."

"I couldn't be happier either," I say and Terra takes my hand in hers.

"Let's go back to bed," Charlie says. "Lucy, is Deck's bed made?"

"Always," Lucy furrows her dirty blond eyebrows. "Never know when one of the kids might come home. I like to be ready."

As we make our way to the stairs Charlie clamps a hand on my shoulder. "Jake's gonna sleep up there."

Right. He caught us. How is that not the most humiliating thing to happen to me tonight? Terra opens her mouth to argue, but I cut her off. "Sounds like a good idea. Thanks Charlie."

I leave the Hawkins family on the landing of the second floor and climb the narrow attic stairs to Declan's room. As I crawl into bed and close my eyes, I try not to think about what my mother said. And I try even harder not to believe it.

20

JAKE

I SLIP INTO MY JACKET AND START TO BUTTON IT UP. NOVA whistles from behind the counter like she's a construction worker and I'm a cute girl. Finn laughs. Terra nods. "Yep."

"Can we not?" Declan says, annoyed. "There's customers."

"He does look dapper," Mr. Hobbs pipes up from his usual spot at the counter. "Lilah always loved a man in uniform. I wore my army uniform when I proposed to her as an insurance policy."

I smile at that. Terra and Nova laugh. He grins and goes back to his bowl of chowder. I tug on the arms of my jacket. I don't like our formal dress uniforms, but Cap said I should wear it to the interview. They called yesterday and told me it was today. I'd already had them push it once because my original date was the day after surgery. I glance at the clock above the counter. I have forty minutes to get there, which is more than enough time.

Everyone else who has applied for the captain's position has had their interview, including Ronan Green. He made a point of telling me how well it went when some of the crew came to visit me at Charlie and Lucy's. At the time, I refused to think about it because I wanted to concentrate on getting better so I could have my own interview. And that day is finally here.

227

"You'll knock it outta the park, Mav," Finn tells me with a confident grin. "Make sure to mention the medal."

"They know about the medal," I say.

"You sure you don't want to wear it?" Nova says. "Don't Army people wear all of them when they attend big events?"

"It's not the Army and I just … would feel like a douche," I confess.

Terra walks around the counter and takes my hand. "You don't need to show off your accomplishments. You're great and they will see it."

I smile at her. "Here's hoping you're right."

"Don't kiss. Do not kiss!" Finn warns and covers his face with his hands. "I'm not ready yet."

"Oh my God, grow up," Nova laughs. "How you did not see this coming, is beyond me. It was written in the stars long ago."

"My wife, the unbreakable romantic," Declan rolls his eyes and heads back into the kitchen. His parting words. "Kiss my sister if you want, but just get going. You're distracting everyone, and they have work to do."

Every single member of his family rolls their eyes in unison. Everyone knows we're dating now. The night after we told Charlie and Lucy, we told Declan and Nova. She squealed with delight and Declan being Declan just nodded. The twins kind of already knew, so we never had an official conversation with them. Logan texted me once and simply said: *do not fuck this up*. Finn had yet to react at all. Until now.

Terra rocks up on her tip toes and kisses my cheek. "Good luck." Then she pulls a perfect, soft gray sand dollar out of the kangaroo pocket on her hoodie and holds it up before slipping it into my left pocket. "My lucky sand dollar will help you nail this."

"You have a lucky sand dollar?" I ask with a confused smile.

She grins. "Who doesn't?"

"Thanks," I reply laughing and then grow serious. "And if you're still working when I get back from this, I'll be pissed. The doctor didn't say you could go back yet. And you can't be mingling in giant crowds yet. Risk of infection."

"Are you Doctor Leclerc or my boyfriend? Pick a lane, Jake," Terra teases but then uses her index finger to make a cross over her heart as she promises. "I'll be hiding alone in my office just fixing the payroll Finn screwed up, I swear. When the lunch rush is over, and the restaurant is dead, I might grab some lunch but that's it. I know the rules."

"Good, Tink," I kiss the top of her head.

Mr. Hobbs finishes his soup and slowly rises off his stool. He shrugs into his raincoat, leaves a ten on the counter, and picks up the flowers wrapped in plain brown paper beside him. "You want a lift, Mr. Hobbs? I have to drive right by Resting Pines."

He looks up at me. "That would be lovely, what with the weather as it is."

I glance outside. It's throwing down rain that is on the verge of being ice. It's official, winter is knocking on the door, trying to get in. I escort Mr. Hobbs out of the restaurant and make sure my umbrella is also covering him as we make out way to my Jeep. He gets in without much struggle, despite it being high and usually difficult for older people.

I wait until he's got the flowers on his lap and his seatbelt fastened and then I drive out of the lot. "I wish I could stay and drive you home too."

"I already have a reservation with Uber Jay," Mr. Hobbs explains. "He lets me call him from my landline and reserve ahead of time. Lilah was his favorite teacher in high school, so I get special treatment. Even after she's gone, that woman somehow still finds a way to look out for me."

I smile at that but also ache a little because you can feel how much he misses his wife like it's a fog that permeates the air around him. I know that feeling. I would have felt that way if something happened to Terra.

"What medal was everyone talking about at the Shack?" he asks.

"I was awarded the medal of valor when I was positioned at a different fire station," I explain. "I rescued an infant from a fire. I was just doing my job."

"Well, there must have been a little more to it, son."

I shrug and turn the windshield wipers up higher. The rain is getting harder. "I happened to be driving home and saw smoke pouring out of the windows of this house. I called my station and found a garden hose to try and slow it, because I'm not supposed to go inside without gear or backup. A woman came stumbling out of the house. She was high on drugs and she was too out of it to tell me there was a baby inside. But as she dropped onto the front on the lawn coughing, I noticed a pacifier fall out of the pocket of her bathrobe so I ran inside and found her infant daughter on some cushions on the floor in the bedroom. My co-workers had arrived by the time I got back out, thankfully, and they could save the infant who had some serious smoke inhalation."

I hate remembering that whole night. I am very well aware that could have been me when I was a kid. I like to remember the stuff after that night and the medal ceremony. "Just before I left that station to come back here, the mother showed up at my work. She was clean and working and taking online classes for an accounting diploma. She was allowed visitation with her daughter, who was also doing well and living with her grandparents. That meant more to me than the medal."

"I understand that," Mr. Hobbs nods and smiles at me. "You know what you did for little Terra Hawkins should get a medal too. But I suppose you're going to say seeing her healthy is enough."

"Yup."

I pull up to the gates of Resting Pines. "Do you want me to drive you in?"

He shakes his head and unclips his seatbelt. "No, thank you. My Lilah is just beyond that first pine."

I hand him my umbrella and after a moment's hesitation he takes it, a grateful smile crinkling the corners of his eyes. "Can I give you some unsolicited advice?"

"Sure," I reply easily, thinking he's going to give me a tip for my interview.

"Wear the medal when you propose to your girl," he says and chuckles to himself. "And the uniform. Judging by the look on Terra's face every time she sees you, you probably won't need it, but it certainly won't hurt."

"Mr. Hobbs, we just started dating," I laugh.

"Uh-huh," He nods. "But you'll need the advice down the road. I'm certain of it. And I wanted to give it to you now, in case I'm with Lilah by then."

He gets out of my Jeep, shuts the door and pops open my umbrella. I sit there and watch him until he disappears out of view just behind the big pine he pointed to earlier.

I would stay even longer. I'm kind of shell shocked by that candid advice, but I have no choice but to shake it off because I have to get to this interview. So, reluctantly, I back away from the gates of the cemetery and drive off.

My interview is in thirty minutes and I'm only ten minutes away, so I'm mentally prepping myself as I maneuver through traffic on Route One. And then my cellphone goes off. I decide to let it go to voicemail, but it rings again immediately. I take a second to look at the screen. There's no name shown there, so it's not a number I have stored in my phone. I ignore it and it rings again. I hit the speaker button.

"Hello?"

"Jake, this is Abbott."

"Oh. Hey." What the hell does Abbott Barlowe want?

"Aspen is bleeding," he says. His tone tight and hard and vibrating with stress. "She is driving herself to Casco Bay Memorial as we speak, and I can't get there. I'm in Colorado on a fucking road trip."

"What? What happened to her?" I hit the brake gently but the car still shudders and swerves a bit because there are puddles as big as ponds on the road right now. I clutch the wheel tighter.

"Something is wrong with the baby," Abbott barks back. "Possibly *your* baby, so she says, but she told me not to call you. She said she would disown me if I did, but she's terrified and alone."

"I..." *have an interview my career depends on.* "I'll head there now."

"Keep me updated," he barks and hangs up.

I move to the left-hand lane and do a U-turn at the next intersection and let out a loud "FUCK."

21

TERRA

"I am not kidding," Nova says wagging a finger in my face. "Sit."

Mom and even Finn are standing behind her with equally stern looks on their faces. I roll my eyes but I know they aren't kidding around. Doc said no work for another two weeks, so I have to listen. Still, I stick out my tongue at them while I walk around the counter and sit down.

"Take advantage of the fact you get to be served for once," Patti Gordon says with a smile. She's sitting next to me at the counter waiting for her take-out order and enjoying a cup of herbal tea while she waits.

We have a deal with Patti; she supplies the ice cream for our milkshakes at a discount if we give her three free lobster roll combo plates a week. She then brings those back to Patti's Parlor and treats her staff to a free lunch. Patti herself is vegan, so we throw in a roll made with just our garlic aioli, lettuce, tomatoes and cucumbers just for her.

"It feels weird," I explain. "I've been serving customers since I was twelve. I love it."

"I know. Me too," Patti replies and lifts the cup of tea to her

233

mouth, the bracelets on her arm jangling loudly. She is a skinny-to-the-point-of-rail-thin hippie who covers herself in a boat load of jewelry. Today she has on four necklaces, all of various lengths and all made of different colored beads. Her wrists on both arms are covered in wire-thin gold, silver, and copper bangles. About forty on each arm. Her ears have three sets of studs and one pair of long dangling feather earrings. "I would be devastated if I couldn't work at my little shop anymore, but remember Terra, this is not permanent. Once your body aligns itself with the energy coming off Jake's kidney, you'll be stronger than ever and will work until you're a hundred. I can feel it. You know my feelings are never wrong."

I smile at her and nod. Patti is also the self-proclaimed psychic of the town and if you ask her just right and bring twenty bucks, she'll read your palm in the back booth at the ice cream parlor. I've never had it done but Nova has. She never did tell me the results.

"Can I take your order, ma'am?" Finn says, leaning on the counter in front of me, pen and paper poised in front of him. He never uses a pen and paper. He's being dramatic.

"Yeah, first of all, I'd like a fried clam roll, no lettuce, with extra garlic aioli and the bun toasted but only on one side,"

His big blue eyes narrow on me in a glare. Finn hates special orders. He's been campaigning for us to put 'no substitutes' on the menus for ages.

"Oh actually, on second thought, I want to make out with my boyfriend later when he comes in here and tells me he aced his promotion interview. I mean really make out with him, tongue and all so..." I pretend to study the menu written on chalk on the wall above the counter as Finn makes gagging sounds at the idea of me making out with Jake, and Patti chuckles. Nova walks over and takes the pen and paper from Finn, hip checking him out of the way. He grabs onto her to keep from tipping over and hitting the floor but lets go like he's been burned as soon as he steadies himself. He is always so weird with Nova. I guess because she's married to Declan? I have no idea.

"How about the usual? No worries about make-out sessions after a lobster grilled cheese," Nova says. "No garlic to worry about."

"Especially if you wash it down with one of those peanut butter chocolate shakes your boyfriend loves so much," Patti adds. "I swear he's the main reason that flavor is our top seller."

I smile because that's the first time someone has publicly called Jake my boyfriend. Someone other than family. It feels like a compliment. Better than one. I smile at her. "A PB and C shake too, please."

Nova nods and walks over to the computer screen on the wall to enter the order in our system. It will pop up on a screen in the kitchen and Javi will get to work on my grilled cheese while Nova makes my shake. My mom is clearing one of the tables when the door opens and Logan walks in. He's got a grim look on his face but that's nothing new.

"Logan, honey. Is something wrong?" Ma asks hesitantly as she stops walking toward the kitchen, a tray of dirty dishes in her hand.

Logan walks over and takes the tray from her hands, and that's when my stomach twists into a knot. He turns and looks at everyone as his mouth opens to speak, and then his eyes land on me and that knot turns to lead. "Has anyone heard from Jake?"

"Not since he left for his interview," I say and my voice is shaking. "What's wrong?"

"Captain called me to ask where he was," Logan says. "Because he never showed up at the interview. And I tried calling him but he didn't answer his phone and so…"

I yank my phone out of my back pocket and start dialing. It goes directly to voicemail. I text. *Jake. Call me. ASAP.*

I look up as Logan walks over to place the tray he took from Ma on the counter. Ma has dropped into a chair at an empty table and is clutching the cross at her neck, her eyes shut tight. Patti reaches over and pats my hand. "He's fine. I know it."

I wish I believed in her "powers" right now.

"Maybe he has a flat tire?" Finn says. "And you know how bad he's always been at paying attention to his phone. It's probably in the Jeep and he can't hear it because he's outside changing the tire."

Or he's dead in a ditch from a car wreck. Or he's got some problem with his recovery from the operation and he's passed out in pain somewhere. "Has anyone checked hospitals? Called the police?"

Before Logan can respond, the door swings open again. This time the bells are announcing Ronan and Nellie Green. Roman is dressed in his formal fireman's suit, just like Jake was when he left. He takes one look at Logan, who is in his work clothes and instantly says, "Are you on a call? Is someone hurt? How can I help?"

It's good to know that his firefighter training supersedes his nature to be an asshole. Logan shakes his head at Ronan and turns to me. "Let's continue this discussion in the back."

As I start walking to the back, Ronan speaks again. "Seriously, Hawkins. I know I am off-duty right now but if you need something…"

"We don't," I reply, my voice too clipped to be anything but rude.

"Well, this is some greeting," Mrs. Green huffs. "Ronan, perhaps we should go to Stan's Seafood for lunch. He will be pleasant to us and I so want to celebrate your second interview going so well."

"The food is better here and you know it, Ma," Ronan replies as Logan and I start walking toward the swinging door that leads to the kitchen. I'm kind of impressed he's willing to admit that since he's never seemed to like us much.

"You had a second interview for the captain's job? Already?" Logan asks, his thick eyebrows pinching.

"Yeah. Me and all the other candidates," Ronan explains. "Surprised they're even still bothering with Maverick, to be honest. Must be a formality."

Nellie Green keeps shuffling into the restaurant. Ma, worry creasing her face, does the unthinkable. "Ronan, have you seen Jake today?"

"He had his interview about an hour after me, so he should be in Portland or on his way back," Ronan explains.

Ma clutches her cross again. Ronan's green eyes bounce around and absorb everyone's faces. "What's happened?"

"Nothing you have to worry about," Logan replies, his tone hard and borderline mean.

My phone buzzes in my hand and I actually jump. "It's Jake."

Nova, Logan, and Finn gather around me as I pull up the message. *I'm fine. On my way to the Shack now. I'll explain everything.*

"Is he insane?" Finn asks.

"Thank God he's not injured," Nova says.

"Is he feeling sick? Was this too much too soon after the surgery?" Ma asks. "Is that why he missed the interview?"

"Maverick skipped his interview?" Ronan exclaims and the douchebag is actually smiling.

"If you're here to eat food, then grab a booth and order some," Logan growls. "Otherwise, door is over there."

Mrs. Green gasps. Ma gives Logan a withering stare. "Logan, customers are customers. And you don't work here anymore."

"I'm sure he has a good reason," I tell Ronan because that smirk on his face, like he's going to benefit from this, is making my blood boil. Even though he probably will. "Maybe he came across an accident on the turnpike and stopped to help. Jake is that kind of guy. I'm literally living proof of that." I smile.

Ronan's smirk grows darker – meaner. "Terra, honey, Jake causes accidents nowadays he doesn't fix them. Or didn't you hear?"

"What does that mean?"

"Tell her what you know, mom."

Mrs. Green nods at Ronan but then walks a few feet over to one of our booths by the window overlooking the sea, and I find myself following her. She shrugs out of her coat, a God awful orange and green patterned thing.

She looks at me with wide innocent eyes. Too innocent. "Oh Terra sweetheart, Ronan was just trying to be funny with a cute play on words. You know because of the accidental pregnancy Jake's responsible for."

Accidental what?

"Terra?" Ma gasps my name.

"Holy shit did he knock you up?" Finn blurts out, his voice loud and filled with fury.

"No! My God, of course not," I say and blush as heat rushes my face. "Mrs. Green doesn't know what she's talking about."

"I don't mean you. I mean Aspen," Mrs. Green says calmly. "I was at the hospital visiting a neighbor. Do you all remember Mrs. Turner? Well when she died, she left her house across the street from mine to her grandson but he died, and now his widow, a cute little girl from Hawaii of all places, is in there by herself fixing it up and anyway, she's all by herself and—"

"Can you get to the point, Mom?" Ronan interrupts and Mrs. Green frowns.

"She had surgery and there's no one in town to visit her so I was visiting her, and I saw Aspen and Jake coming out of the obstetrics department together, a couple days after your surgeries actually. You were both still patients I think," she pauses to put her purse down in the booth. "And then the other day, when I was visiting my neighbor again, Aspen was walking across the parking lot alone and there was no denying the bump. It's the cutest thing, so I stopped to tell her and pat it. She didn't say Jake was the father. Was actually quite rude to me, but what else is new?"

"Aspen is not carrying Jake's baby," I let out a sharp, high-pitched laugh. I realize I have never made a sound like that before but no one has ever said something so completely ludicrous to me before. "There's no way."

"Why do you care?" Ronan asks, annoyed for some reason, like this has anything to do with him.

"Because he's my boyfriend."

Ronan blinks. "What? Since when? Anyway Aspen's baby has to be his."

"It isn't," I bark, fully aware I sound like River on the verge of a meltdown.

"Logan…" Finn says his twin's name slowly, in a low voice.

It draws all our attentions because it's ominous-sounding and as soon as I lock eyes with Logan, my heart starts to break. A fissure … like a windshield when a rock nails it just so. "Logan?"

"Terra, can I talk to you in the back. Alone?"

"Oh my God…" Ma never ever takes the lord's name in vain. That is proof that this is as real and devastating as it feels.

Without a word, I walk slowly toward Logan because I feel unsteady and tears are blurring my vision. He's holding open the door to the kitchen. I walk straight through it and into my office. I shut the door and continue walking to my desk. Finn and Declan have been in here more than me lately, so it's a disaster. Invoices and unopened mail are piled on one corner. My framed pictures that were evenly spaced on the other corner of the desk are jumbled together. One is even tipped over. I don't care. I don't care about anything.

Logan slips inside, closing the door firmly behind him. I can't look at him. I can't. "It's true?"

"Not necessarily," Logan replies. "I mean yes, she is pregnant and yes it might be Jake's but last time I checked, he didn't know. She wouldn't do the paternity test."

The tears spill down my cheeks. Logan walks toward me. I raise a hand, palm out, and finally look at him. "Don't. You should have told me."

"He should have told you," Logan corrects. "Terra, you know this wasn't my secret to tell, and I told him not to get involved with you without telling you."

"I can't … I can't believe this is happening," I sob. I feel betrayed. I know he didn't cheat. I know, without anyone explaining it to me, this baby is from that random hook up months ago, but I still feel deceived.

"Terra, look, he should have told you, but if it isn't his," Logan pauses and scrubs his face with his hand and then leans against the door. "He didn't want to blow things up with you if there wasn't a reason, you know?"

"How long have you known he might have … Aspen might be having his baby?" I ask. "Since that night you brought Chewie over and lectured me on the ride home?"

He nods. "I couldn't tell you. You know it."

"He lied to me," I whisper and Logan immediately shakes his head.

"He didn't lie. He just excluded this information, because it would do nothing but hurt you," Logan argues back firmly. "Terra, how Jake handled this, keeping it quiet, isn't any different from how the family handled my problems. No different from what I did to him. What we all did."

"I can't be here. I want to go home."

"Mom and Dad's?"

"My place. My kidney is fine. It's my heart that's sick now, and Mom and Dad can't help heal that," I reply and wipe at a tear that wants to fall. I'm not sad. I'm more frustrated and humiliated and just a whole bunch of emotions I need to sort out. "Can you drive me?"

"I have the ambulance and Lester waiting in the parking lot. It's against procedure," Logan explains, but he must see the desperation on my face because he nods. "Okay. Just this once."

I walk toward the door and he opens it and follows me out. We leave through the back door and as soon as we reach the parking lot, a car is pulling into the lot. Tom's Range Rover. Oh my God, this day can bite me. He pulls up right beside us, rolls down the passenger window, and smiles. "Hey you! So great to see you up and around. I called your mom and dad's place a few times to check on you. Did they tell you?"

"Hawkins! We got a call!" Logan's partner hollers with his head out the window as he starts the ambulance.

Logan's eyes grow wide and fill with regret. "I'm sorry, Ter."

"Don't worry about it. Go! Be safe," I say and turn back to Tom. "Can you give me a ride home? I don't have my car."

"Of course, T," he unlocks his doors and I climb in.

As we're driving away from the restaurant, Jake's Jeep passes us. I turn and look the other way, but I'm sure he sees me.

22

TERRA

"Hey wasn't that your donor guy?" Tom says and starts to hit the brakes.

"Do not stop driving. Please," I beg and wipe another tear away. Tom's whole face twists with confusion but he nods and does what I ask, thankfully.

Tom asks me a bunch of inane questions as we drive about my operation and my recovery, and I answer them like a robot. My eyes never leave the familiar scenery blurring by outside the passenger window. When he finally pulls into the parking lot of my building, I unbuckle my seatbelt and reach for the handle. "Thank you."

"Wait! That's it?" Tom asks, baffled. "Can I at least help you up the stairs? Maybe come in and talk?"

"Honestly, Tom, I don't want to hear anything you have to say." How he seems startled by this is beyond me. "You weren't there for me when I needed you."

Tom's dirty blond eyebrows knit and his mouth tips downward in a frown. "Terra, I couldn't give you a kidney but I paid your bills. Doesn't that earn me a second chance? I still care. I always cared."

"Not enough," I reply and run my hands into my hair. I close my eyes.

"Tom, you never had to give me a kidney, you just had to make me feel like I wasn't a burden. But you couldn't do that and honestly, I shouldn't have been settling for just that anyway."

"Lupus is a hard disease to wrap your head around if you don't have it," Tom argues back defensively. "You seemed so normal, and then boom. Suddenly, you weren't."

"I was never normal," I reply and sigh. "But I deserved someone who could grasp that and who never made me feel like you did. I was settling with you, and I'm not doing it again."

"Really? So that's it?" Tom looks genuinely hurt, and I feel a flutter of guilt but I know it's misplaced. "You can't cut me any slack? Your deductible was almost eight thousand bucks, Terra. You'd rather be alone than with a guy who helps you out with that?"

"I'm not alone," I reply and swing open the door. "I have someone I love who I think loves me. He's just … I just…"

"Sure, now that you have a good kidney again, I'm sure it's easy for a guy to date you now," Tom snaps. "We never would have had problems if you hadn't gotten sick."

"I was always sick, you fucking twat waffle," I hiss, finally done with any crumb of civility I was holding onto. "Bye, Tom. Don't ever contact me again."

I jump out and walk away, never looking back.

23

JAKE

I WATCH HIM WALK RIGHT BY ME FOR THE FOURTH TIME TONIGHT without even acknowledging my existence. Keribo and Murphy, who had gone on a Dunkin' run with him, both greet me as they walk by. Logan, nothing. I'm not the adult I thought I was. This hurts exactly like I thought it would when I was seventeen and scared I'd lose him if I went for their sister. The difference is now I'm angry.

I understand why Lucy looked at me with disappointment yesterday when I walked into the Shack. I know why she wouldn't talk to me and just shook her head. I understand why Finn told me, "Just fuck off for a minute. I'm kinda pissed at you." I know why Declan asked me to leave and Nova didn't stop him. Terra was publicly humiliated because I didn't tell her the truth. But Logan knows why. He knows what a spot I was in. He understands how I was trying to respect Aspen's privacy and wishes, how I'd planned on telling Terra as soon as I found out if it was mine. He fucking knew.

And he didn't stand up for me? And he's shunning me?

The three of them are halfway up the stairs that lead to the private quarters when I stand up and turn to face him. "You know what Hawkins? Fuck you."

All three of my co-workers, including Logan, freeze and slowly turn back to face me. I may not be the future captain of this place, but I am a lieutenant, and that is not how I should be talking to any of them. But that broken, little, teenage boy I've put on a shelf like an artifact in a museum is back in action, and I can't seem to help it.

"You two should talk this out," Murphy says. She's always been one hell of a smart woman and tells it like it is. If I'd been promoted, I would have recommended her for my lieutenant's position. "I don't know exactly what the issue is, but the man just gave your sister an organ, so I'm Team Jake."

She grabs Keribo by his arm and drags him away, leaving Logan standing alone on the stairs. "You're really pissed at me?"

"Yeah I am," I say, my body tense with rage. "You knew my plan. You know the position I've been in. And you just let everyone throw me away like I planned this? Like I wanted her to find out this way?"

"That's not why I'm not talking to you, Maverick," Logan replies calmly. "I'm pissed off at you because it's been twenty-four hours since Terra found out and you haven't talked to her. At all."

"Because she took off with Tom," I reply and just saying his name makes acid churn in my gut. "She doesn't want an explanation or she would have stayed to hear me out."

"Of course she fucking does," Logan barks back at me as he storms down the stairs to the counter I'm stuck at for another two weeks of shifts. "She's Terra. Stubborn as a mule. Completely able to carry the weight of the heaviest emotional baggage in the world unless it's her own. Then she cowers and turtles and lets it crush her to smithereens."

He's right. I know this. I've watched her do it time and time again with everything from her lupus diagnosis to the way she cut me off entirely for years after that stupid closet non-kiss. "Tom wants her back."

"Tom rejected her in her time of need."

"People make mistakes. I have, obviously. If she can't forgive him, why should she forgive me?" I ask. "I mean seriously, she hates Aspen so much and she thinks that she's going to be in my life forever now, bonded by a baby."

"I heard the baby is okay. Abbott told Declan, but is it yours?" Logan asks.

"No. It's not, but I still think it would be easier to forgive Tom, if she was going to forgive either of us, and she'd get more out of forgiving him," I explain what has been rolling around in my head for the last twenty-four completely sleepless hours. I drop back into the chair behind the desk, defeated. "He's got a good education, a stable job, and he's from a great family."

"Hey asshole, you're from a great family too. Ours." Logan glares at me with more anger than I've seen on his face in a decade. And he always looks angry. "The fucking sick joke of this whole situation is you use every excuse to reject her because you don't think you're good enough for her, and all this time she has never felt like she was enough for you. God, you two are a fucking disaster."

Logan shakes his head, his brown hair rustling so he reaches up and shoves it back off his forehead. He starts for the stairs again as the door to the firehouse opens. It's almost seven-thirty in the evening. The weather outside is horrendously dark and windy, and so chilly the rain they are predicting may actually turn out to be snow. We don't usually get walk-ins after sunset, so it pulls both our attention.

Charlie Hawkins is standing there in his flannel jacket and jeans and work boots. Hands shoved in his pockets and shoulders hunched. His favorite Boston Eagles baseball cap covering his salt and pepper hair. His expression is grim. More so than normal and my heart skips a beat. "Is it Terra? Is she okay?'

"Is it Ma?" Logan panics.

Charlie shakes his head and his expression lifts just a little. "Boy, you two sure know how to go from zero to catastrophe in record time. Everyone is fine. I'm here to chat with one of my sons."

He walks right over to stand at the desk and then he says. "The unofficial one. Jake."

Logan blinks. The words leave me feeling confused, but my heart is swelling just the same. Charlie gives me a smile. "See you later Logan. Oh and your child, the one with fur, had an accident on your ma's hand woven rug. She is not impressed."

"I'll get Finn to watch him next shift. And I'll pay for cleaning," Logan says with a sheepish smile. "See you later, Dad."

He disappears up the stairs. Charlie watches silently until he is out of sight and then he turns to me. His smile from earlier is gone, but he doesn't look mad. "Look, kid. You fucked up."

"I know."

He puts both elbows on the counter and marries his hands. They're thick, wide, rough hands made up mostly of nicks, scars and callouses. Charlie Hawkins has worked hard his whole life using those hands, and he wouldn't want it any other way. "We all still love you. You need to know that. Even Lucy, who is letting her anger get the best of her right now. She still loves you. And not just for what you did for Terra with the whole donation thing. We loved you long before that, son, and we'll love you long after no matter how this plays out."

This whole conversation will be really comforting sometime in the very near future, but right now it's just surreal and I can't seem to grasp it's even happening. Charlie isn't a talker. He's a jokester on a good day, a grunter on a bad one, and a stoic observer on the average ones. This … I have never ever seen this.

Not when Logan ended up in rehab. Not when Declan tried to kill himself. Not when Terra was diagnosed with lupus. Never. He is generally the strong, silent man who gets things done. He's booked plane tickets to rehab, he'll spend seventy-two hours next to a hospital bed. He'll remortgage his life's work to get any one of his loved ones out of trouble, but he doesn't do *this*. Talk. Share feelings.

"Do you have feelings for Aspen again? Still?"

"No. She's a friend and that's it. What happened was…"

He untangles his hand and holds one up to stop me from continuing. "I don't need to know any details. I just know that I've watched Terra push you away for what feels like eons, and I've watched you let her. I recognized it because Lucy did the same thing to me back in the day."

"Really?" I almost smile. "But you two have been together forever."

"Married when she was twenty-five and I was twenty-four," Charlie says and then he grins. Big, bold and sheepish. "I would have married her right after high school if she would have just dated me."

I laugh. I know little tidbits about their life before kids but not details. "She wouldn't date you then? Why? Because you were younger?"

He chuckles. "Nah. I was way better looking than any guy in her year. Every girl in school wanted me, but Lucy always played it cool and I was too worried she'd shoot me down to take a chance and ask her out. While I was building my courage, Nellie Green asked me to the Sadie Hawkins dance and I said yes. Turns out Lucy was gonna ask me but I had no clue and then … well Nellie told everyone we were an item after that, and Lucy believed her. She also hated Nellie, even back then, so I was in the dog house. Then she ran off to college. Not something I had in my future because I knew I was taking over the family business."

I nod. He grins again. "Never stopped thinking about her, though. Every summer she came back I turned on the charm and she pretended she didn't care. It was a very long, very frustrating dance. And then she came back from school engaged."

"What?" I almost shout because I'm so shocked. I knew nothing about this. If any of the Hawkins kids know about it, they never mentioned it.

Charlie leans closer and lowers his voice. "To Stanley Dyck."

I gasp. "Stan, the owner of Stan's Seafood?"

Charlie nods. "At that time, he was a baker. He made bread and rolls and had a little shop on Seaside Avenue. Lucy worked with him. I convinced my dad to change suppliers. Buy our rolls from him because she was the one who took and delivered the orders. I knew she was miserable. I knew she was making a mistake. She knew it too, but she was willing to let me go over foolish pride and stupid hurt feelings she used like a shield. The week before her wedding, when she delivered our rolls, I asked if she wanted to see the sunset from the water. Took her out on the boat, told her flat out I was her only shot at happiness, and kissed her like I wanted to do for over half a decade."

"You dog!" I laugh.

"She called me something more spirited and slapped me across the face," Charlie recalls and winces at the memory but then the grin is back. "But the next day word got out she'd broken off the engagement, Stan had fired her immediately, and so I walked right over to her house with flowers and offered her a job and a husband. She took both."

"Oh my God, this story is amazing." I think of the wedding pictures they have framed on their mantle, the one next to the picture of Terra dressed as Tinkerbell. They got married on the fishing boat by Charlie's brother Jimmy, who is a priest. They both look positively elated in the photo.

"I have a point to rambling on with our little rocky road to true love," Charlie says quietly. "And it's that if you love her—and I know you do—don't let her go easy. That Tom kid already did. You haven't yet. And if Aspen's having your kid, we'll figure it out. The thing I know about love is that it's complicated, it's messy, but when it's true and real, it makes space."

"It's not mine," I tell him. "We found out when we were at the hospital when she had that scare. I was going to tell Terra everything yesterday but she left with Tom."

Charlie nods. He doesn't look relieved or anything, which I find interesting. He really truly believes that baby or not, his daughter loves me and will continue to do so. That gives me a sense of calm I haven't felt since I moved back if I'm honest with myself.

"If you love my daughter the way I think you do, you'll tell her. *Really* tell her. Tom or no Tom." He turns and starts back toward the door. "Tell Logan bye and you two be safe tonight. Oh and son, don't ever make me see your naked ass in my house in the same room as my daughter again. Got it?"

"Yes, sir," I feel my face heat as I watch him go. When the embarrassment subsides, my head and heart are filled with a lot of emotions, but for the first time in a while, none of them are bad.

24

TERRA

ALL I WANT IS TO MAKE IT THROUGH THE DAY WITHOUT BURSTING into tears. I thought maybe coming to my happy place, the beach, would give me a better start to the day than staying in bed until my alarm went off, staring at the ceiling while my body fills with despair like high tide climbing up the beach while I'm chained to a brick on the shore.

The sun has just crested the surf, and the weather is cold but not freezing. The rain that started last night turned to flurries, but it didn't really stick everywhere. The roads are clear but lawns and such are lightly coated. I'm wearing so many layers I don't feel cold at all as I crest the board walk and make my way over to one of the benches in the snow dusted sand. I take a moment to dust off the name plate with my mitten clad hand. *Eammon C Hawkins & Saoirse F Hawkins.*

"Hi Nana and Pa," I say softly and then sit. There's very little wind, which is a blessing, and the sun has escaped one of the multiple clouds for the moment so I close my eyes and feel its warmth on my face.

I love seeing snow on the beach. High tide, like right now, is my favorite because I love the idea of solid and liquid of the same form meeting. I have no idea why, but I've found it fascinating my entire life. I remember being five and my parents would bring us down here at the beginning of December and we'd build a snowman on the beach for Ocean Pines annual beach snowman contest. But my brothers would do all the work and I would just watch the waves as they creeped higher and higher until finally touching the snowy edges and melting it, reclaiming more and more of the beach.

"I knew when you weren't at home that you'd be here."

The voice makes me jump, and I turn expecting to see my mom or Nova but it's Aspen Barlowe. I don't even bother to waste the energy glaring at her, I simply turn away and focus on the ocean again. She doesn't take the hint and walks across the snowy sand to join me. Ironically, she's the only person I ever shared my fascination with beach snow with.

"I guess it's a good sign you feel well enough to walk down here," she says quietly after a minute.

"I guess it's a good sign you're out here stalking me and not on bed rest or still in the hospital," I reply coolly.

"Baby is fine. Normal spotting, I guess," Aspen replies. "I should really read a pregnancy book. But you, the kidney is playing nice? Adapting well?"

"I have some fatigue and my staples don't come out for another couple of days, but everything is right on track for how it's supposed to be." I tell her because I'm hoping she won't keep talking if I explain things.

"Medically sure," Aspen replies and that forces my eyes off the ocean and to her pink-cheeked face. "But we both know not *everything* is how it's supposed to be."

"Because my almost-boyfriend knocked you up?"

Aspen's blue eyes lock with mine, and the sadness emanating from them is palpable. "Your boyfriend, the man you've loved your entire life, did not knock me up. It's official."

I let that sink in. And it does. It sinks like a stone. "Oh. Okay. Well … it doesn't change much. I mean, for me. I guess it changes a lot for you."

"Oh my God Terra, give it up!" Aspen yells so loud that I jump. When I turn to face her again, she looks positively furious. "Do you want me to say it? Do you need me to? Fine. I can do it. I couldn't admit it as kids because I was so jealous and hurt I couldn't see straight, but I can now and I will. Problem is I don't think you'll actually hear it. You only hear what you want, just like you only see what you want."

"What the hell are you talking about now?" I snap back. "You know I used to think your non-linear babble was adorable and I was so proud of myself that I usually understood you, but now … now it's not cute. And I don't get you anymore because we are not friends."

"And we are not friends because IT'S ALWAYS BEEN YOU!" Aspen screams that last part, right in my face. Then she lifts her mitten covered hands and mimes like she's trying to scratch my eyes out or ring my neck or something. Hard to tell with the mitts but the message is not friendly. "Jake Maverick has always wanted you. Always. From probably the minute he started hanging out with your family. Definitely from the time he was locked in a closet with you. I always saw it and I was always madly, deeply, truly jealous of it. I never had what you had, Terra. Not the unconditional family support, not the adorable smile, not the perfect grades, not a perfect boy's unwavering attention."

She pauses and takes an audible breath, exhaling heavily in frustration. "And as much as I loved you, I was jealous that you didn't see it. Jesus if any boy looked at me the way Jake Maverick has always looked at you, I would have gone to any lengths to make him take the chance he was too scared to take. You were so insecure, you just shut down. So I tried everything in my power to take your place. I thought if I had the balls you didn't that would be enough to get him to love me. But it wasn't."

"Have you been drinking?" I'm trying to make a joke but there is nothing funny about this.

She points to her stomach and the tiniest bump is visible. "Hello? Baby. Stone cold sober."

"Then you're delusional."

"I'm not the only one who sees it now, Terra. Everyone sees it. Your entire family. Hell, even Miss Patti paid my herbal tea at Dunkin' the other day because, and I quote, 'I know that Maverick boy is in love with Terra Hawkins and, well dear, we spinsters need to stick together.'"

I fight so hard to control the laugh that wants to erupt from my chest that I snort right in Aspen's perky, currently rage-y, little face. Her eyes widen and then she bursts out laughing and I do too. But I'm already shaking my head. "This town is mad. Full of lunatics who don't know what they're talking about, and apparently you're one of them."

She stops laughing and so do I. We catch our breath and she reaches out and covers my hand in my lap with her own. She gives it a small squeeze. "He hasn't said it, but he came back for you. And he gave you a goddamn body part, Terra. We dated for a year and I can now officially say the most he's even given me is an orgasm."

"He gave me a couple of those too," I whisper scared to see the reaction that confession will bring to her face. I know we have barely talked for years but … I don't want to hurt her.

"Your family is all he has," Aspen says flatly. "You're his friends and his family all rolled into one. But he's never thought of you as a sister. He was excellent at pretending he did though, as you know. If this baby was his, it wasn't going to mean he was mine. He would have still been yours if you wanted him. So ask yourself that, Terra. Would you have still wanted him if this baby was his?"

"Yes." I confess it without hesitation because the one thing that has never faltered in my life, no matter the obstacles or troubles, is that I look at Jake Maverick and I feel good.

Her curls, unable to do their usual bounce thing because they're crushed under a knitted hat, shake on her shoulders as she jumps up and stands in front of me. "Then what the hell are you doing running from him right now?"

My eyes stare past her at the rumbling ocean, water crashing forward and wiping the snow off the sand. "Aspen, I spent my whole life waiting for him on some level. And where is he now? One text. He sent one text that said *Are you with Tom? Is that it? Are we over?*"

"You want him to just show up at your door, bang it down and claim you cave man-style?" Aspen cocks an eyebrow as she shoves her hands in her pockets.

"Not exactly," I bite back a smile. "But I want to hear all this from him. I deserve an explanation, from him, not you, and I deserve to know how he feels in his words."

"You know how he feels, Terra. You are the smartest person I know," Aspen counters. "And that's why you also know he's still terrified of real feelings. You're the psych major, Terra, not me. His childhood was a cycle of abandonment. Deep down, whether he admits it or even realizes it, he thinks people leave him no matter what he says or does. He's disposable. Unworthy. His feelings don't matter. They don't change anything."

I look at her, my eyes sliding own to the bump under her coat. "Can I ask… if not Jake then..?"

"I told Jake I'd never tell," Aspen smiles sadly. "But please know, no matter what this town says, and I'm sure there'll be a lot said, I know who the father is. It was Jake or one other person and … so I know. But I'm the only one who needs to know."

"Okay," I nod. I move my eyes back to hers. "Do you wish it was Jake's?"

"Hell yes," Aspen says flatly. "He would have been a solid parent."

Tiny little snowflakes start to slowly drop from the sky all around us. I stand up too. "We should go before my new kidney and your baby become popsicles."

"Good idea. See, you aren't a complete idiot," Aspen winks. I roll my eyes at her but I'm smiling. As we walk the rickety board walk, now a little bit slick in spots from the condensation turn icy, we both reach for each other's arms at the same time.

"Ronan Green," Aspen whispers it so softly it takes me a second to register it. My step falters and I stare at her.

"Ronan, engaged-to-be-married Green?" I whisper back and she nods. Her eyes are sad, and I realize instantly she has feelings for him. "Why won't you tell him? Because of Courtney? They're toxic. Everyone knows it. You might be doing him a favor."

"Nellie Green as a grandmother? That's not doing my baby any favors," Aspen replies and she pulls me so we keep walking. "Anyway, Ronan knows I'm pregnant now like the whole town does, so the baby might be in my belly, but the ball is in his court."

We take a few steps in silence and I watch her. She looks stressed and when she opens her mouth, I speak before she can. "I won't tell a soul. Not Jake or anyone. I promise."

She smiles gratefully. Our eyes connect again. "Do you remember your high school yearbook quote?" she asks me out of the blue.

"I know yours was 'As you slide down the banister of life, remember me as a splinter up the ass.'" I reply.

"And yours was 'I love you Jake Maverick so come and get me when you're ready,'" Aspen says, and I burst out laughing.

"No it wasn't, you asshole," I'm laughing so hard it actually makes my incision ache so I try to stop. "Mine was, 'Every day of your life is a second chance.'"

"Yeah, but looking back, it sure as hell feels like what I said fits too, huh?" Aspen says as we reach the sidewalk at the end of Winona Avenue. "Well, it could fit, if you let it."

"Oh my God, keep this up and you're going to be a great mom," I say lightly, like it's a light-hearted joke, but it makes her smile soften and her eyes water. I walk to my truck which is parked in front of her car on the side of the road.

"Thanks," she says, but I read her lips more than hear the words, her voice is so soft. Her car beeps as she unlocks the door but she pauses, her hand on the handle as I open my door. "You remember Jake's senior quote?"

"Never say good-bye because saying good-bye means going away and going away means forgetting," I recite without even having to think about it.

"It's from *Peter Pan*," Aspen reminds me. "Go to him, *Tink*."

25

TERRA

I TEXT HIM AS SOON AS I WALK IN THE DOOR TO MY APARTMENT. Well, actually while I'm resting on the stairs between the second and third floor. Exertion still knocks me on my ass. Doc says it's all normal.

I'm not with Tom. You and I are not done, but we need to talk. Are you free?

Thunder booms above me as I send the text, and I don't know if that's the universe's way of clapping for me or a warning signal. A couple minutes later, I find the energy to climb the rest of the stairs. Mostly because the rain started to fall in heavy, icy drops all around me. I unlock my front door and step inside, managing to avoid getting drenched as thunder claps again and lightning flashes through all my windows. I take off my coat and mitts and walk through the apartment to the living room. The French doors that lead to my balcony rattle with the wind, which is blowing the sheets of rain sideways.

That is fall in New England for you. One minute snow flurries, the next a hurricane-esque rain storm. As a therapist, sometimes I want to give Mother Nature meds. There's a hard knock at my door which startles me as I stare out the window and contemplate starting the first fire of the season in my fireplace.

I walk to the door and stretch up on my toes to see through the peep hole. Jake. How did he get here so quickly? My heart starts to gallop as I unlock the door and open it.

"How'd you get here so fast?"

"What?" He looks confused. "I drove here as soon as my shift was over."

"Have you read my message yet?"

"No. I'll read it when I'm done telling you something. And if you don't like what I have to say, you can blame Mr. Hobbs," he says gruffly as the rain pours down around him.

It's suddenly all so real. This thing with us, this moment right now is either the beginning or the end. I have no idea which it will be or what Mr. Hobbs has to do with it. Frozen in confusion, I stand in the doorway, wind and water whipping around us. "Mr. Hobbs? The seventy year-old sweetheart who eats chowder every Wednesday?"

Jake nods. "I just want to make it clear to you the reason I did it. The reason I came back, the reason I donated a kidney, it wasn't for Logan or Finn. It wasn't so your parents would accept me more or to solidify my spot as an extra in the Hawkins family saga," Jake is soaking wet now. His onyx hair hangs into his eyes, dripping fat wet drops of water. He doesn't seem to notice. "I did it because I knew if anything happened to you, I would become Mr. Hobbs."

"What?" I don't get it. How would my death make Jake a seventy year-old man?

He takes a step toward me. He's so close I have to tip my head back to keep eye contact, and the drops of water falling from him are hitting my shoulders and face now as he looks down at me. "If you died … I would spend the rest of my life longing for you."

My heart and soul have spent the last twenty-four hours trying to find a path for us. A way we could hold onto what I thought we were building. Never in a million years did I ever dream he'd say this. Because now … now there is no path to take. I've been teleported directly to the destination. No matter what has happened or will happen in the future, I'll be Jake Maverick's forever.

"I am madly in love with you," I whisper as I blink back tears.

"Then will you let me inside? I'm about to drown out here," Jake says softly and I laugh. It's wildly jarring but so is this entire conversation, in the best possible way. I move to the side, and Jake's giant body slips into my hallway. I close the door behind him and then I walk right up to him and wrap myself around his soaking wet body. My arms loop his neck and pull his lips down to mine but before the kiss can start, he speaks. "I love you too, by the way."

"I got that message. Loud and clear," I reply. He's so wet and now I am too, and I don't care. I kiss him, slowly, languidly, and it's perfect, just like we are. He wraps his arms around me and hugs me tightly to his body, my feet lifting off the floor. My stitches start to ache and I wince against the kiss so he puts me down.

When our lips slip apart, he buries his face in my neck. "I have to let you go. We both need dry clothes now. And to talk about the whole Aspen thing."

"Or no clothes. That's always an option," I tell him, my lips ghosting over the side of his long, thick neck. "And we can talk after."

"See Tink, you're full of good ideas," Jake replies arms still holding me up as he walks us back to my bedroom.

We undress each other, and touch each other's naked bodies, with a new level of intimacy. Because we're both laid bare in so many new ways. And as we tangle in the sheets, the rain water making our skin slick, turning to sweat as we lead each other to climax with our hands and our mouths.

An hour later, I'm curled up beside him, my head on his chest listening to his heartbeat, and my fingers trail across his abdomen. My heart clenches every time it glides over one of the puncture-type wounds healing from the operation. If we stay together until we're old and gray, I don't know if that will ever stop happening, that pinch of gratitude and guilt.

"So… Aspen…"

"I know the baby isn't yours," I say and tilt my head on his chest to look up at him, hooking my leg over his massive thighs as I do. "Aspen and I talked it out."

"All of it out?" Jake questions.

"Yeah. I … I think I forgive her," I say quietly. "And I forgive you. I mean you don't need it, actually. I understand you couldn't violate her trust."

"Thank you for understanding," Jake says softly. "It's her whole life that gets changed by this kid. And yeah, it would be mine too but only by choice. That's how it is for men, so I couldn't flip the switch on that change before she was ready. And I trust you, Terra. Even though you two had issues, I knew you wouldn't say anything, but if I told you I was scared I'd lose what we were starting."

"I'd have been hurt, angry, jealous. But I would have found my way back to you," I confess, my voice a whisper. "I belong with you, Jake."

"You do," he pulls me up, closer to his face and kisses me. Our tongues tangle lazily. When he breaks the kiss, he reaches up and pushes my overgrown bangs out of my face. "Also, I belong to you, Terra. I always have even when I was too scared to admit it. A child wasn't going to change that."

"Are you sad the baby isn't yours?" I ask, holding my breath because I don't know what I want the response to be.

His hand stops making lazy circles on the base of my spine. His eyes hold mine as he speaks. "No. Terra, I've never wanted children. I would have been there for this kid one hundred percent if it was mine and I would have loved him or her, truly I would have. But I don't feel loss because it wasn't something I was hoping for or trying for. Does that make me an asshole?" He's searching my face, nervous energy radiating off of him.

"Do you remember when I was almost kicked out of school because I refused to do that stupid baby project?"

Jake smiles. "The one where they gave us those creepy electric dolls that would cry and fuss and we had to pretend we were parents for seventy-two hours? And you refused to participate even though they threatened you with suspension and your mom grounded you."

I nod. "I didn't want kids back then. That was why I did it. I didn't think it was fair to force someone to do something, to pretend they were a parent, when they knew in their soul that they would never be."

"But you were sixteen."

"Yeah. When did you know you didn't want kids?"

"Always."

"Exactly," I climb up so I'm lying flat on top of him skin-to-skin. "In the end, they didn't expel me because I gave them some five page research paper I wrote filled with the statistics and complications of women with lupus having children. Mom even ungrounded me when she read it. But that was just a convenient excuse. Fact is, I just never wanted them. I still don't."

He kisses me again, slowly, lightly, but it lights a fire in me anyway.

"Of course, that doesn't mean I want to stop going through the baby-making motions."

"Oh no, we shouldn't stop that. It's a good skill to have," Jake says laughing. "We should practice it a lot as soon as the doc gives us the go-ahead, which better be soon, or I will lose my Terra-loving mind."

He wraps his arms tighter around me. Holding me to his chest, he whispers into my ear, "You're my everything, Tink. All I will ever need."

And my heart wants to burst. I had no idea, none at all, when he walked back through the door of the lobster shack that he would save my life in so many different ways.

EPILOGUE
JAKE

IT'S USUALLY FUN WORKING THE TOWN'S HALLOWEEN PARTY. I remember my first couple of years when I started at the fire department in Ocean Pines it was one of my favorite events, like Illumination Night but better because the kids were adorable in all their costumes. There were a bunch of events in the center of town at the gazebo and the local businesses gave out candy. We did too from the firetruck and let kids sit in the driver's seat.

But tonight … tonight was pure and utter hell. Because I was working seven p.m. to seven p.m., and at five o'clock the surgeon gave me the all-clear for full duty and all other strenuous physical activities. Including sex. And yeah, I asked it bluntly, because I wanted the answer to be clear. But there was no time to find Terra, who had had her appointment earlier in the day and was also cleared. So we had to wait another twenty-four hours.

Logan is off tonight but he shows up with River who is the absolute most adorable Han Solo I have ever seen. Of course he's got his favorite sidekick, Chewie, with him and he's dragging that Ewok stuffie I gave him as well as a little black bucket filled with candy already. "You should have dressed up as Leia," I tell Logan who gives me a look that says 'fuck off'.

"I told Daddy to be Jabba the Hut but he said no," River informs me and I laugh and bend to scratch Chewie behind the ears.

"Your dad would be the best Jabba ever," I announce and Logan's 'fuck you' look gets stronger.

"Riv! Your grandpa is dressed up as a lobster!"

I lift my eyes from Chewie and my frustration at working turns to pure rage. Terra is walking across the street to the fire truck in a costume. She's dressed up as Tinkerbell. But not the cute, goofy looking Tinkerbell she was dressed as at seven. She's dressed in a much more adult version. Nothing too sexy, just a glittering short green dress and a pair of sparkling sky blue wings. She's got on heels, and her dirty blonde hair is piled up in a little bun with sparkly makeup on her face, and she looks incredible. I want to lift her off those heels and fuck her against the side of the truck right this very second, which is absolutely not going to happen. Fuck my life.

"Jake, babe, you look totally flustered," she comments, pure fake innocence dripping off her words as she bats her eyelashes.

Logan groans. "Come on Riv. Let's go see Grampy."

"You look pretty Auntie!" River proclaims.

"That's an understatement," I reply.

Logan glares at me. "Do not have sexual thoughts about my sister in front of me."

He growls it low enough and so close to my face that River doesn't hear. I smile and reply. "Sorry. Too late."

"Barf," Logan takes River's hand and Chewie's leash and walks off toward the restaurant. Terra sticks around, smiling smugly at me.

"You are making the next twenty-four hours impossible," I tell her.

I walk over to kiss her cheek but she puts a hand on my chest and stops me. "There's time for that later. You have somewhere to be right now."

"I do?"

"You need to head over to city hall," she points to the big red brick building on the other side of the town square. "The battalion chief loves our lobster bisque, clam roll combo. He comes in once a month to grab it when he's out this way meeting on committees in Portland. Yesterday was that day, and I couldn't help but explain to him how one of his officers saved my life."

"Terra…" I'm conflicted about the idea that she got involved in my work problems.

"He's not from around here, Jake. He's works in Augusta so he hadn't seen Mrs. Green's blog, and apparently you didn't tell them why you postponed the first interview," Terra gives me a brief but stern look of disapproval. "Anyway, now he knows and Aspen also called him and explained she was having a pregnancy emergency, and you came to help her over the interview and, well, he agreed to have an informal interview with you tonight."

"I can't … Are you serious?"

"She's serious," Captain D'Amato walks up beside us. "He's here with one of the other battalion chiefs who would have also been at your interview, so get your ass to City Hall, first floor conference room, and have a little chat."

"Like this?" I look down at my work clothes. They both nod.

"Go, Jake! There isn't going to be a third chance," Cap says in his sternest Cap voice. I nod and with one last look at Terra, who gives me an encouraging smile, I jog across the square.

The interview seems to go well, all things considering, but the rest of my shift is torture. I just want to be with Terra. The next evening, when it finally ends, I drive straight to Terra's apartment as I call her on speaker phone. "Tink," I say as soon as she answers. "It's sex time."

I hang up without giving her a chance to respond. I take the stairs to her place two at a time and not only did she get up, but she beat me to the door and has it open before I can knock. And she's wearing that damn costume again. Holy shit.

"Any word on the interview?" she asks as my feet hit the landing.

"I told you last night. It went well," I remind her. "It's gonna take time to hear anything more, but I'm confident. And now let me thank you for making that happen. And for wearing this outfit again."

I scoop her up and kick the front door shut behind us. I press her up against the wall and kiss her, my tongue sweeping into her mouth. I'm pushing my hard cock into her and she's rocking back against it while she pulls at my shirt, trying to yank it off.

"You have to tell me if anything is too rough," I pant. "We can go as soft and slow as you need."

"What I need is to be fucked, long and hard, Jake," she whispers against my ear before sucking the lobe into her mouth and giving it a little nip.

I move us off the wall and carry her into the living room, almost knocking myself out on all her sloping ceilings. This apartment is smaller than a clown car for a body as tall as mine, but right now it doesn't matter, all that matters is getting inside her. I hate taking that costume off her because fuck, it's hot, but I do. Because naked Terra is my ultimate fantasy.

I lay her bare on the couch and undress standing above her. She watches me with rapt attention and her fingers find their way between her legs. Watching her touch herself as she watches me undress is making my body turn to fire. I'm ready to explode just rolling on the condom. I crawl on top of her but after a long, deep kiss she pulls back. "Let me take the lead."

I nod. She tells me to get up, I do, and she gets up too and then pushes me down onto the couch and says. "Lie down."

Then she climbs on top of me and turns to face my feet and

without hesitation, lowers herself down on my cock. I watch her ride me, and hold her hips, but she's too far away, so I sit up, wrap my arms around her and cup both her breasts, rolling her nipples between my fingertips and peppering her back with kisses. Her hips move faster. I am tingling everywhere. I move one hand past her belly to her pussy and find her clit. She lets out the hottest little moan and her back arches and she comes. I can't, I won't, without seeing her face. So I pull out when her hips slow and flip her around and push her down on my cock again. I tip my head down and our lips meet and then our foreheads press together and I force my eyes to stay open as I come so I can see her. My girl. The one that got away, the one who let me come back.

ACKNOWLEDGMENTS

Thank you to my husband, Jack, who refuses to let me give into imposter syndrome or fear. Love you. Thanks to my mom and dad for never telling me to go outside and play when I was a kid, holed up in my room reading or trying to write. And for taking me to Maine every summer of my life. Thanks to Sarah Jillain, AKA the Beast of Fryman, for being my confidant, cheerleader, beta reader and gut-check. Thank you to my agent Kimberly Brower for all she has done and continues to do for me on this wild journey.

Thank you to all the established, brilliantly talented indie authors who let me email them with a million newbie indie questions. I could not have done this without you Lex Martin, Sarina Bowen, Stephanie Kay, Rebecca Jenshak, Kat Mizera, Jami Davenport, Tiffani Lynn, DeAnna C Zankich and so many more I'm sure I'm missing because my brain is fried. But please know, if I missed you here I'm still overwhelmed with gratitude. Massive love to Jen Obirek, her man, and the late, great Lisa B. Kamps who answered all my firefighting Qs. Katie Kenyhercz, thanks for your amazing editing work on all my messy drafts. Claudia Fosca Stahl, thank you for lending me your sharp eyes. I am forever grateful. The hardest part of writing an 85k novel is the eight to ten sentences on the back cover so thank you to Romance Rehab for the blurb help. And Mignon Mykel at Oh So Novel, thank you so much for your cover magic.

Thank you to the readers – extra big shout-out to those who jumped on the ARC team - but all of you have given me the strength and courage to believe in my storytelling and share it. I hope you enjoyed Terra and Jake's story and the Ocean Pines world. There is more to come…

OTHER BOOKS BY VICTORIA DENAULT

Blindsided

The Hometown Players series

The San Francisco Thunder series

Subscribe to Victoria Denault's newsletter